Praise for the Otter Lake mystery series

"Delightful . . . with laugh-out-loud moments, a touch of romance, and a fun, sassy style. Readers will enjoy every moment spent in Otter Lake."

—Diane Kelly, award-winning author
of *Death, Taxes, and a Shotgun Wedding*

"A frolicking good time . . . with a heroine who challenges Stephanie Plum for the title of funniest sleuth."

—*New York Times* bestselling author Denise Swanson

"Time spent with the folks in Otter Lake is well worthwhile, with writing that is witty, contemporary, and winning." —*Kirkus Reviews*

"Wonderfully entertaining!" —*RT Book Reviews*

Also by Auralee Wallace

Skinny Dipping with Murder
Pumpkin Picking with Murder
Snowed In with Murder
Ring in the Year with Murder

DOWN THE AISLE

With

MURDER

Auralee Wallace

St. Martin's Paperbacks

This is a work of fiction. All of the characters, organizations, and events portrayed in this novel are either products of the author's imagination or are used fictitiously.

DOWN THE AISLE WITH MURDER

For information address St. Martin's Press, 175 Fifth Avenue, New York, NY 10010.

ISBN: 978-1-250-15147-6

Our books may be purchased in bulk for promotional, educational, or business use. Please contact your local bookseller or the Macmillan Corporate and Premium Sales Department at 1-800-221-7945, ext. 5442, or by e-mail at MacmillanSpecialMarkets@macmillan.com.

Printed in the United States of America

St. Martin's Paperbacks edition / May 2018

St. Martin's Paperbacks are published by St. Martin's Press, 175 Fifth Avenue, New York, NY 10010.

10 9 8 7 6 5 4 3 2 1

Chapter One

"I want to be just like that maid of honor when I grow up."

"You can't be serious."

"One hundred percent."

"I'll start drawing up the papers for our friend divorce."

I exchanged looks with Freddie, my best friend, business partner, and—on this particular night—professional party pooper.

We were at the Dawg, the only bar slash restaurant in Otter Lake, "Live Free or Die" New Hampshire. A town that had everything the postcards promised. Long docks stretching into the water. Nights with a billion stars. And tonight—for one night only—a mechanical bull all done up with enough lipstick and glitter to make Cowboy Barbie proud.

Normally the bar was a subdued-looking place. Everything was made of wood and smelled of beer and grease. It was a comforting atmosphere. An atmosphere that was pretty much gone now. Whoever had been in charge of decorations for the party had gone pretty heavy on feathers, strings of plastic beads, and the color *pink*.

But then again, it was a bachelorette party.

"I hear ya, Erica," Rhonda said. She was the third business partner in our Otter Lake Security Triumvirate. "That Lyssa really knows how to party."

"Well, get up there then," Freddie said. "Nobody's stopping you. I'll even take pictures. We'll put it on our OLS holiday newsletter next Christmas."

I looked over my shoulder at the woman on top of the bull with the plaid shirt tied at her waist. Judging by all her shrieking, she was having a blast. A small gathering of male locals watching her from the bar seemed to think so too. They hadn't been deterred by the PRIVATE PARTY notice on the door. In fairness, there wasn't really any place to go in Otter Lake on a Friday night except for the Dawg. But she didn't seem to care if they were watching. She was in that rodeo to win it. And given the amount of shooters she had thrown back it was all pretty impressive.

"Nah, I said I want to be like that *someday*. Today is not that day."

"Chicken," Freddie said, jiggling his baby finger in his left ear. Lyssa's shrieking was pretty loud.

"Yes, yes I am."

In fairness to me, I had once accidentally flashed the entire citizenry of Otter Lake holding Betsy the Beaver—the town mascot—in my arms. On a stage. Under a spotlight. So that might have left me with some issues about putting myself out there.

"Aw, does that mean you won't sing with me later?"

Rhonda asked, her ginger eyebrows coming together to form a sad peek. "I saw them setting up a karaoke machine."

"Sorry."

"Freddie?" she asked, turning her sad face to his.

"Sure. What are you thinking? Miley Cyrus's 'Wrecking Ball'? Katy Perry's 'Roar?'"

Rhonda's eyes lit up. "Are you serious?"

"No."

"Not nice, Freddie," I said, giving him the side-eye before taking another sip of my beer. "You know, with the bull and the karaoke, I'm actually kind of amazed Lyssa was able to throw together this party so quickly," I said, leaning back in my chair. "Candace is one lucky bride."

That's right. Candace, ex-PR person for MRG Properties—the company attempting to turn small-town Otter Lake into a cottage playground for New Hampshire's rich and famous—was getting married. To Joey. An ex-con, who kind of looked like a hot werewolf. He was really big and had a lot of thick dark hair. He was also a sweetheart. As for the ex-con bit, he had stolen a few cars back when he was barely eighteen trying to pay off his younger sister's medical bills. Candace had become his pen pal when he was locked up. And the rest was history—a weird, somewhat murderous, convoluted history.

They had only been seeing each other for about six months, but that was enough for them to decide to tie the knot. I was trying to keep an open mind about the whole thing. I certainly wasn't in any position to be giving relationship advice. Besides, Candace and I were becoming fairly good friends now that she had gotten past me once accusing her of murder, and I had gotten past her dating the on-again, off-again love of my life, Grady Forrester, and I didn't want to ruin all that with my unasked-for opinions.

"Still feeling guilty, I see," Freddie said.

"Guilty?" The hand holding my beer bottle froze halfway back down to the table. "What are you talking about?"

Freddie rolled his eyes so far back into his head his eyelashes started to twitch. It wasn't a good look.

"He means about you being Candace's maid of honor," Rhonda threw in.

"What?" I practically shrieked. "That's ridiculous. Candace never wanted me to be her maid of honor."

"Right," Freddie said. Blinking. I think he might have hurt himself. That's what happens when you overdo the sarcasm.

I looked over to Rhonda. "Help me out here."

"*Well . . .*" She had said it in that really high pitch people use when they want to tell you the thing they know you don't want to hear, but won't because you might . . . I don't know, punch them or something. "But it's okay. We all know you have issues with weddings."

"I do not have issues with weddings," I said, before taking another sip of beer. "And for the record, Candace never once brought it up with me."

Freddie nodded. "Yeah, that might have been because every time the topic of the wedding came up, you looked like you were going to throw up."

"That is so not true," I said with an exaggerated scoff.

They exchanged looks again.

"It's not. Maybe . . . maybe I just have resting nauseous face. Did either of you think of that?"

Neither answered.

I sighed. "Okay, fine. Maybe I don't *love* hearing about all the wedding details. I mean, all that talk about flowers, centerpieces, and color schemes."

"But—"

"Chair covers. Napkin rings. Bridesmaid dresses."

"She's got quite a list," Freddie said.

"DJs. Wedding party gifts. Rice—"

"Rice?" Rhonda asked.

I blinked. I was kind of glad she had derailed me there. The wedding train had run away with me. "Yeah, rice. You know, to throw at the couple as they leave the church."

"Nobody throws rice anymore," Freddie said.

"Sure they do."

"No, they really don't. Pigeons eat it and then their stomachs explode."

"Come on," I said, leaning back in my chair. "I have never seen a pigeon explode."

"That's because people stopped throwing rice."

Rhonda chuckled.

I should have seen that coming. "Okay, I'm pretty sure that's an urban legend. But the point is . . ." What was my point? "The point is I like weddings just fine. And why are you so argumentative tonight?" I asked Freddie. "It's a bachelorette party. We're supposed to be having fun. You need to get into the spirit." I waved a hand at Rhonda. "Give him your hat."

She reached for the piece of tinfoil on her head. It was molded into the shape of a very specific part of the male anatomy.

"Rhonda," Freddie said, "you put that penis hat on my head, and I will stab you where you sit."

Rhonda's eyes widened.

"He didn't mean that," I said, giving her hand a pat. I turned back to Freddie. "Are you all right?"

"Peachy," he said, taking a sip of beer and looking away.

Hmm, *peachy* was not a word anyone used when they were actually peachy. Maybe he was just tired. Freddie had really been hustling to get our business, Otter Lake Security, off the ground, and all that work was finally starting to pay off. An insurance company had given us a gig spying on a disability claimant. Our target had been in a head-on collision and was suing the other driver's insurance company—the company who hired us—for damages. Apparently he was too injured to work, but they suspected he was doing some pretty physical renovations on the cabin he had just bought. They wanted both pictures and video of the claimant doing the work, so they could take him to court and end his lawsuit. We were the only security company in the area, so we got the job. Luckily we didn't know the guy. That might have made things awkward. Rhonda, an ex-cop, was the only one of us technically allowed to do the spying work given that she was technically the only one of us who had a private investigator's license. New Hampshire law required us to have at least four years' experience working in the field with a certified professional. Rhonda's experience as a police officer counted.

"I do feel bad for Candace though," Freddie said, dragging his eyes away from the table filled with the party's signature cocktail. I hadn't tried one yet. I wasn't sure about the rapidly disintegrated cotton candy they were topped with. "This isn't her type of party. She isn't a bull-riding, bead-wearing, shot-drinking bride."

"I'm sure it's . . ."

Freddie pushed himself to his feet.

". . . fine," I finished. Not sure why. He obviously wasn't listening to me.

"I'm going to get another beer and free Joey's nonna. You guys want one?"

"Free Joey's nonna?" Rhonda asked, straightening up. "What?"

"She's caught in the chairs again."

I whirled my head around. Okay, that was weird. I mean, it wasn't like Joey's grandmother wasn't welcome or anything, but she did look like she was in her eighties, and I was thinking a bachelorette party wasn't exactly her bag. Especially given that she did indeed seem to be trapped in a circle of chairs. Guess she didn't have a lot of upper-body strength.

"I heard that the bridesmaid you so love much insisted they bring her because she was *so* cute," Freddie said, shaking his head. "I don't think she knew what was happening to her."

I frowned. "How long has she been stuck in the chairs?"

Freddie shrugged. "Five, ten minutes."

"Five, ten minutes?! Why didn't you get up sooner?"

"I was almost done with my beer. I thought I'd save myself a trip."

My eyes widened.

"Oh please, like you wouldn't have done the same thing. Do you guys want another beer or not?"

"I . . ."

"Suit yourselves," he said, shuffling off.

I looked over at Rhonda. "What was that all about?"

She shrugged. "No clue."

"I haven't seen him this negative about everything since his emo period in high school."

Rhonda chuckled. "Remember when he used to wear all that black eyeliner?"

I smiled. "And Mrs. Applebaum thought he was a Satanist and crossed the street whenever she saw him coming?"

"Good times. Good times," Rhonda said with a nod. "But *we* can still have fun."

"Of course we can," I said.

We clinked beer bottles.

"I am happy for Candace," I said. "I know it's quick, but she and Joey really do seem happy."

"I know! When it's right, it's right," Rhonda said with a nod. "That's the way relationships should be. Easy. No drama. Just two people finding each other, making it work." She dragged out the last part of the sentence as her eyes grew in horror. "Not that that's always the case. I mean, sometimes getting through problems and drama just makes a couple—"

"Please stop," I said, holding up a hand.

"I'm just trying to say that you can't compare relationships. Just because you came back to town around the same time Candace arrived, and since then, well, Candace is getting married and you and Grady are still—"

The look on my face cut her right off.

"I'm making it worse, aren't I?"

I nodded.

"You know it comes from a place of love, right?"

"Your love hurts, Rhonda."

Yup, when I had originally decided to move back home to Otter Lake, a big part of me hoped my new life would involve Sheriff Grady Forrester, but that hadn't exactly worked out. I mean, I was glad that I did it. I loved being closer to my family and friends— most days—but it still hurt a little that Grady and I hadn't found a way to be a couple. I had thought maybe back at New Year's, Grady and I had a chance to get back together, but he preemptively dumped me with this whole spiel about taking some *time* to think about things—and then I *may* have kissed Matthew Masterson, a really handsome, kind architect like a couple of hours later because, well, he's a really handsome, kind architect, and my feelings were pretty hurt. Let's just say, I heard secondhand from Rhonda, that Grady hadn't taken the news of that event particularly well. We hadn't really talked since. Not because I didn't want to . . . but based on past experience, well, everything I said to him to try to make things better usually made things worse. And I couldn't take things being any worse. As for Matthew, well, he had decided to go back to New York for a couple of months. Not directly because I had been messing with his head . . . just, maybe, indirectly, a little bit. And really, absolutely nothing had happened with either man—or any man—since, and that was six months ago, but like I said, I was still totally cool with romance. For other people.

"I'm sorry, Erica, I didn't mean to—"

"It's fine. I'm fine," I said, waving a hand in the air. "I'm happy for Candace."

Rhonda sighed. "Well, it's a good thing someone is."

"Huh?"

Rhonda tipped her beer bottle in the direction of a young woman sitting at the bar with waist-length dark hair and a miserable expression. There had been some speculation that Joey's family wasn't exactly thrilled about the upcoming nuptials. And by family, I meant Joey's sister, Antonia. His parents had died in a car accident when they were kids. Candace wouldn't confirm or deny any rumors about whether or not any of this family strife was true, given that she never had an unkind word to say about anyone, but she had looked pretty stressed whenever the topic of Antonia had come up. I was thinking there had to be some truth to the rumor given that Antonia looked like she might start angry-crying any moment. "I hope she doesn't use that face for the photos." I shook my head. "I feel so bad for Can—"

"Speak of the bride!" Rhonda said, jumping to her feet.

I whipped my head around before getting up too. "Candace!"

"Hi," she said with a cute little wave.

"Hey!" I said in a voice that reached a level of brightness that I had never achieved before. And it wasn't at all because I was feeling guilty. I mean, fine, yes, in all honesty, I had maybe got the sense a month or two ago that Candace was thinking about asking me to be her maid of honor. Her sister had been her first choice, but Bethanny was studying in Australia and couldn't swing the airfare back on such short notice. And I would have said yes if Candace had asked, but I was not a good choice. I didn't understand all the nuances of weddings. But with all Freddie's talk about the party not being right for Candace . . . well, maybe I *was* feeling a little guilty. "There you are." I leaned in to give her a hug. A short hug. Her tinfoil penis hat poked me in the side of the head—which felt very wrong.

She readjusted her headpiece. "Are you guys having a good time?"

"Are we having a good time? We are having the best time!"

"Where did Freddie get off to?" she asked, looking around. "I wanted to say hi."

"He's just getting another beer. But who cares about us," I said with a *pshaw*-type wave of my hand. "Are you having a good time? Your friend Lyssa seems really nice," I said with lots of nodding and smiling. Probably too much smiling and nodding. "I mean, I haven't actually met her yet. But she really knows how to throw a party."

"Yup," Candace said with a somewhat pained-looking smile. "She's always been good at that." She shot a look at the bar. "You don't think . . . well, I'm not sure Big Don's happy about all this."

"What?" I shrieked. At least it felt like a shriek. This tone of voice felt very unnatural. "No. Big Don loves this sort of thing." I shot the Dawg's owner a quick glance. Okay, so he might look a little like a grizzly restraining himself from going on a bloody rampage . . . but, well, it was unlikely that he would do anything like that. "It's fine. Fabulous, really."

"It's just . . . I haven't seen Lyssa in so long. I thought maybe she—well, this is just a lot like the frat parties she used to take me to."

"But bachelorette parties are always over-the-top, aren't they?" I said, giving her arm a squeeze. "I mean, I wouldn't know. I'm terrible at this sort of thing. I'd probably plan something boring at the bowling alley."

"Oh! Girls' bowling night!" Candace said with even more pain in her smile. "That sounds so fun."

"No. No," I said. "That's fine for any old night. But this is your wild last night out as a single lady."

She smiled weakly. "You're probably right. I should just go with it."

"Candy!" a voice shrieked from across the room.

"I'd better get back," Candace said, jerking a thumb in Lyssa's direction. "We're having trouble getting people to ride the bull. Lyssa's talking about putting together a posse to just grab people and plunk them on." She looked back at me. "Are you going to ride?"

I waved my hands out in front of me. "Oh, no, no, no."

I watched as a montage of embarrassing Erica Bloom moments passed through Candace's consciousness. I could tell that's what it was by all the cringing she was doing. She knew about the beaver. "I get it," she said with a smile. "Rhonda?"

"I think I'll pass too. My groin's still bad from when I got cross-checked playing hockey last—"

"Candy!" Lyssa once again shouted from across the room.

"I'd better go," Candace said, smile crumpling.

"Yeah, we'll catch up with you in a bit."

We dropped back down into our seats as Candace walked away.

Rhonda shook her head. "I've never seen a woman look so unhappy wearing a tinfoil penis hat."

I sipped my beer. I wanted to argue, but I couldn't. This was terrible. Sure, I wasn't super into weddings, but Candace was. And she had every reason to be happy. She and Joey were deeply in love. She should be having the time of her life . . . at a bowling alley . . . without a tinfoil hat.

I put my beer back down when an idea hit me.

That's what this party was missing. A toast!

I could totally do that.

A toast couldn't be that hard. I was fine with drawing attention to other people. And Candace needed reminding of why we were all here in the first place. Two great people had found love and were getting married.

I pushed myself to my feet just as Freddie returned to the table.

Sure, I wasn't naturally talented in the way of public speaking, but this wasn't about me. It was about Candace. I tapped my knife against my beer bottle. Hard. The music was pretty loud. "Everyone? Everyone!" The din quieted just a bit. "If I can have your attention—"

Lyssa and her group of men were still talking and laughing.

"Everybody!" I tried again.

"What are you doing?" Freddie asked.

"Trying to breathe some life into this party," I said.

"Oh well, I can help with that. Hey, Lycra!" Freddie shouted.

Lyssa turned around.

"Erica here wants to ride the bull!" Freddie shouted, jerking a thumb at me.

"Freddie!"

"What? Someone other than Lyssa needs to do it. And you said you wanted to be more like her," he said, stepping aside for the posse. "I'm helping you grow as a person. You're welcome."

I tried to wave off the group of people coming for me, but it was too late. I was already being lifted into the air. I looked down at Freddie. "You're going to pay for this."

"Meh. See you on the other side."

Chapter Two

That had been a long night.

I gingerly rolled over in bed, and curled my duvet under my chin. My shoulder hurt. I hadn't landed the dismount. Not even a little bit. In fact, I was thrown so hard from the bull, I rolled off the mats and into the jukebox. But at least it didn't start playing. That's the type of thing that makes a story legend. And just when I thought the party couldn't get any more uncomfortable for Candace, the stripper showed up. He wasn't a professional. Nope, not a lot of professional strippers in Otter Lake, so Lyssa had convinced a local, Chris Williams, to dress up as a UPS worker and do a little dance for everyone. I say convinced but from what I knew about Chris, well, let's just say I think he'd win the vote for *most likely to end up drunk and naked at a bonfire*. And even though he was still in his early twenties, he already had a real head start on his dad body. Big Don kicked him out before he had been able to deliver his package to Candace, thank God.

It really hadn't been her type of party.

But that was all over now.

Today was the big day, and judging by the light blazing through my closed eyelids, it was going to be sunny. Perfect day for a wedding.

Just then my phone rang. I didn't even have to look at it to know it was Freddie. My ring tone had been changed to . . . ah yes, that must be the theme song for *Teenage Mutant Ninja Turtles*. He liked to keep his personalized phone signature fresh.

I rolled over, eyes still closed, phone at my ear. "Why are you calling me so—"

"She's dead," Freddie said, cutting me off.

"Who's dead?" I asked.

"Somebody's dead?" another voice asked.

"Wah!" My eyes flew open.

Twins. Hovering. Right above my face.

"Who was that?" Freddie asked.

"Kit Kat and Tweety are here," I answered once I could speak over my beating heart. The twins were the only other inhabitants on my mother's island. They were in their seventies now, but still built like wrestlers. They also had matching white perms and dentures. For some people, they might come off as a little rough around the edges—they always had a dirty joke ready to go, and occasionally took out their teeth to frighten misbehaving children—but they were good people, salt of the earth. But speaking of earth, their place had burned to the ground about a year ago, so they had moved into the retreat until it could be rebuilt. It had been the obvious choice. I mean, they had co-existed on the island with my mother for nearly thirty years in peace and harmony. We were like family. That

being said, living in these close quarters had its challenges. "They're both here. In my room. Watching me
sleep, apparently."

"Well, that's not creepy," Freddie said in my ear as
Kit Kat yanked the pillow out from underneath my
head.

"You weren't sleeping. You're flopping around that
mattress like a fish on a dock. Now who is dead?"

I cleared my throat and blinked hard a couple of
times before I answered. Nothing was working right
yet. "I don't know. Hang on. Freddie, who is dead?"
To an outsider it might seem strange that I wasn't a
little more alarmed by Freddie's death announcement,
but he called me at least once a week with a celebrity
death.

"Tell the twins to go away," the voice on my phone
said. "You know I don't like competing for attention."

I sighed and looked back at the twins. "I don't know
what's going on. Can I meet you in the kitchen after I
talk—"

"Are we going to find any bacon in the kitchen?"
Tweety asked.

Son of a . . .

That. That right there was probably the number one
challenge of us all living together.

Meat.

In the past, my mother had allowed meat on the
premises for the guests, but after she'd lost her last
cook, she decided to take on all the cooking herself—
with some hired help from town—which meant *no
meat*. For anyone. Well, except for my evil fur-sibling
of a cat, Caesar. I had grown accustomed to my
mother's cruelty-free ways, and I was mostly okay with

eating my meat products off the island. The twins, however, were not. To make matters worse, my mother had taken it on as her personal mission to cure the sisters of their diabetes. This was resulting in some *tension* in my living situation.

"I forgot the bacon." I scratched absently at my shoulder, eyes closed. "Actually I didn't forget. I just didn't buy your bacon. I was at a party. Where was I supposed to keep it? I didn't know how long I would be out, and—"

Suddenly my pillow whapped me in the face.

"Hey!"

"Told you she didn't get it. That's why she wasn't answering our texts."

"Getting bored here," my phone drawled.

I snatched my pillow back again and tucked it safely against the wall. "I'm sorry, okay? Can you please now—"

"Did you at least bring us back something from the party?" Tweety asked. "I betcha there was lots of food. Dessert? Man-shaped cookie?"

"Yeah, no, I did not bring you back a . . . cookie." I frowned. "You know what? You two are going to need to go now."

"Fine, but if I slip into a diabetic coma, I want you to know, Erica, that it's your fault." Kit Kat shut my door hard enough to make my clock—a frog with fishing poles—rattle against the wood wall.

"Got it," I said, rubbing my face. Nope, this was so not the life I had imagined for myself when I'd decided to move home. No, in that life, Grady would be bringing me naked coffee. Or coffee naked. Whatever.

I ran my hand down over my face. "Okay, so who's dead?"

"What's her name? Lycra. The maid of honor."

"You mean Lyssa? Candace's Lyssa? Are you sure it wasn't, like, Alyssa Milan—"

"Of course Candace's Lyssa!"

"Hey, don't you yell at me. I just woke up."

Freddie sighed.

"And how could she possibly be dead? What happen—"

"Erica, honey, are you awake?" my mother asked, pushing my door open and floating into the room in a purple and pink caftan, holding two large glasses of something green. "Have you seen the twins?"

"Oh my God, is that your mother now?" Freddie groaned. "When are you going to get your own place?"

"I'm trying," I snapped back before looking at my mother. "I think they're in the kitchen."

"No, I was just there," she said with a dramatic sigh. "They're hiding from me again. They're like big, white-haired children."

"Well, they don't really like your smoothies."

"I know they don't like the smoothies, but—"

My mother cut herself off when she saw me pull my phone away from my ear as it shouted, "Helloooo?"

"Is that Freddie?" she asked. "Why is he calling so early?"

"I can't do this," Freddie said in my ear. "Be at your dock in fifteen. We need to get over there."

"Over where?"

"Candace's!" He hung up.

"What's going on?" my mother asked.

I shook my head against my pillow. "Apparently Candace's maid of honor is dead."

"Oh no, that's terrible. Is Candace all right? Well, of course she's not all right. She's supposed to be getting married today."

I sat up and swung my feet onto the floor. "Maybe Freddie has it wrong— Ow!" I whipped my ankle back up to see a razor-thin slice in my skin. "Morning, Caesar," I grumbled. The fur beast had taken to sleeping on the floor by my bed since I'd moved home. Some might think he was being sweet, but really it was because he knew I was slow and stupid first thing in the morning.

"I hope so."

"Freddie's coming to pick me up. I guess we're going over there to see if there's anything we can do."

"Of course. But darling . . . ?"

I blinked at my mother, still trying to process the news.

"You haven't forgotten about the retreat, right?"

I froze for a moment. "Of course I haven't forgotten." I had totally forgotten. These days I helped out as much as I could with Earth, Moon, and Stars. It was the least I could do since I had been living rent-free in my mother's lodge for a year now. Real estate was hard to come by in Otter Lake what with MRG buying up all the property for development.

My mother had a best-selling author slash guru coming this week, and she was kind of nervous about it. All of our cabins would be up and running—a few attendees were even camping. On top of that, we had to bring some professional vegan caterers in to help with the cooking. If it went well, though, she might be able to attract even more big names in the self-help field.

"I'll be around to help. Promise."

"I've already had the first guest arrive," she said.

"Already?"

She nodded.

I pulled a light sweater over my head. These spring mornings were still pretty cool. "What's the theme of this retreat anyway?"

"Oh, Zaki is just going to be promoting his new book. I doubt you'd be interested."

Zaki. I don't think he had a last name. He was too rock star. I looked up from the shoe I was trying to tie to meet my mother's eye, but she was engrossed by staring at the . . . ceiling? "What's his book called?"

"Oh . . ." She twiddled her fingers in the air like she was trying to remember the name by . . . summoning a spell? "I think it's called *Why Are You Still Single?*"

My chin dropped to my chest. Okay, granted, my brain was half asleep and the awake part was still reeling from Freddie's news, but— "Did you say you are having a retreat called *Why Are You Still Single?* but you doubt I'd be interested?"

She nodded.

I looked around my room just to make sure I hadn't woken up in an alternate universe.

My mother swatted at my arm. I guess Freddie wasn't the only one who occasionally overdid the sarcasm. "Well, are you?"

"Of course not."

"There you have it," she said, swirling her hands.

"But since when do you care about whether I'm interested or not?" My mom had once tricked me into attending a talk on the benefits of colonics. I definitely wasn't interested in that one.

"Darling," she said, throwing her hands about some more. "You're the one always saying I should respect your boundaries."

"But every time I say that, you say, *That's just your fear talking, Erica.*" I shook my fist in the air. *"Break down those walls!"*

"I do not."

"You do t— You know what? I've gotta go." I shoved my phone into my back pocket. This was just too weird, and, apparently I was off to deliver maid-of-honor condolences. It . . . was a lot of *morning* to take all in one shot. "Have you finished that list of supplies you wanted me to pick up?"

"Not yet. I probably won't get to it until tomorrow, but you'll help me get the cabins ready later?"

"Don't worry, Mom. I'll be there . . . or here." I shook my head. "Then . . . not now. When I get back I mean."

She shot me a concerned look.

"I'm just going to stop talking until I get some coffee."

"Do you think we should have brought something?"

I was standing on the edge of Candace's property by the dock. I adjusted the little French bulldog in my arms so that I could take the goggles from his face. Stanley was Freddie's dog, and he took him almost everywhere. Freddie said it was because if he left him alone for too long he'd pee everywhere, but really it was because Stanley was his baby.

"Like what?"

I watched him drop the anchor at the back of his boat, *Lightning*. It was so big, it needed the extra stability or it might drift off with Candace's dock attached to it. On the bright side, Freddie had gotten us here in just under fifteen minutes. The roar of the engine would have woken the entire town by now, but at least he didn't have the sound system going.

"I don't know, like flowers or . . . Oh! A casserole. That's what people do."

Freddie stopped what he was doing to look at me.

"You know, because grieving people can't feed themselves?"

"When would we have found time to make a casserole?"

"I don't know. I just feel weird showing up empty-handed."

"And you couldn't have thought of this before we got here?"

"I'm sorry. I—"

"Don't worry. It's fine," Freddie said, getting back to securing the boat. "Worse comes to worst, I'll order them a pizza or something."

"A pizza?"

"Pizza makes everyone feel better, Erica. Sometimes you have to think outside of the box."

Nope, Freddie's mood had not improved from the night before. In fact, if anything he seemed even more down. He had barely spoken the entire boat ride over. I had racked my brain trying to think of something *I* might have done to upset him, but everything had been great between us. I mean, sure we spent most of our waking hours together—which might be a lot for some people, but for us it was usually pretty fun times. We were like some classic buddy duo. Like . . . like Harold and Kumar . . . or Eddie Murphy and the blond guy in that cop film I'd never seen . . . or Abbott and Costello . . . didn't really know much about them either. But, you know, like that.

"Freddie, are you sure you're okay?"

"Yup," he said, walking over to me and stooping to clip a leash on Stanley. The old pup was already half asleep in the sun. He then picked him up and headed for the path that led to the cottage.

"Well, okay then."

I followed Freddie up the path that led to the cottage. Candace had been renting the place for over a year now. The owners had pretty much moved to Florida, but weren't quite ready to sell. The cottage was tucked back into the woods. It was a cute little place. You couldn't even see it from the water, so it had lots of privacy.

"So is Sean still coming down even though the wedding's . . . off?" I mean, I was assuming it was off.

Sean and Freddie had been in a long-distance relationship for the last six months. They had met on New Year's, and things had been going really well despite the distance. Like really, really well. Like so well, they were going to have to find a way to shorten the distance between them kind of well.

"Bean . . . Sean was never coming to the wedding."

"What? Why not?"

"I didn't invite him."

"You didn't invite him? Why wouldn't you—"

"He's got exams this week." Sean was in medical school. "I just didn't want him to feel like he had to come."

"Oh." I pushed my bangs back from my eyes. "So is everything all right between you t—"

"Why are you asking so many questions?" Freddie said, whirling around.

"I . . . don't know," I said carefully. I mean, of course I knew. I was trying to figure out what had turned Freddie into such a scary, scary man, but given that he was acting like such a scary, scary man, bringing it up seemed unwise.

"Oh, stop looking like a scared little animal. You know you're my favorite. I'm just having an off day. All this stuff with Lyssa," he said, turning back around to resume his walk.

Sure . . . except that didn't explain last night.

We walked a few more steps before I asked, "So what exactly did Joey say happened again?"

"Just that it was accidental."

I frowned. I thought it was kind of weird that Joey had wanted us to come over. I would have thought Candace would want to be with her family right now. It made me wonder if there wasn't something more to Lyssa's death.

"Hey," I called out to Freddie just before he made the clearing. "If it comes up, we should probably offer Candace Otter Lake Security's services if, you know, she has any questions about Lyssa's death."

Freddie didn't turn. "I guess."

"You guess?" I called after him. "You love this sort of thing."

He stopped walking.

"Okay, that sounded bad. I know you don't love people accidentally dying. You just love being in the thick of things."

"Whatever." He shot a look over his shoulder. "Just remember, *pro bono is a no-no.*"

Freddie had insisted *pro bono is a no-no* be our number one rule at Otter Lake Security. It hadn't taken much for Rhonda and me to agree. We had once spent the majority of a day looking for Mr. Coulter's glasses. He was convinced he had dropped them in the woods behind his house. They were on top of his TV. All we got for our trouble was a piece of apple pie. It was good pie though.

"Well, yeah, but we could make an exception just this once."

"It always starts with just one exception and then—" Freddie cut himself off and cocked his head.

I heard it too. Voices.

"It's a sign, Joey."

"It's not a sign."

"It is. You just don't want to see it."

It was hard to tell with all the trees, but I thought I could make out Antonia, Joey's sister, standing on the lawn. I couldn't see Joey though. "And would you please just come down from there, so we can talk."

"No, Candace has wanted this weather vane up on the roof for months now."

"So why do you have to put it up today?"

"Because it's the one thing I can do for her that will maybe cheer her up."

Freddie and I took a couple of steps forward, so we could get a better view. It was hard to say why we were creeping, but . . . Antonia sounded angry, so I guess we were eavesdropping. We had a bad habit of doing that.

"Hey, maybe we should . . ." I jerked my head back toward the boat.

"Joey asked us to come, remember?" Freddie whispered. "We'll just wait for an appropriate moment to interrupt."

"But—"

"I'm not going all the way back to the boat."

I rubbed a hand over my face.

"Joey . . ." Antonia pleaded.

"Keep your voice down," he said. "Candace will hear you. We can talk about this later."

"I don't want to talk about this later. And I don't care if *Candy* hears it."

Freddie and I exchanged looks. I did not like how she said Candace's name at all.

"Toni, you're my baby sister, and I love you," Joey said. "But you're killing me here. Enough."

"No, it's not enough." Uh-oh, Antonia's tone had turned ugly. "You need to listen to me. She is not right for you. You need to call off this wedding before it's too late."

Just then we heard a thump—

I grabbed Freddie's arm.

—and the sound of something tumbling off the roof?!

"Joey!"

Chapter Three

Freddie and I ran out onto the lawn to see Antonia crouched by Joey lying tangled up in a bed of ferns.

"Joey! Are you okay?" I yelled as Freddie and I ran over, Stanley clutched in his arms.

"I'm fine. I'm fine," Joey said, holding up a hand. "Hey guys."

"What were you doing up there?" Freddie asked.

"I just wanted to get that weather vane up," Joey said, pointing to a giant rusted steel chicken that had impaled itself with its north arrow deep into the earth. It was still vibrating from the impact.

"You could have died," Antonia said, voice catching.

He ruffled her hair. "Nah, don't you worry. Take more than that to get rid of me, kid."

"Silver bullet," I whispered, elbowing Freddie in the ribs.

He didn't react.

"You know, because you're always saying that Joey

looks like a werewolf . . . and silver bullets kill were-wolves?"

"A woman has died, Erica."

My jaw dropped. Did he just . . . *dead shame* me? Now I *knew* something was wrong. We were each other's safe places. If Freddie and I couldn't even make inside werewolf jokes at the most inappropriate times . . . well, I didn't know who we were.

Joey untangled himself from the foliage and hauled himself to his feet. "Thanks for coming," he said to Freddie and me.

"No problem, but are you sure you're okay?" I asked, looking him over.

"Maybe we should take you to the hospital," Antonia said. "Get you checked out."

"I'm fine. Really," Joey said, making eye contact with all of us in turn. "It's Candace we need to be worried about. I . . . I don't know what to do to make this better."

"Don't worry. We're here to help," Freddie said. "What do you guys like on your pizza?"

Joey and Antonia both shot him a look of confusion.

"Maybe later," Freddie said quickly. "So where's Candace at?"

Joey looked back at the cottage. "Inside. She's really upset. I mean . . . of course she's upset." He shook his head and climbed the steps to the front door. "This was not how this day was supposed to go."

"Are her parents here?"

Joey stiffened. "I think maybe I should let Candace tell you about that."

Antonia followed him. As she passed me, I could

have sworn I heard her mutter, "She didn't even come outside to see what happened."

Joey shot her a warning look before opening the door for us to step inside. "Have you guys met my sister, Toni?" he said, waving a hand at the young woman who had also pushed past him and dropped onto the couch. She looked like she was about to angry-cry again.

"We haven't actually spoken," I said. "It's nice to meet you. Too bad about the . . . circumstances."

She tried to give me an acknowledging smile. I think. It was hard to tell. It could have been a "I hate this town and everybody in it" smile too.

"I'll, uh, take you to Candace," Joey said.

"Wait," Antonia snapped, popping up. "Where's Nonna?"

Joey stiffened again and looked around the room.

"Nonna?" I asked, looking too. "She's here?" I don't know where I thought she would be. Still at the bar maybe?

"She wanders," Joey said quickly. "She was sitting in here when we went outsi—"

"There she is," Antonia said, pointing out the window.

I looked and there was the same woman I had seen last night shuffling across the back lawn . . . waving an umbrella at a squirrel? In fairness, the squirrel looked like a jerk. It was standing on its hind legs chittering pretty loudly—just out of the umbrella's reach.

"She's a really sweet woman," Joey said, as she made another swipe for the squirrel. "She's just got a thing about tree rats."

"Tree rats?" I asked.

"It's what she calls them. I'd better—"

"Candace is in the bedroom?" I asked. We'd been over enough to know the way.

He nodded.

"You go ahead. We'll just . . ." I pointed to the back.

Candace's rental cottage was decorated to match her personality perfectly. There was lots of yellow and sky blue everywhere and it had a sunflower motif carried room to room. It also smelled vaguely of cupcakes. Candace liked to bake—which was probably some of the reason why we liked to visit so much. Well, that, and, you know, Candace was a really nice person.

I knocked lightly at the bedroom door before peeking my head in. "Candace?"

Oh boy. I had seen Candace cry before. New Year's. It was a big, messy, ugly drunken cry. I was kind of expecting the same thing today, but this was much, much worse. There she was sitting up in bed looking kind of like a bunny . . . whose puppy just got run over by a truck. If that made any sense. Probably not. But she was both adorable and sad. Killer combination. She wasn't crying at the moment, but was right on the cusp of that tear-filled eyes and trembling-lip cry. She had her curly blond hair piled up in a messy bun on the top of her head and was wearing flannel pajamas. Her nose and eyes were bright, bright red. I gathered she hadn't heard us come in—or heard Joey tumble off the roof—because of the earphones she was wearing, but she spotted me now.

The sight of Candace had me tempted to call my mother. This type of situation was right in her comfort zone. I could see it now. She would probably rush right over to the bed, pull Candace onto her lap, and rock her like a baby while smoothing back her hair. That's what Candace looked like she needed. I just wasn't made that way. I think my mother rocked it all out of me.

I sat on the edge of the bed and patted her shin through the quilt she had over her. "Candace? Freddie and I are here."

"She's sad, not blind from a fever," Freddie snapped before tagging on a, "Hey." He then put Stanley on her bed.

"Thanks for coming, guys," she said. "You didn't have to do that."

"Of course we did. How are you doing?"

She shook her head and fresh tears rolled down her cheeks. "I just don't understand any of this."

I grabbed a tissue from the nightstand and started dabbing her face before I realized it was probably best to just let her do it. She was blinking like I had poked her in the eye. "Do you know what happened? To Lyssa, I mean?"

"Not really. It doesn't make any sense. Amos came by from the sheriff's department this morning." Candace looked at me with teary confused eyes. "They think that maybe she went swimming. She had had a lot to drink. She may have gone out too far and . . ."

I didn't know what to say. I looked to Freddie for help, but he was scrutinizing a kitten figurine he had picked up from Candace's dresser.

"It's my fault. I rented them a place on the water," she went on. "I lost track of her for a bit, so I texted her. She said they were headed there. I should have made sure. I just thought . . ."

I patted her leg again. "It's not your fault."

Freddie didn't look over but he asked, "Who's 'them'?"

"Sorry?" Candace asked.

"You said you rented *them* a place. Who's them?"

"Lyssa and her boyfriend, Justin. When she got here, she said they had broken up." Her face twitched all over with the effort of trying to hold back fresh tears. "She really likes . . . liked him, but thought maybe he was too young. Apparently he just showed up in town during the party and texted her. She said she needed to talk to him. She threw her hands in the air. "I don't know where he is now. Where he lives. Anything." She shook her head. "I need to tell him, right?"

"I'm sure the sheriff's department is looking for him. Don't worry about that right now." I patted her leg some more. Just in a slightly different spot. I didn't want to leave a bruise.

"Are they sure what happened to Lyssa was accidental?" Freddie asked.

"What . . . else could it have been?" A look of horror spread across Candace's face. "You don't mean—"

"Nice work, sport," I hissed at Freddie before turning back to Candace. "No, he doesn't mean anything. Ignore him." Thankfully, Freddie was back to ignoring us too. He was flipping through a binder of some sort on Candace's dresser. A big white binder. I mean, I kind of wanted an answer to that question too, but I knew better than to just ask it. Besides, given our history, Freddie and I always had murder on the brain. But this had to have been be an accident. The alternative was just too grim.

Lyssa was just so full of life. To think that maybe someone . . .

No. Just . . . no.

"They were able to identify her with all the pictures from the party last night, so I don't have to"—Candace swallowed hard—"see her. She doesn't have any family really." She pressed the tissue to her eyes. "I should have gone to find her. And why would she go swimming?"

"I don't know," I said, shaking my head. But I could find out. Or at least try. "If you want, Freddie and I could go over to the sheriff's department and—"

Freddie cleared his throat, but I ignored him. A new thought had suddenly occurred to me. "Wait, you said earlier that Amos came by? You mean, Grady didn't come himself?"

She shook her head. "I wish he had. I mean I know with our history . . ." Again, Grady and Candace had dated during one of Grady's and my *off* periods—a nine-month period—which was longer than all of our *on* periods put together, but that was all ancient history. "Amos is just so sweet, but I tried to ask him some questions and . . . well, I'd like to hear Grady's take, you know?"

Freddie and I exchanged looks. We did know. That was weird. Sheriffs of small towns were usually raised better than to not show up personally when someone has died.

"What about the wedding?" Freddie suddenly asked. "Where does everything stand?"

Candace's hands flopped from her lap onto the bed. "I don't even know where to start. Obviously, we can't get married today. Joey's already called the guests. But there's so much more to do. And every time I try to start, I just think about Lyssa and . . ." Her breath hitched.

"You two were pretty close, huh?" I said gently.

Candace sniffled back something and looked up at me with red-rimmed eyes. "I feel horrible for saying this, but no . . . I mean, not exactly."

"I just assumed because she's your—was your maid of honor that—"

"She just called me out of the blue not too long ago wanting to visit. We got talking about the wedding and she just kind of took over just like she always used to do back when we were roommates in college. It didn't seem like a bad idea. I didn't really have anyone else I felt comfortable asking."

"Oh," I said with a nod. I was willing to bet the expression on my face was the resting nauseous one Freddie and Rhonda had been talking about at the party.

"And now she's dead." She didn't say it was her fault, but the look in her eye told me it was what she believed. This was bad. Not only was Candace's big day ruined, but she blamed herself for Lyssa's tragic death. We were going to need reinforcements.

"Do you want us to get your parents? Are they staying in town?"

"They were supposed to fly in today."

"Today?" I couldn't keep the surprise from my voice. "That's cutting it close."

"They're not exactly fans of . . ." She picked at the quilt covering her lap. "I called to tell them about Lyssa, and . . . then that whole conversation just turned into a big fight."

"What? Why?"

"The same reason Joey's sister thinks we shouldn't get married." After walking around the bed a bit, Stanley dropped himself by Candace's hip. She gave his head a scratch. "It's too soon."

"I bet the ex-con bit doesn't help either," Freddie said.

I looked over at him again. He was very lucky he was just out of striking distance.

"They want me to postpone the wedding by a couple of months, but they know I can't do that."

"Why not?"

"Joey's nonna," Candace said.

"The woman taking on that squirrel out back?"

Candace forced a smile. "It's the only thing Joey really wanted for the wedding. For his grandmother to be there, remembering who he is. She has dementia and heart problems, so she's leaving to live with Joey's aunt in Italy. We don't know how much time she has left. I don't know, maybe we'll just have to do a courthouse wedding—"

Freddie gasped.

"I know," Candace said, bursting into tears. "It's awful, isn't it? But I don't know what other choice we have." Oh boy, she was really sobbing now.

"Please," Freddie said. "Please don't do that."

"I'm sorry," Candace said, waving her tissue in the air. "I'm so sorry. I don't mean to cry like this."

"It's okay." I suddenly found myself patting Candace all over. Legs, arms, shoulders, head . . . like I could pat her back together again. What was Joey thinking, inviting Freddie and me over? We were both really terrible at giving sympathy.

"But you know," Candace said in the unnaturally high squeaky voice. "This isn't about me."

"You're the bride. Everything is about you," Freddie muttered and went back to flipping through the binder. Suddenly, I felt alarm bells go off deep in my consciousness, but I didn't quite know why—

"It's about poor Lyssa. How could I even think about getting married? And Joey and I have had such a fairy-tale relationship. We have been so blessed. I have so much to be thankful—"

"You have no idea how much you're going to be thankful for," Freddie further muttered.

Both Candace and I gave Freddie strange looks that time, but he was still absorbed in the binder.

"Really," Candace, said, dragging her eyes away from Freddie. "It's times like these that you need to count your blessings. The only tears shed today should be for Lyssa, not for my wedding."

"Right you are," Freddie said, snapping the binder shut.

"Um, sorry?" I asked. "I think it's okay if Candace feels a little sorry for herself."

"Not anymore."

"What are you talking about, Freddie?" Candace asked.

"I'm saying you don't have to cry about the wedding anymore," Freddie said. "It will be fabulous. Erica and I will take care of the whole thing."

"We . . . will?"

"We've got everything we need right here," he said, tapping the front cover. "It will be magical and beautiful and romantic and all that other crap. How does a month from now sound?"

"Oh Freddie, you are so sweet," Candace said, crying even harder at his generosity. "But I couldn't ask you to do that. Besides, Nonna's leaving in just over two weeks, and I'm not sure I can even think about the wedding right now."

"You don't have to think about the wedding. Didn't I just say that?" Freddie asked me of all people. *I didn't know!* I was busy reeling. "Two weeks, that's not much time. But doable. I assume you already have your own glass slippers?"

What . . . what was happening here? I was pretty sure he knew nothing about planning a wedding. Or replanning . . . or rescheduling . . . whatever! In fact, when Candace announced she was getting married a couple of months ago, Freddie had gone on about the fact that she'd better not ask him to plan it. That it was such a gay-man stereotype—I inwardly gasped. Of course! He was just covering for the fact that he'd really wanted to plan the wedding all along! It made perfect sense. Freddie loved telling people what to do and dressing up. He was a wedding planner at heart. He probably wanted to do the bachelorette party too! That's why he hated it so much. He probably planned this whole th— Okay, that was going too far. I didn't think he orchestrated Lyssa's death. I was getting carried away. "Freddie," I hissed, jumping to my feet, "what are you doing?"

"Erica's right, Freddie. You are such a sweetheart," Candace went on, "but there's too much involved. It can't be done."

Freddie's eyes widened. "Can't be done?"

Oh God, by making it a challenge, she was just making it worse. "Excuse us for just a second," I said back to Candace with what I hoped was a reassuring smile then straight-armed Freddie to the other side of the room. "What exactly do you think you are doing?"

"It's not a big deal."

"Freddie, weddings are a big deal. A very big deal. Especially to people like Candace who started their wedding binders back in high school," I said through my teeth. God, the binder was huge. I don't think I put that much effort into, well, anything. I once started a vision board, but I couldn't decide on the color of background I wanted, and it all just fell apart from there. "You don't know anything about planning a wedding. I certainly don't know anything about planning a wedding."

"Listen. I know you have issues with weddings—"

"I do not have issues with weddings!" I shout-whispered.

"But it's just a party," Freddie said. "A party she was planning to have at the town gazebo. Her vendors are mainly local. We can get them to postpone. The hard work is already done. It'll be a piece of cake." A smile touched the corner of his mouth. "Wedding cake. Get it?" Oh sure, now he was in a better mood.

I scowled at him. "This is the most important day of Candace's life. We cannot screw it up."

"Of course we're not going to screw it up. That's why we're doing this, because what *will* screw it up is a dead nonna attending the ceremony."

"I . . . I don't think that would happen."

"You know what I mean. Besides," he said under his breath, "someone in this cursed town should be happy and in love."

What the heck was that supposed to mean?

"And look at her," Freddie hissed, waving a hand at Candace. "Does she look happy and in love to you?"

Candace sniffed. "Guys, you are so sweet, but . . ." *And* she was crying again.

"She needs us, Erica."

"Really," Candace called out through her tears, "I couldn't ask you to do this."

This was not happening.

This couldn't be happening.

How was this happening?

I swallowed hard and faced Candace. "You're not asking," I said, forcing what I hoped was a convincing smile to my face. "We're offering."

"Oh Erica . . ."

"Nope," Freddie said, holding his stop hand up. "No more crying. You're going to need to pace yourself with all those tears. Save some for the wedding of your dreams."

"But . . . what about Lyssa?"

"Lycra—I mean Lyssa—would want you to be happy," Freddie said with a smile.

"But I don't think I could . . . I mean, until I know what happened . . ."

"No problem. It's like Erica said. We'll do that too. Pro bono," he said, shooting me a look.

I struggled to keep my face neutral. Offering our services to look into Lyssa's death was so not the same thing as offering our services to take over the wedding. We were way better at handling death than we were at handling love.

"Do you really think it's possible?" Candace asked. "Erica?"

I looked back and forth between Freddie's unreadable face and Candace's devastated one now with just a little bit of hope.

"I . . . uh . . . guess we can." I said, making extra sure I was nodding my head up and down and not shaking it side to side. "Yup. We'll do it. Will plan the wedding and find out what happened to Lyssa. No problem."

Chapter Four

I could totally do this.

I just needed to sit down somewhere nice and quiet and make a list.

Number one on the list?

Kill Freddie.

I mean, what was he thinking?

He wasn't thinking. That was the truth of it. It wasn't that I didn't want to help Candace. I did. She was my friend. And as Candace's friend, I would recommend not putting Freddie and me in charge of her wedding. Again, the investigation was one thing. We had looked into deaths before, and likely this was just a tragic case of death by misadventure. But the wedding . . .

Freddie had taken full advantage of my state of shock on the way out of Candace's, and we had divvied up the preliminary tasks before he'd dropped me back at the retreat. He was supposed to get in touch with as many of the guests as possible to see if they could come in two weeks then call the town offices and find out if the gazebo was still available. I was supposed to call the DJ, cake baker, and florist to see where we were at. We'd figure out the rest after that.

I sighed and plopped myself down at the picnic table under the shade of trees. A couple of crows squawked at me. I guess this was their picnic table. Well, they could just, "Bite me," I called up to the trees.

I ran a hand over the front of Candace's binder. Okay. Again, I could do this.

Really, this was all part of being friends with Freddie. He was unpredictable. I knew that. And he apparently also liked to keep secrets about things that were bothering him. Yeah, I still wasn't over that either. But, again, at least he was in a better mood. Too bad I was in a much, much worse one.

And what was that whole *somebody in this town should be happy and in love* thing? I really, really hoped something hadn't happened between him and Sean. It would explain a lot, but . . . they were good together.

I sighed.

I couldn't help but think inviting me to get involved in wedding planning was a little like asking a goldfish to do the tango. I mean, I had grown up at a feminist retreat. I seem to recall my mother referring to marriage as state-sanctioned slavery at some point. What did I know about . . . about . . . those little pillows that you tie the rings on to? Did people actually do that at weddings? Use those little pillows? For the ring bearers? Was that a thing? I didn't know. I didn't know anything about weddings!

But, again, it was time to rally. I didn't have time to explore my feelings about weddings. I was suddenly very busy.

I took a deep breath.

I just needed to make some phone calls. Being the small town Otter Lake was, everyone would surely be willing to help Candace out.

I opened the binder and flipped to the first tab as a cicada buzzed in the tree above me. Mrs. Roy. Check. The florist. That seemed like good place to start. I mean, I knew Mrs. Roy. She was a bit of a rambler, but a sweet lady. She wouldn't have a problem postponing two weeks. Sure, there might be some financial considerations, like an added fee or something, but— no, this was Otter Lake. Candace was one of us. We could make this happen.

I pulled out my phone and dialed the number in the binder.

"Pansies and Posies."

"Hi, Mrs. Roy, it's, uh, Erica Bloom calling. How are you?"

"I'm lovely, dear, but I've just heard the news about Candace's maid of honor." Of course she had. It had been a few hours now. The whole town would know. The ladies' society was probably already working on a needlepoint commemorative pillow. "It's awful. Just horrible. I bet you're calling to sort out the flowers."

I felt my shoulders drop in relief. Mrs. Roy had gotten straight to the point. Maybe this wouldn't be so bad. "I am."

"Of course, dear. I'll help any way I can."

"Great. That is so good to hear. I was worried—"

"But first," Mrs. Roy said. "Tell me, Erica, is she really . . . dead? The maid of honor, I mean?"

Okay, I guess we were taking one little tangent on our way over to the point, but that was to be expected. "Yes, unfortunately. She—"

"I just wanted to be sure. Everybody is so upset, but it seemed so unlikely her being thrown from a horse like that."

"Horse?" I frowned. "Oh. No. I mean, there was a mechanical bull at the bachelorette party, but that's not what happened."

"Are you sure? I heard that she went flying off and slammed right into the jukebox. Snapped her neck."

"Nope. Nope. I think that was me you heard about actually. Minus the snapped neck."

"Oh, that makes more sense."

I blinked a few times. "Right." I took another breath. "So about the flowers for the wedding—"

"But wait, it doesn't make any sense then. If she didn't fall off the horse, how did she die? Was it the polly?"

"The polly?" I scratched my temple. "Wait . . . do you mean molly? The drug?"

"Yes, but I don't like to call it molly. I know it sounds silly, but I had a cousin named Molly. Lovely woman, Molly. It just wouldn't feel right."

I clutched my head. "I understand. But it wasn't—"

"It's such a waste."

"You mean . . . the death?"

"Well, I meant the name, but that's awful too. Drugs take too many young people. You shouldn't go into the city."

"Okay," I said slowly before blurting out, "but it wasn't drugs. I think she might have drowned."

"Drowned? That's awful. How did she drown? Oh," she said with the sound of lots of realization dawning. "Alcohol must have been involved. I've been to a bachelorette party or two in my time. I know what goes on."

I planted my elbow on the picnic table and dropped my forehead against my palm. This . . . this had to be what having a stroke felt like. "I really don't know. Now about the flowers—"

"Are they sure Tommy wasn't involved?"

I jerked up. "Tommy? Tommy Forrester?" Grady's cousin. "Why . . . why would anyone think that?"

"Oh, I just heard they were cozying up toward the end of the night."

"Really?" That must have been after I left. "Is your source legit?" Otter Lake had a thriving rumor mill, but while output was plentiful, quality was questionable. I mean, look how they had mangled Lyssa's cause of death. Maybe they had somehow mistaken Tommy for Lyssa's boyfriend, Justin.

"Margot has all the best information, dear. And you know that Tommy's never been quite right in the head since you tried to implicate him in Dickie Morrison's murder."

"Tried to implicate him? I did no such thing. He—"

"Well, however it happened, he hasn't been quite right since then."

Tommy had been involved in some shady business when I had first come back to town a couple of years ago. A rogue employee of MRG Properties had paid him and his buddies to cause trouble around town to help encourage some of the more reticent seniors to sell their properties. It hadn't amounted to much more than minor vandalism and noise violations, but the scheme blew up in their faces. Everybody around town ended up knowing what Tommy had done, and right around the same time one of his closest friends was murdered. The whole thing had left him a little messed up. Rumor had it the only time he left his home was to go to the Dawg. To drink. Alone. It was sad. I mean, Tommy had always been a bit of a douchebag, but—

"Plus I heard Amos found a condom at the scene."

"What?" I near whimpered.

"Oh yes, took it away in one of those little baggies."

"I—"

"I thought you'd already know that. Are they doing a postmortem?"

"I'm . . . not sure . . ." *Why would I know that?* was the rest of that sentence.

"I thought Sheriff Forrester might have told you. Nobody can really tell if you're on again or off again."

"We're off and—"

"And rumor has it Freddie has found a way to hack into the department's computer system."

"What?! That's ridiculous." Please, God, let it be true that that was ridiculous.

"Well, I just thought I'd ask."

I closed my eyes and took a steadying breath. "Now about the flowers for the wedding, I see that Candace ordered white peonies—"

"That's right. They're just beautiful."

Finally . . . *finally,* we were getting to the flowers.

"Well, the wedding is being pushed back two weeks and—"

"And all the peonies will be dead."

"What?"

"Well, maybe not completely dead. But brown and limp."

"All the peonies in the world will be dead?"

"No," she said with a chuckle. "Just all the ones from my gardens, and the ones I ordered."

"Well, can't we order some more or—"

"On such short notice? In that quantity? Oh no. Why are those two in such a hurry to get married anyway? They've only known each other for six months, and two weeks seems a little inappropriate given that a member of the wedding party has died."

"Joey's nonna's not well and—"

"Oh, I see. That makes sense. And, you know, on second thought, maybe it's a good thing. Candace and Joey are such a sweet couple, and the town needs something to celebrate. It seems like it's just been murder after murder ever since . . . well, I guess since the time you came back to town."

"I . . . I . . ."

"This town needs a win."

"Right. Well, it won't be much of a win without—"

"Carmen!" Mrs. Roy snapped.

Carmen? I looked up at the trees. The crows sitting up there didn't seem to know who Carmen was either.

"Carmen! You walk away. Those cupcakes are not for you."

I blinked. Oh, that's right. Mrs. Roy had a hound dog named Carmen.

"Sorry, dear. *Carmen!* It's really sweet of you to help, but—*Carmen!* I love this dog to bits, but she is going to be the— *I see you thinking it. Don't you think it.*"

"Mrs. Roy?"

I could hear Carmen howling in the background.

"Erica, I have to let you g— *Don't you make me get up!*"

"But what about the flowers? A wedding needs flowers."

"Don't worry. We'll figure something out. Oh! You know, I've been meaning to experiment with tree-branch bouquets and—"

"Tree-branch bouquets?"

"Come by and we'll talk. That's the lovely thing about nature. No time is a bad time to create something beautiful! I'll text you. *Oh, now I'm on my feet. You're only getting one treat now. Not two. That's what happens when you don't listen to Mommy.*"

Click.

I thunked my forehead onto the picnic table.

It's just a party, he had said.

The hard work is already done.

It'll be a piece a cake.

Killing Freddie was moving right back up the list.

Chapter Five

"It's murder."

"Rhonda?" I rubbed my hand roughly over my face. I really needed to stop waking up like this. Correction, other people really needed to stop waking me up like this at—I cracked one eye open and peered at my clock—six in the morning. "What's going on?"

"Lyssa *was* murdered after all."

And here I had been thinking things couldn't get any worse. That must have been my mistake. The universe heard me thinking that yesterday and took it upon itself to show me who was boss.

I had gotten pretty much nowhere with the wedding planning. I couldn't get a hold of Vivienne—she was making the cake—and the DJ Candace had hired was booked solid for the next four months. I had spent the rest of the day buzzing around the retreat trying to get the cabins ready and directing the vegan caterers my mom had hired. A couple more guests had also arrived early.

And now there was this.

Murder.

All sorts of unpleasant emotions washed over me. I mean, yes, I didn't know Lyssa, but . . . murder? There had to be some sort of mistake.

"How do you know it was murder?"

"Freddie called me and told me."

"He what?"

"He called me and—"

"Yeah. Yeah. I got that," I said, squeezing my eyes shut tight. "Why didn't he just call me?"

"Don't know. I'm just the messenger."

Okay, that made zero sense. Zero. Even when we were annoyed with each other, Freddie and I were still joined at the hip. And by the sound of Rhonda's voice, I wasn't entirely convinced that she didn't know the answer to that question. "Rhonda—"

"Anyway, he wants you to meet him at the sheriff's department. You're going to tag-team Amos for some answers. I obviously can't do it. I've got to get out to the site for the insurance job. You're still bringing me lunch today, right?"

"Yes, but—"

"And don't be too hard on Amos. He's such a sweetheart."

"I know. But Rh—"

"Got to go. Bye!"

I let out a grunt of frustration and dropped my phone from my ear. What was going on here? Since when had I become the third wheel? Not that Rhonda was the third wheel . . . but yeah, she kind of was because Freddie and I were best friends first. I mean, I could have accepted being a threesome of best fr— Actually, no, that sounded wrong, but the point was still valid.

I hauled myself out of bed. I needed to get going. And not because I was at Freddie's beck and call, but I really wanted to know what had happened to Lyssa too. Not just for my curiosity, but for Candace. She needed answers.

I pulled on some clothes and tiptoed down the hall. I didn't want to wake my mother. She needed her sleep. I stopped in the kitchen to write her a quick note saying I'd be back asap then headed for the door. I could get some coffee at the Dawg before I made my way to the sheriff's department.

I opened the big wooden door to the lodge, slowly and carefully. It was the screen door that led outside that was going to be the problem though. It always made this screeching sound when the spring stretched. I opened it as slowly as I could and eased my way onto the porch. I then turned and carefully guided it back into place so it didn't make its signature *bang!*

Made it.

I turned. Now, all I needed to do was—

"Holy, fricking . . . Zaki!"

Man. Zaki.

I mean, man—guessing it was Zaki—just sitting on the porch.

It had to be the best-selling guru author we had been expecting. He was wearing a relaxed black T-shirt and jeans and was sitting on what I was guessing was a meditation mat. Those seemed like self-help guru-type identifiers. He also had a really nice watch. That was probably the best-selling part.

Totally hadn't seen him at all.

"Good morning," he said with a smile.

"Good morning," I said, shaking my hands out. They had been balled into fists probably because I had just done a jerky sort of shadow-boxing dance on the spot. "You . . . you must be *Zaki*!" I fake-yelled his name in intimation of my earlier exclamation then chuckled awkwardly.

He smiled. "My apologies. I didn't mean to startle you."

I smiled back. Best I could. I was very startled. "Why are you . . . ? I mean, I'm so sorry you've been sitting out here. We didn't realize—"

"My flight was early. It is such a peaceful morning. I didn't want to wake anyone."

I nodded. I couldn't help but wonder how he had gotten over to the island. Either Red had been up early or Zaki was a good swimmer. He had the build for it.

"You must be Erica, the ever-powerful and honor-able ruler. I've been looking forward to meeting you."

I blinked. "I am? You are?"

He laughed. It was a nice sound. It went with his nice face. He looked a little like a middle-aged Indian George Clooney. "The meaning of your name. It is a hobby of mine. I often look up the meanings of people's names before I meet them. Helps me to remember."

"Right," I said with a slow nod. "Cool."

"You seem to be headed out. Is that the case? Or would you care to join me?" He gestured to a free mat by the wall. "I was about to meditate."

I waved a hand out. "Thanks, but meditation isn't exactly my thing. I've always had a monkey brain, you know," I said, hopping my fingers around in the air. "I can't stop my mind from jumping around."

He laughed again, and I swear the birds stopped singing to listen to the sound. "Well, the practice of meditation has been known to help with that."

"Guru sarcasm," I said with a slow nod and a smile. "Nice."

His eyes twinkled. Actually twinkled. Like he could do it on command.

"Thank you for the offer and—and I'm sorry to, uh, scream and run—but I do have to get going," I said, hurrying down the first couple of steps.

"Enjoy."

I stopped. "Well," I said, hopping back up the steps. "Thank you, again, but I wouldn't describe this as the type of day one would enjoy." I wasn't quite sure why I had taken the time to clarify that.

"Would you like to talk about it?" Zaki asked, gesturing toward the mat.

"Oh no, no, no," I said, waving a hand in the air and trotting back down the steps. But strangely, part of me did want to talk to him. He had a certain . . . charisma? Maybe all the best-selling types do. "I should really get going."

"Of course."

"Right," I said, nodding but not moving. "I'll be back though."

"Seeing as you live here."

I wagged a finger at him.

He smiled.

"Okay, bye."

"Good-bye, honorable Erica."

A minute or two later, I was gliding along the lake. It really was a beautiful day. I passed a couple of other boats, one with someone waterskiing. I didn't recognize any of the people, but shot them all a friendly wave anyway. They might be holiday renters—the summer season was just starting—or maybe new neighbors in one of the luxury homes MRG had built. Either way, life was too short not to be friendly—

—and bam, just like that I was picturing poor Lyssa riding that bull.

It just seemed impossible that she was gone.

I started replaying the night in my mind—I had been doing that a lot since I'd heard she was dead—trying to see if there was anything I missed. But nothing stood out. Lyssa had been so happy . . . and full of life. Again, I didn't know her, but I did envy the way she had just grabbed that bull by the horns. She didn't care what other people thought of her. She was just . . . free.

I sighed, then blinked and looked around the shoreline.

Um . . . where was I going?

In all my thinking about Lyssa, I hadn't been paying attention, and, for some reason or another, I seemed to be headed for Grady's house!

Stupid subconscious.

I didn't often drive by Grady's part of the lake. Didn't really have any reason to. Most of the time, I was only going back and forth between the island and town or Freddie's—and I didn't need to go by Grady's to get to either. So it would have looked pretty weird if I did go by there a lot—probably like I was stalking him or something. So even if I really wanted to know what he was up to, or say, just wanted to see his place because, I don't know, it made me feel closer to him or something ridiculous like that, I usually resisted. I mean, I didn't want to be weird to the outside world . . . even if things were really weird in my head.

But it was cool. There was no way he'd be home. With everything going on, he would have been at work at the crack of dawn—if he didn't sleep at the sheriff's department overnight, that is. So maybe just this once I could drive by . . . and if I just so happened to look over at his place, well, that was cool too.

Totally normal. Not at all sad.

And if I slowed down a little—which I totally was right now—well, that was just responsible. I had seen at least one snapping turtle near Grady's dock, and I didn't want to hurt any turtles, even if a snapping turtle would most likely hurt me given half a chance.

I slowed the boat just a little more as I got closer. Yup, still looked like Grady's place. No visible differences. Not sure what kind of difference I was expecting to see. A sign maybe that read ERICA, COME BACK TO ME? No, no, that would be weird. I mean, not so weird that I wouldn't do it, but still weird. I'd have to talk to him about it . . . after doing other things. Oh my God? What was wrong with me?

I gave my head a good shake then—

—uh-oh.

Was that Grady sitting on his porch?

Suntanning?

Grady didn't suntan. He had a lot of trouble with any activity that involved sitting still and, well, relaxing. But he looked very relaxed. Sunglasses on. Face tilted up at the sun.

That was very strange.

Why wasn't he at work?

I frowned. And you know what else was strange? He wasn't watching my boat go by. What kind of sheriff didn't stare suspiciously at every person who passed by just to keep an eye on things? Grady had always been on alert when we were together. Well, not that time he had visited me in Chicago, but . . .

Oh no.

What if he had a woman in there?

No. No. That didn't make sense. Why would he be sunning himself on the porch with a woman inside? Unless she was showering. Or making them a snack. Wine with, like, a little sampler tray of delicious things . . . like spicy cheese and fruit! Oh my God, I hate those chicks who know how to make sampler trays. Although it was a little early for wine and a sampler tray. What if she was making them coffee and eggs! I hated those women too. Well, technically, I was probably one of those women. Coffee and eggs wasn't a big deal, but . . . but I knew what I meant!

I gripped the steering wheel. This was why I shouldn't drive by Grady's. It was none of my business if he had some culinary-type woman inside. It wasn't even my concern if he was wearing sunscreen. I really hoped he was wearing sunscreen though. You didn't mess around with—

Wouldn't you know, just as I had the thought, I spotted him squirting some sunscreen on his chest and rubbing it all over his pecs and stomach, and even lower to—

Well, wasn't that just terrific.

Good luck getting that image out of my head anytime soon. Thanks a lot, Grad—

Just then a boat horn ripped through the air.

Crap!

I wrenched the wheel to the right. I had been heading straight for another boat. Anchored. People picnicking.

I waved a sorry hand in the air, but seriously, wasn't it a little early for a picnic too?

Now, what were the chances Grady hadn't opened his eyes for that?

I looked back at his cabin.

Zero.

Definitely zero. He was sitting up in his chair, staring directly at me by the looks of it.

I sighed.

Okay, well, the last thing I wanted to do was talk to Grady right now what with his chest all shiny and glistening—Freddie was right, he often pointed out that Grady's physical perfection was annoying—but I also didn't want him thinking I was just doing a drive-by like the weirdo I was.

I steered the boat toward his dock before slipping it into neutral.

Well, this was going to be awkward.

We hadn't actually spoken in a long time. I didn't include the five times he had said, "Erica," in his very formal greeting voice when we bumped into each other on the street.

As I said, after things had come to a head at New Year's, it was like we had both given up. For me, it felt like the more I wanted things to work, the worse I made everything, and I just couldn't do it anymore because every time I thought the pain couldn't possibly get worse, I discovered I was wrong. I had had to embrace a "some things are just not meant to be" outlook since then. I mean, wasn't it Einstein who said doing the same thing over and over again and expecting a different result was the definition of insanity? Well, I had been beating my head against the Grady wall for years now . . . and I probably had the brain damage to prove it.

I got out of my mother's boat and tied it off to Grady's dock. I could see out of the corner of my eye he was coming down from his porch to greet me . . . or maybe preemptively arrest me given that he had already probably guessed Freddie and I were looking into Lyssa's death. Wouldn't be the first time.

My heart thudded in my chest.

I couldn't move from my spot beside the boat on the dock.

Nope, I couldn't seem to even take a step.

He would have to come to me.

"Hey, Grady."

"Erica."

Chapter Six

"Were you . . . going swimming?" I asked.

"I was."

"Good. Good." Many moons ago, Grady used to swim by my mother's dock to see if I was there, but that memory was kind of *ouchie,* so best not to dwell on that.

We nodded at each other.

"So . . ." I said, swaying a little on the balls of my feet, "kind of thought you'd be at work." Dammit! I had totally just blown my "coming to see him" alibi for my creepy drive-by crime.

"Nope. Not at work."

"Right."

"You've probably already guessed why I'm here."

He raised his brow in question.

I frowned at him. "Candace's maid of honor drowned yesterday?"

He nodded. "Right. Right. I was really sorry to hear that."

"Yeah, Candace was sorry to hear it too. Especially from Amos." Okay, that felt a little like an unnecessary cheap shot, but that didn't stop my mouth from saying it.

Grady sighed. "Probably was pretty rough for Amos too, but it is part of the job."

I frowned at him. "Okay, what is going on here?"

"What do you mean?"

"A premature death happened in your town, less than forty-eight hours ago, and you're talking about it like . . . like it's some natural disaster halfway across the world."

He frowned. "No . . . I mean, I do feel terrible for Candace."

"But what about you?"

"You think I should feel bad for myself?"

"No, what about your responsibilities in this matter?"

"Oh," he said with a big nod. "I don't have any."

"You don't have any?"

"Not right now."

"Not right now?"

Even when we were standing two feet away from each other we had problems communicating.

"I'm on vacation."

"You . . . you don't go on vacation," I said, looking at him sideways. "Especially not when something like this has happened."

"Well, I've had it planned for a while, and—" Just then he leaned toward me, hand outstretched, fingers reaching for my temple. What was he doing? I couldn't let him touch me. Grady's touch had a powerful effect on me. I might start crying or declaring my undying love for him if he touched me. So before I could figure out what he was doing, or what I was doing, I swatted at his hand, stepped back, forgetting about the bit of rope lying behind me on the dock, and fell hard onto my butt. At least I didn't shout, *Who are you? And what have you done with my ex-boyfriend?*

"Erica!" he said, reaching a hand down to me. "Are you okay? There was just a deerfly and—"

I waved his hand away. "I'm fine."

"Are you sure?"

I popped to my feet. "Just bad . . . flip-flops."

He nodded. "Anyway, I wish I could help you out with the investigation—I'm guessing that's why you're here. But I'm off for the next two weeks. Sorry."

"Okay, seriously, what the hell?"

Grady's eyes widened, but the smile returned to his face. "What? I don't understand."

"You're sorry you can't help *me* with the investigation?"

"Well, OLS is a legitimate business now, and you have Rhonda working with you, so I guess . . . I trust you. Where is Freddie?" Grady said, looking behind me as though he might suddenly appear.

My jaw dropped.

"You trust us?" I repeated.

"Yeah, I guess I do," Grady said with a shrug.

"Liar," I near shouted. "Okay, what is really going on?"

Grady laughed some more. "Okay, look, I can see that you are a little surprised, so let's just say . . . I got some good advice not so long ago and I've decided to run with it."

"Advice."

"Yeah, advice. You know, I'm trying not to sweat the small stuff."

Okay, I wasn't exactly sure what to make of Grady's whole new attitude toward life, but I didn't exactly like how it made me feel. Grady and I hadn't stood this close to each other in a long, long time and here we were just behaving like perfectly neutral acquaintances. Okay, well, one neutral acquaintance, and one freaking-out acquaintance. Actually no, this Grady wasn't even an acquaintance. He was a brand-new person. Like a stranger. And while it wasn't like I was expecting him to fall to his knees overcome with emotion—well, okay, maybe I was hoping for that—and I certainly didn't want to fight, this whole *beige* thing we had going on was not pleasant. It was actually kind of painful.

"Murder," I suddenly said.

"Murder?" Grady asked.

Finally I had him repeating something *I* was saying.

"Murder is not small stuff."

"I didn't think the cause of death had been established yet," Grady said with a frown. Then he shrugged. Shrugged! "But your sources could be better than mine."

I scratched my forehead. "So let me get this straight, crime-fighting is on holiday because the sheriff's on vacation?"

"Amos can handle it with—"

I started laughing.

Grady didn't join me though.

My laugher died. "Oh, you're serious."

"You don't have to worry. Amos isn't alone. I've asked Sheriff Bigly from North Country to watch over this case."

"But . . . but what about Candace?" I asked. "You don't care at all about her?" Okay, some people might find that strange coming from my mouth because, you know, Candace and Grady dated, and Grady and I dated, but in my mind it made perfect sense. One because Candace was a really good person, and two, I would expect him to have a little more regard for his exes.

"Of course I care about Candace. I thought . . . didn't I just say that I felt bad for Candace?"

"Who cares how you feel."

Grady raised his eyebrows as a hint of a smirk came to his mouth.

"No, I just mean, don't you want to do something about it?"

"I can't fix all the world's problems."

"What world? I'm talking about Otter Lake!"

"Do you want to come in for a coffee?" Grady asked, jerking back a thumb.

I put a hand to my head. "No. I . . . I think I gotta go."

"Okay, well, good luck."

I shook my head side to side. "You need to stop saying stuff like that. You're really freaking me out."

"Sorry," he said, putting his hands up.

"Stop apologizing too," I said, getting into the boat and untying it from the dock.

"Okay, well, I guess I'll see you around," Grady called out. "Oh, and say hello to your mother."

Chapter Seven

"Amos, calm down, buddy. We're not here to cause any trouble."

The young deputy behind the desk shook his head. "I know why you're here, and I'm not supposed to talk to you. In training they taught us that the more you say the higher the risk of saying something you don't mean to, so it's better if you say nothing. Besides, Grady—I mean, Sheriff Forrester—has said several times—"

"Oh," Freddie said, raising his eyebrows politely. "Is Grady here? We'd be happy to speak with him if he has a moment."

He just shook his head.

Amos Brian had to be the cutest deputy of all time. He was in his mid-twenties, but he looked like he was about seventeen. Fresh-faced. Apple-cheeked . . . although right now those apples were on fire.

I had met up with Freddie just outside the sheriff's department. He didn't seem so much grumpy today as . . . distant, maybe? Before I even got the chance to tell him about Grady, he had rushed inside. I mean, *Say hello to your mother?* That was something that needed to be discussed in great detail.

"Is he coming in later?"

Amos shook his head again.

"Could you elaborate—oh," Freddie said, smiling and wagging a finger at him. "I see what you're doing. Just like you said, don't want to say anything you shouldn't. Clever. Isn't he doing a clever thing, Erica?"

"Totally clever." I felt bad for Amos. He tried so hard. But we needed to help Candace. And the town. We all needed answers. "Otter Lake is really lucky to have you."

He blushed harder. "Whenever you two walk in the door, I feel like I'm going to be sick."

Freddie and I exchanged looks. Not exactly the way I wanted to be thought of, but I guess it came with the job.

"Amos, it's okay. Look, we'll leave you alone. Nobody wants to get you in trouble. And I for one think it's totally unfair that Grady's off . . . what? Picking up coffee? Leaving you to answer all the questions about . . . what happened last night."

"Oh, he's not picking up coffee."

Freddie raised an eyebrow.

"He started his vacation today."

Freddie did a comic double take. "Vacation? Grady never goes on vacation. Well, he did that one time he went to visit Erica in Chicag-o," He got all tripped up on the last bit there, drawing out the *o* while giving me a nervous sidelong glance. Grady's trip to Chicago was a bit of a sore subject for me. You know, because everything was perfect and we totally fell in love, but then Grady said the words *I love you* at the airport, and I didn't because I have intimacy issues apparently and I lose the ability to speak when I'm feeling strong love-type emotions and then, well, everything devolved into a big pile of crap after that, and he started dating Can— See? This is why I didn't like talking about Chicago!

Again, I could have given Freddie a heads-up on the whole vacation thing if he hadn't been in such a rush to . . . what? Not be alone with me?

"Well, where did he go?"

Amos swallowed, making his Adam's apple bob. "Can't tell you that either."

"That's okay," Freddie said. "You don't have to. This is Grady we're talking about. He'd never go far. He's probably just camping in the mountains somewhere brooding, and thinking his lonely, handsome-man thoughts."

I blinked. "Lonely handsome-man thoughts?"

"Yeah, you know. In a flannel shirt."

"He's actually suntanning on his porch right now."

He blinked at me. "Well, you could have mentioned that."

"I tried. You—"

"Doesn't matter." Freddie plunked an elbow on the counter and leaned toward Amos. "So does that mean you're in charge now?" He picked up a pen and lazily twirled it in his fingers.

"No. No, we've called in Sheriff Bigly from North Country."

"Oh well, we'd be happy to talk to Sheriff Bigly," Freddie said.

Amos's eyes grew very wide. "You don't want to do that."

"How come?"

"Sheriff Bigly's heard the stories."

"What stories?" I asked. "You mean like 'Freddie and me' stories?"

Amos nodded vigorously.

I bit my lip. That couldn't be good. Hopefully it wasn't the grave-digging one. We really didn't come off too great in that one.

"Besides," Amos went on, "now that it's not looking like a case of death by misadventure after all—"

Freddie dropped the pen.

Amos immediately realized what he had done. But he also realized it was too late to take it back.

"So, it was murder," Freddie said.

"Nothing's official yet. Promise me you won't spread it around town."

Freddie looked at me. "When I went to the gazebo to check out the location, I saw all the police tape and I thought to myself—"

"Wait," I said, holding up my hands. "Lyssa died at the gazebo?"

Freddie nodded.

"The location for the wedding is a crime scene?"

"I know it's a bit of a hiccup," Freddie said. "But—"

I threw my hands in the air and spun away. Well, this was just fantastic. Candace wasn't going to want to get married where her maid of honor died. I mean, I didn't think like a bride, but that had to be a hard no.

"We don't even have the official cause of death yet," I heard Amos say. "Everybody's just assuming it was drowning, but—"

I looked back at Amos. I was suddenly really concerned that he might throw up. I think he was worried about the same thing because he snapped his mouth shut.

"Amos?" Freddie asked.

No response.

"Are you okay?" I tried.

He nodded his head but kept his mouth firmly shut.

Freddie and I exchanged glances.

"Does . . . this mean you're done talking to us?"

He nodded again.

"Let's go," I said, grabbing Freddie's elbow and pulling him off the counter.

He whirled his head around and mumbled through his teeth. "What are you doing? He won't be able to pull off this silent treatment forever."

"Mercy ruling." Yes, we needed answers, but I didn't want to get Amos fired. "We've got enough for now."

"Oh!" Freddie said, jabbing a finger in the air. "Not quite. Amos, when do you think we can get at the stuff Candace left in the gazebo for the wedding?"

He shrugged.

"Dude, I've got a wedding to plan, and Candace has all the chairs and some plastic containers in there with decorations and stuff. I need to get in."

The young deputy just looked apologetic.

My guess was Otter Lake being the small town it was would have to call in a special forensics team to go over the crime scene.

Freddie sighed. "Could you at least ask Sheriff Bigly?"

Amos frowned but then nodded.

We said our good-byes—well, Freddie and I did, Amos just nodded some more—and we left.

"Death by misadventure," Freddie said once we were outside.

"What?"

"That's how I want to go." He trotted down the steps to the sidewalk. "But not until I'm like really, really old. Although that will probably make the misadventure part a little trickier to get into. You should do it with me," he said. "Maybe we could go parachuting while juggling knives or something."

"I'm not going parachuting with knives," I said, pushing my bangs back from my face. "But at least you're in a better mood."

Freddie stopped to face me. "What are you talking about?" he asked with a squint. "And when are you planning on cutting your bangs?"

"What's wrong with my bangs?" I flipped them back again. "I'm going for a windswept, layered kind of look."

"You look like a sheepdog."

I pointed at him. "And that right there is exactly what I'm talking about."

Freddie just stared at me blankly.

"How you've been acting."

"How have I been acting?"

"Mean. You've been mean. And why didn't you call me yourself this morning?"

Freddie scoffed. "I was busy and I was already talking to Rhonda about the insurance case and—"

"No. No. No. That is not it." I planted my fists on my hips. "You need to tell me right now what's got you in this mood. It must have something to do with me because—"

"Erica," he said with the type of smile that just made me insane, "I hate to break this to you, but not everything is about you."

"What?" I said, throwing my hands in the air. "I never said it was about me!"

Freddie shot me a sideways look.

"Okay, fine, maybe I did say that." Like two seconds ago. I shook my head. "I don't believe this. First it's you. Then my mother was acting all sketchy. Then there's *vacay* Grady. What is going on in this town?"

"I have no idea what you are talking about," Freddie said. Suddenly his eyes were looking a lot like my mom's when she lied. All wide. And childlike. "Name one time I have been mean to you."

"You just said I looked like a sheepdog."

"Yeah, but that's because I care."

I curled my hands into fists. "Would you just tell me what's going on."

"There is nothing wrong with me," he said. "I am, however, slightly concerned about you."

We stared at each other for a moment.

"You know what? Fine. Don't tell me," I said, waving a hand at him and walking down the steps backward. "I know I'm not crazy. You know I'm not crazy. But if you want us to pretend like I'm crazy, so you can keep whatever secret it is that you're keeping, then it's fine by me. This crazy person has a lot to do, thanks to y— Whoa!" With all my crazy talk, I didn't realize that I was about to run right into Mrs. Shank walking her dog.

"I'm so sorry. I didn't see you there."

The poor woman had dropped into a defensive crouch.

"Are you okay?"

She nodded quickly then picked up her dog and hustled away.

No, I wasn't crazy. I just scared women in the streets . . . and their little dogs too.

"Cut those bangs, Erica," Freddie called after me as I stomped down the street. "You're going to hurt someone."

"It wasn't the bangs!"

After the sheriff's department, I just kept walking all the way to Candace's place. I had texted her earlier asking if I could come by. Not only did I want to check in on her, but I also wanted to talk to her about the night of the bachelorette party while her memory was still fresh. Normally, this was the type of thing I do with—he who shall not be named—but that wasn't about to happen. Who did he think he was? *Cut my bangs.* Maybe he needed to get *his* bangs cut.

It was a good forty minutes from the sheriff's department, but I needed time to think . . . and to kick rocks. Yeah, the kicking-rocks thing was going much better than the thinking.

I was not crazy. There was definitely something wrong with Freddie. Or he who shall not be nam— whatever! It was my internal rant. I could call him what I wanted. And I was almost one hundred percent convinced that whatever was going on had something to do with Sean. But why wouldn't he tell me? That right there was the part that was making me nuts. I felt like a cat standing in front of a closed door. I just had to know what was behind it. Besides, Freddie was supposed to be the relationship I could count on. And vice versa. No matter what was happening in either of our love lives. So none of this made sense.

I shook my head and kicked another rock. Whatever. Freddie could keep his secret. I needed to focus on Candace. Candace was the one with real problems. Compared to Candace's problems, Freddie and I just had like . . . pumpkin-spiced-latte problems. With Lyssa's death—now a murder—Candace was going to need our support more than ever. We didn't have time for this ridiculousness.

A small chill ran over me as I turned a corner to the small dirt service road to Candace's place. The sun was hot today, but there was no humidity yet and the trees were thick and tall.

It wasn't much farther though.

I could already see the laneway markers for the drivew—

Wait . . .

Who was that?

I froze and squinted at the trees opposite Candace's cottage.

I could just barely make out a figure. Just standing there. Not moving.

I could have been mistaken—it was hard to tell given all the tree branches—but it looked like a woman.

"Hello?" I called out, taking a few steps forward.

The figure looked over to me, but I couldn't make out the face. The windbreaker the person was wearing had a hood. She . . . or he . . . did wave though.

I waved back. Must just be a hiker . . . but given everything that had happened . . .

"Can I help you?" I called out, hurrying my steps. But the figure had already turned and was walking deeper into the woods. I was quickly losing sight of her.

Should I follow?

Didn't seem like a great idea safetywise. But what if that person was a lead? This was why Freddie and I were supposed to do this kind of thing together. That way we wouldn't die alone. Nobody wanted to die al—

"Erica?"

"Wah!"

I whipped my head around.

Candace. Standing in her front door. "Are you okay?"

"I'm fine," I said quickly. I would probably look more fine if I wasn't clutching my heart. "I just . . . I saw someone in the woods."

"Who?"

"I don't know."

Candace's eyes scanned the forest. "People do hike out here. There's a pretty popular trail."

I nodded. "It's just with . . ."

"I know," Candace said. "Come in."

Chapter Eight

"I'm sorry again if I scared you," I said, accepting the mug of tea Candace was handing to me. "It probably was a hiker. I mean, she waved when I called out to her, or him . . . whoever."

She sat in the chair across from me on the sofa and curled her legs underneath her. "No, I'm sure you're right." I looked Candace over. Her hair was brushed today and she didn't look like she had been crying, but the bags under her eyes hinted that she wasn't sleeping.

"But you should probably mention it to Amos."

She nodded and pulled a pillow on her lap. "He and Sheriff Bigly are coming over later. I will."

I nodded and looked around. "Where is everybody?"

"Joey and Antonia took his grandmother to the doctor," Candace said, taking a quick glance at her phone. "She was having a rough morning."

"Oh." I wanted to say *So they left you here alone?* But I restrained myself. It felt pretty judgey.

"Joey wanted to stay, but Antonia . . ." She shook her head. "I told him I was fine."

"Are you really though?" I asked, blowing on my tea. "Now that we know for sure . . ."

"That Lyssa's death was suspicious?" She took a deep breath. "I don't know. Amos said they need more information about her—and I want to help—but I don't know what more I can tell them. I mean, it's been years since we were really close. And even back in college, we weren't ever really . . . confidants. You know what I mean?"

I frowned. "Not exactly."

"Well, Lyssa was always lots of fun and over-the-top. That's why I was so drawn to her. I was kind of shy," she said with a small shrug. "But I can't help but think she used all that . . . *personality* as a way to keep people at a distance."

"Why?"

"From what I could piece together, her childhood was pretty rough." Candace shook her head and looked out the window. "She didn't get along with her adoptive parents. The only time she ever really told me about it was when I got back to the dorm one night and found her superdrunk." She picked at a loose thread on the pillow in her lap. "She had just contacted her birth mother for the first time."

I waited.

"Her mother wanted nothing to do with her. Hung up as soon as she knew who it was."

I let go of the breath I didn't know I was holding. "Wow. That's rough."

"Yeah, but then the next morning, she was back to

her usual self. When I brought it up, she pretended like she didn't know what I was talking about, and we were off to the next party."

It was hard to reconcile the version of Lyssa I had created in my head with this new information. Maybe she wasn't as free and confident as I had thought.

"I just wish I could have been a better friend to her, you know?" A tear slipped down Candace's cheek. She quickly brushed it away.

I nodded. "What about her boyfriend? Justin? Has anyone been able to track him down?"

"Still haven't heard from him. The police haven't located him. I can't even find any pictures of him online."

I frowned. "Really?"

"Yeah, it's weird." Candace grabbed her phone again. "Lyssa was always pretty big on social media, but now it's like she's been scrubbed clean."

I came over and sat beside her. We spent a few minutes trolling the usual sites, but Lyssa was nowhere to be found, except for a few old pictures from Candace's pages.

"That is weird."

"And that's not all," Candace said. "I've been going over that night again and again, and . . ."

"And?"

"Well, Lyssa had this bag. Like a purse. But it was kind of big." Candace sized out the shape with her hands. "She wouldn't let it out of her sight. She insisted she take it to the Dawg. I didn't think anything of it at first. But now . . . it seemed out of place."

"You told Amos about all this, right?"

"I told him, but . . ." She sighed. "I feel terrible saying it, but I'm worried about whether he's up to this job."

I nodded.

"I hope this Sheriff Bigly is more like . . ."

"Grady?" I asked, raising an eyebrow.

She shot me an awkward smile.

"You can say his name, you know."

"I know. I just didn't want to be . . ." I could see the struggle to find the right words play across her face. "I hope this doesn't sound wrong, but I'm just so happy that I found Joey. It's like finding . . . home. I want that for you too. Whoever it's with." Her eyes darted up to mine. "Does that sound bad?"

"No, not at all. Thank you," I said, giving her hand a pat. "I kind hope for the same thing."

We sat in silence for a moment.

"You never know," Candace said in a slightly lighter tone. "Maybe this vacation of Grady's will be good for him."

I looked at her, eyebrow raised. "You think?"

"Oh yeah," she said with just a bit of a smile. "He needs to relax." Her smile broadened. "Like we get it, dude. You're sheriff." She rolled her eyes. "Of the fun police."

I burst out laughing. I couldn't help it. I was surprised to hear Candace joke that way. Not just because of the circumstances, but because she was normally so . . . nice.

"You know," I said suddenly. "I'm really happy you've found your home in Joey. That's amazing."

"Thanks," she said, before taking a shaky breath. "But you and Freddie are the amazing ones. I just wanted to say . . . I know how much is involved in this wedding. If for whatever reason, you guys—"

"The wedding's going to be great, Candace," I said.

"But I want you to know if you want out—"

"Out?" I near shouted. "Never. And don't you worry. We're not going to let you down."

Chapter Nine

We were so going to let Candace down.

I had stayed with Candace until Joey got back. His grandmother was okay. Apparently it was normal with her condition for some days to be worse than others. After that I walked back into town. I figured I'd go by Tommy's next to find out what he knew about the night of Lyssa's death, and then maybe after that drop by Vivienne's to check out the wedding-cake situation. Unfortunately, before I even got started, my mother sent me an emergency text with the list of last-minute items I needed to pick up. And what a list it was. I was kind of worried the retreat would be over by the time I picked all of it up. She had even included paper plates and plastic utensils in the items. She had to be freaking out. I mean, things were bad if my mother was going plastic. She thought disposable dishes were a third-degree environmental crime. It was probably for the best, though, that I put off going to Tommy's. I kind of didn't want to go without Freddie. Not that I was

afraid of Tommy or anything. But he could be . . .
unpredictable.

I was still really confused about that whole situation. Had Lyssa lied to Candace about her ex-boyfriend coming to town because she didn't want her to know she was really hooking up with Tommy that night? Was Justin ever even in Otter Lake? Or maybe the rumor mill had just messed this one up—thought Justin was Tommy. No matter what, I needed to get over there tomorrow. I needed to know who she was with that night. With or without Freddie.

By the time I had finished getting everything and made it back to the boat, the sun was starting to set. Thankfully, while there was a lot on the list, most of it was pretty straightforward—except for the item on the back. She wanted me to pick up spare camping supplies from the twins' friend Alma. Trying to get something out of that woman without staying for supper had an off-the-charts difficulty level. But I had managed it with a promise to play euchre some other time with her, her husband, and their middle-aged son who collected beetles in little glass cases. I think Alma hoped we'd hit it off and get married someday. I'd just file that under *Problems for Another Time*.

I needed to hurry back to the island if I wanted to make it for the official meet-and-greet campfire—which I did. Not because I was interested in what Zaki had to say about why it was that I was still single or anything. I just wanted to get my hands on some vegan marshmallows. They were better than one might think.

Just before it really got dark, I eased my mother's boat alongside the dock. I loved these long June evenings. Soon the frogs—those little spring peepers—would be singing their hearts out. Hey, maybe Candace would like a twilight wedding; then we wouldn't have to have a DJ, we could just listen to the frogs. Nah, that was weird. Again, I really didn't think like a bride.

I climbed the log steps dug into the hill of the retreat, hands loaded down with supplies and a tent bag slung around my neck. With my hands tied up, I had about a million mosquito bites by the time I made it to the top, but life wasn't all bad. As I crested the hill, I spotted Kit Kat and Tweety in their rocking chairs with tin cups. The sight of their matching perms and dentures glowing a soft white in twilight always put a smile on my face.

"Uh-oh," I heard one of them announce as my feet crunched over the gravel path. "Here's trouble."

"Caesar," the other one ordered, pointing at the cat at the top of the porch stairs. "Go get Erica. I don't think she's going to make it."

A moment of silence followed.

"Because then she'll be the thing the cat dragged in?"

"Exactly."

The sound of cackles filled the air.

"Good one," I called out.

"We know."

Their tin cups clinked together.

I stopped at the foot of the lodge steps. I couldn't seem to get either one of my legs interested in climbing them. They felt like they had walked an ultramarathon today. Besides, Caesar would never let me pass. His enormous orange and white body looked like a capsized cruise ship on the landing. He could barely tilt his head up far enough to give me his signature evil look through his furry slitted eyes. There was no way I was going to be able to step over him without getting cut.

I lowered my bags to the ground and dropped myself onto the bottom step. I needed a moment to catch my breath before I went round back. I also wanted to make sure the campfire was good and under way, so I could lurk a bit without my mother reading too much into it.

Again, I was just in it for the marshmallows, but . . . if I did pick up a word or two of wisdom from the bestselling guru, you know, so be it.

"You look like you could use a drink."

"Just throw some this way," I said. "I'll open my mouth."

"Your mother didn't think you'd be back this soon," Tweety said.

Kit Kat nodded. "Said you might be having dinner with Alma."

I nodded. "It was a close one, but I escaped."

Apparently Caesar didn't like the vibe I was giving off because he heaved himself up, walked approximately five, six steps down the porch and then capsized himself once again.

"Is that my mother's all natural iced tea? Or gin?" I shot a nod to the cup in her hand.

"Iced tea."

I crawled up the porch steps and reached for her cup. She handed it to me, but said, "You should just take that stuff inside and get to bed. You look like you could use a good night's sleep."

"Then you need to figure out this whole thing with Candace's bridesmaid," Kit Kat added. "People are scared."

"Some are locking their doors for the first time ever."

I took a sip from the cup. "I know, but I'm okay. I was actually thinking I might check the campfire. I met Zaki this morning. He was pretty interesting."

"Your mother thinks so too," Tweety said just under her breath.

"What?"

"Nothing. Nothing," Kit Kat said with feigned lightness. "But you're not thinking of actually taking part, are you?"

"Well, I don't know about taking part," I said. "Maybe . . . just have a little listen."

The twins exchanged looks again.

"What is going on with you two?"

Kit Kat looked at her sister. "I told Summer she should have told her before—"

"I know. I know," Tweety said. "But she wanted to wait for the perfect moment—"

"But Erica's not an idiot. She's going to figure it—"

Tweety just held up a hand for her sister to stop.

"Um, hello?"

The twins raised their brows in an identical expression.

"Would you like to share with me what my mother should have told me?"

"Nope," Kit Kat said.

"Not our business," Tweety added.

I sighed. I knew better than to argue with that *nope*.

Besides, I was sure whatever it was my mom was up to, I'd find out soon enough. I *knew* she had been acting funny. She had probably saved me a spot front and center for this retreat then used reverse psychology with the whole "you wouldn't be interested" bit, so that I *would* be interested. Well, that was fine. I could play along. Just this once. But I was only going to listen to what the others had to say. There was no way I was participating.

"Well," I said, pushing myself to my feet. "I might as well go on back and see what's waiting for me."

"You never know," Tweety said. "You might learn something."

I frowned at her.

"She means like how to make a relationship work," Kit Kat added.

I frowned at her too. "I got that."

"You never know, maybe Zaki will say something that will finally help you get yourself together," Tweety said with a big nod. "You could meet a nice new man, or figure out what to do with an old nice man, so we can have a little—"

"Stop," I said with a point.

"Baby," Kit Kat finished. "We want a baby."

"We're not getting any younger, you know," Tweety said with a knowing look.

The identical look came to her sister's face. "Neither are you."

"Uh-huh." I looked at the cup in my hand before passing it back. Why couldn't it have been gin?

I slung the tent bag around my neck and picked up my many bags.

"Good luck," Kit Kat said.

I threw them a nod. It was the only part of me that wasn't laden down with supplies.

When I turned the back corner of the lodge, I was greeted by the sight of a large group of women all seated around the campfire pit three or four rows deep in a mishmash of chairs. They were listening to someone talking. I could only see the back of him, but it was definitely—

Freddie?

I walked a few steps closer to the group to hear him say, "So, my name is Freddie. I'm not normally a big sharer, but you all seem like a nice group of ladies."

A small chuckle ran over the crowd.

"Anyway, back to me," he said, waving his hand out. More laughter.

"I could really use an outside perspective on this particular problem I'm having. You see, I'm having trouble balancing—"

"Erica!" my mother suddenly shouted.

"Erica!" Freddie said, whipping around.

Then the group of women turned around and let out a collective, "Erica?"

So much for lurking in the background.

I waved a hand in the air. "That's me."

Chapter Ten

"Darling," my mother called out as she rushed over to me. "What are you doing here?"

"I live here."

She laughed. It had a slight edge to it. "I just meant that I thought you'd be having dinner over at Alma's."

"Yeah, no, I got out of it."

"Wonderful. Wonderful," she said with a smile that died almost instantly. "Listen, darling, I wanted to talk to you about something before—"

"Is it about Freddie? Did you invite him to the retreat?"

"Freddie?" she said, looking back at the group . . . looking awkwardly over at us. "Oh no, he just showed up. He wanted to know if you were here, and when I said you weren't, he said he thought he might stick around."

"Oh," I said, before shaking my head. "What did you want to talk to me about?"

She shot a quick look back at the fire. "Maybe now

is not the best time. We can talk later." She snatched the plastic bags from my hands. They were so heavy she nearly took one of my fingers with her. "I'd better get these inside." She was already rushing away. It looked like Zaki was headed toward her to help with the bags, but she called out, "Please continue without me. Sorry for the interruption."

"They are so cute together," I heard a woman say.

They?

Obviously that woman didn't know my mother very well. She never dated. She was married to her work.

I dropped the tent bag from my shoulder and headed for the fire.

"Freddie," Zaki called out, "would you like to continue?"

"No, thanks," he said quickly. "I'm good."

"But you wanted an outside perspective on—"

"I said, *No, thanks. I'm good.*"

Freddie's *No thanks. I'm good* was one step away from *I said, Good day, sir.*

I knew I wasn't crazy. There *was* something wrong with Freddie.

Something he didn't want me to know.

Well, that was just too bad, Vlad—I mean, Freddie—our relationship didn't work that way.

I walked my way around the back of the circle to the opening, so that I could get to where Freddie was sitting on a log by the fire. I sat down beside him as Zaki invited another woman to share her story.

"Fancy meeting you here," I whispered.

"I just dropped by, and . . . well, I thought it might be interesting."

"But you're not single."

"Well, no . . . but my poppo is a big fan of Zaki's," Freddie whispered quickly. "I was going to ask him for his autograph."

Hmm, yes, Freddie's grandmother did have *fangirl* tendencies when it came to celebrities. He once stood in line for two hours to get Tom Selleck's autograph for her birthday, but he got his wires crossed, and it turned out it wasn't Tom Selleck sitting at the desk at all, but David Hasselhoff, and the whole thing fell apart from there. But regardless, it all seemed very convenient.

We quieted down as Zaki strolled past us. Because there were so many people listening to the talk tonight the inner ring of the circle around the fire was pushed pretty far back. Zaki was strolling around it, hands clasped behind his back.

Once he had moved on, Freddie leaned toward me and whispered, "I mean this whole thing is kind of silly, right?"

"I don't know. I just got here."

"Well, I've been here longer than you," Freddie whispered, voice superheavy on the charm. But it was distraction charm, I could tell. "And I can already tell you why everybody is single."

I frowned.

"Like the woman talking right now? She's still single because she thinks," he whispered, adding air quotes, "that she intimidates men, but really it's because she feels she has to bring up the fact that she's a doctor in every conversation."

I didn't answer. Nope. I would not be distracted. Freddie *was* going to tell me what was going on with him this time.

"Oh, then there's that lady there," Freddie whispered, pointing at a lovely woman, maybe in her late thirties. "Attractive. Nice. Seems like a really sweet lady? I call her Old Yeller."

Still no answer from me.

"Yeah, her normal speaking voice is a yell. It's very jarring. Watch." Freddie waved at the woman.

"Hey, Freddie!"

Well, that got the crowd's attention.

"Sorry," she said.

Everyone turned back to listening to the doctor. Except us.

"And that one there," Freddie whispered, pointing at a woman maybe in her late fifties. "I call her Eeyore. 'Cause she's so sad."

I couldn't help but look over for just a second. The woman in the white T-shirt and khakis did seem kind of downtrodden. She was sitting by herself at a picnic table occasionally lifting her eyes up to people passing by. But I would not be distracted!

"She's too sad for love." Freddie then whacked my arm. "And then there's the hypochondriac." He pointed at a woman swatting frantically at mosquitoes. "Nobody wants to date a hypochondr—"

"Did you and Sean break up?"

Freddie's eyes darted around my face.

"Because I'm trying to think of some other reason for why you're behaving the way you are, and why you would come to this retreat, and I got noth—"

"Erica?" Zaki said with a small laugh. It wasn't the nice one that had made the birds stop singing earlier. "Is everything all right? Would you two like to share with the group?"

"Oh, I . . ." I stopped to clear my throat. Yup, everyone was looking at me. "Would you excuse us for a second?" I grabbed Freddie's elbow and pulled us both to our feet. "I'm so sorry to interrupt. Everything is fine. We're not really . . . participating. Please carry on."

"What?" Freddie said in a lowered voice as I dragged him down the path that led out of the circle. "You're not going to tell them about Grerica?"

I stopped and blinked at him.

"You know, you and Grady smushed together," he said, making a smushing motion with his hands. "Maybe they could help."

"That's it," I said, holding my hand out. "Give me your phone."

"Why?"

"Do you have it on you?"

He pulled it out of his pocket. "Of course I have it, but—"

I made a lunge for his hand, but he snatched it away. "What do you want with it?"

"I've had it, Freddie. I know you are hiding something, but it's *me*," I said, patting my chest. "We don't hide things from each other. I can help."

Freddie frowned at me like . . . like I had just sprouted antennae or something.

"Give me your phone," I said, holding my hand out again. It had to be that he was too embarrassed to talk about it out loud. "You don't have to say anything. I just want to see when the last time you texted Sean was."

"That . . ." Freddie said, drawing the word out into many syllables, "is not going to happen."

"No. Enough is enough," I said. "Help me, help you."

He laughed . . .

. . . which made me just *a little bit* mad. "Give me the phone."

"No."

"Why not?"

" 'Cause."

"But you go through my phone all the time!"

"That's different."

"How is it different?"

"It just is," Freddie said. "End of story. I'm going back to the bonfire."

"Um, we are in the middle of a discussion here."

He took a step back. "I think we've pretty much covered everything."

"We've covered nothing," I said a little too loudly. A few heads turned.

"Well, I'm going back." Freddie took another couple of steps.

"I see what you're doing," I said, matching his steps. "You think if you make it back into the crowd, you'll be safe. That I'll let this drop. But I'm not dropping it, Freddie. Our friendship—"

"Is starting to scare me." He shot me a smile before turning to head back towards the bonfire. "Love you."

I trotted over to catch up to him. "I'm getting that phone," I whispered. "Whether you like it or not. Hey, maybe I'll even change your ringtone while I'm at it."

He chuckled again. "Oh, okay."

"What's that supposed to mean?" I hissed.

"You outsmart me? I think we all know who is the Road Runner is this relationship and who is Wile E.

Coyote." Freddie then held up a hand and waved at the group as we returned to our seats. "Now hush."

Now *hush?*

Hush?

I dropped to my seat and blinked at the fire, not really seeing it.

He . . . he had gone too far.

My eyes dropped to the phone clutched in Freddie's hand, then I raised them up to his face. He was completely ignoring me. There was no way he was going to put it down, but maybe if I just hit the underside of his hand, the phone would pop in the air, and I could grab it. If I did it just right, no one would even notice. Then what could he do? He wouldn't make a scene in front of all these people.

I'd show him who was the Road Runner in this duo.

I reached my hand underneath Freddie's and—

Just then he looked at me. "What are you—?"

I hit his hand and the phone spun into the air. It landed in the dirt a couple of feet away.

Well, that got everybody's attention.

"Sorry. Sorry," I said getting to my feet. "Not sure what happened there. I'll just—"

But Freddie was already on his feet. "I got it."

"No, I'll get it."

"I said, I'll—" In his haste, just as Freddie was reaching for the phone, his foot kicked it even farther away. And before I even realized what was happening, he had the phone and—

—we were running duck, duck, goose style around the fire.

"Erica! Freddie! What are you doing?" my mother shouted from . . . somewhere? "Stop it this instant!"

When I turned to look at her, my bangs flopped into my face. Unfortunately I hadn't stopped running though, and I didn't see the little bit of stump sticking up in the dirt. I pitched forward and smashed into Freddie.

"Watch the fire!" my mother screamed, even though Freddie was really nowhere near it as he flew Superman-style into the air before landing belly-first on the hard-packed dirt. The impact sent his phone flying from his hand.

I scrambled over the top of him and snatched it up.

"Aha!" I shouted a moment later. "Now we'll see who's the Road . . ."

Oh . . . wow.

Would you look at all those people staring at me with . . . horror. I had forgotten all about them in my moment of victory.

I rose to my feet.

Well . . . that had escalated quickly.

And now everything was going so slow.

"We broke up, okay?" Freddie finally said, yanking me back into the moment. "Sean and I broke up. Are you happy now?"

He got to his feet and brushed the dirt from his front.

"Freddie, I . . ."

Suddenly it was very quiet.

Yup . . . nothing but the crackling of the bonfire.

"Right," my mother said, fluttering to stand by Zaki, eyes very wide. "I think what Freddie and Erica have demonstrated for us just now is . . . the bravery it takes to really get in touch with one's feelings. Isn't that right, Zaki?"

He didn't answer. He looked a little stunned, actually.

"Also . . . conflict resolution! They have found a way to resolve their differences in a healthy—"

Zaki quickly shook his head.

"No, that wasn't very healthy, was it?" my mother said, furrowing her eyebrows into two worried little peaks.

"Marshmallows!" she shouted. "Who would like more vegan marshmallows?"

Freddie and I remained frozen as the rest of the crowd recoiled away from us toward the picnic tables.

Once they were gone, Freddie looked at me and said, "Well, I hope you're proud of yourself."

"I . . . I am so sorry." I was too. I had just been so hurt that Freddie was freezing me out that—"I went too far. I don't know what came over me. I've just been so worried about you and—"

"Whatever, Summer."

My jaw dropped again.

Had he just compared me to my mother?

"You know," he went on, "given everything that has happened, I think, perhaps, we should consider spending some time apart." He nodded. "A friend break."

"You can't be serious."

"Yup. I am."

"Freddie . . ."

"I think maybe I should focus on replanning the wedding, seeing as you were so unhappy with that. And you can handle the investigation."

What . . . was happening here? I took a step toward him, but he stepped right back. "But . . . you love murder investigations."

"Yes, but we all know you are more comfortable with murders than weddings, so this just makes the most sense."

I stared at him a moment. I couldn't believe this was happening. Freddie and I were like two peas in a pod. We were like nitro and glycerin. We were like . . . like . . . maybe I didn't know what we were like anymore. "Okay. If that's what you want. Fine."

"Good. I'm glad that's settled."

"Me too." I flicked my head to get my bangs out of my eyes and stomped toward the lodge.

I heard Freddie groan. "But while we're apart would you just get someone to cut your bang—"

"Break started," I called back over my shoulder.

"But you are going to seriously hurt some—"

"Break! Started!"

Chapter Eleven

I woke up the next morning with a splitting headache. A big, big part of me was holding on to the hope that what had happened at the campfire the night before was just a bad dream, but I knew that wasn't the case.

I, a grown woman, had chased my best friend around a campfire in front of a whole bunch of strangers so that I could go through his phone without his permission.

Oh no . . . and don't tell me I . . .

I sat up in bed and looked at my reflection in the mirror over my dresser. Yup . . . that wasn't a dream either . . . I had angry-cut my own bangs. That fourteen-year-old girl on YouTube said it was like totally no problem to do it yourself, but she was wrong.

I flopped back onto my bed.

This . . . this . . .

. . . was not my fault!

Okay, maybe the bangs were my fault . . . and maybe I hadn't exactly been on my best behavior, but

I had been driven to it! All of it. I wasn't sure that I believed that even as I was thinking it, but I thought it was worth hearing myself out. Fine, okay, yes, I never should have demanded Freddie give me his phone, but a person could only take so much! He had been miserable for days and wouldn't tell me why. He had started this whole thing. I . . . had just finished it.

And I was going to finish this investigation too.

Oh, I knew what Freddie was thinking. He was thinking that there was no way I could find out who killed Lyssa without his help, but he was wrong, wrong, wrong. I didn't need him. At least not the way he needed me. I mean, good luck, Mr. Ng, planning Candace's wedding all by yourself.

I rolled out of bed. I needed to get out of here. Yes, I was fully aware that I should apologize to my mother, Zaki, and, well, everyone at the campfire last night, but I just couldn't. Not yet. I should have known that going to the retreat was a bad idea. I mean, *Why are you still single?* I think the answer was pretty obvious. I chased people around campfires!

I needed to get out of here. Soon all the retreat guests would be up and wandering around staring at me . . . from safe distances . . . probably wondering what happened to my hair, and if I was still in the possession of sharp scissors. I didn't need all that. And it's like I always say, there's no better distraction than solving a murder. Okay, I had never said that, but the scary part was I could, and it would apply to my life.

I jumped out of bed, threw some clothes on, and grabbed a baseball hat. This time I was going to be smarter exiting the retreat. No leaving through the front door for me. Nope, I would climb through my window. Just in case Zaki was meditating out front again. I couldn't face him today. I could still see the look of horror on his face.

Fifteen minutes later I was zipping across the lake.

Yup, forget the town. It was time to rack up some wins for Erica.

And I knew just where to start.

Tommy Forrester.

I slipped the boat into neutral and drifted toward Tommy's dock. Not too long ago Tommy had had two docks and two boats. That's when he'd been involved with the shady business with MRG incentivizing seniors living on the lake to sell sooner than they may have been originally thinking. But I guess a lot had changed since then. He was back to just one boat, and it was in pretty rough shape—along with the rest of his property.

I took my time tying my mother's boat off. I was hoping that Tommy had heard me coming and was awake. Not only was there a very good chance Tommy was sleeping one off, but I didn't really know how Tommy was doing these days. And Mrs. Roy had made it sound like he wasn't doing too well.

I walked the length of Tommy's dock to the front lawn of his cottage. It could have easily been mistaken for a junkyard though. Rusted-out box spring on the front lawn. Beer bottles—lots of beer bottles—everywhere. Seat of a toilet lying across the front path. Nice. Nice.

Now, Tommy's place hadn't been in great shape the last I'd visited him. Actually, some people might have called it a break and enter. I prefer the term *look-see*. But it was nothing like this.

Suddenly my toe hit a large rusted-out steel drum, making a loud clang.

I was really starting to think that Tommy needed some help from, like, a family member or someone to turn things around. A cousin perhaps. Too bad his only one seemed beholden to nobody and nothing—except for his desire to get his relaxation on.

That had actually been one of the worst parts about last night—resisting the urge to call Grady. Even though we were in the place we were . . . and he was in the place he was, which was *La La Land* apparently . . . I couldn't help but think he would understand why I had freaked out the way I did. Well, maybe not understand—that was asking a lot—but at least give me one of those kisses on the forehead that says *Hey, you're still a good person. I still like you.* I really needed that right now. Not that that would work through the phone, but . . . whatever.

I picked my way over the rusted-out mattress spring, hands out to the side for balance.

I totally had this, though.

I mean, yes, I obviously had my failings as a person, but the one thing I did know how to do was question people. Maybe it was even because of those failings that I was so good at it. People felt safe with me. Like I wasn't judging them.

Generally speaking, people usually liked me.

Just then something white zoomed across my field of vision.

What the . . . ?

I turned to see Tommy standing on his back porch in just boxers holding a bucket in one hand getting ready to whip another golf ball at me with the other.

Yup, generally speaking, people liked me . . .

. . . just not maybe Tommy Forrester.

But I didn't have time to think about that right now.
I needed to—

Duck!

Chapter Twelve

"What the hell, Tommy?!" I called out from behind the steel drum.

"Get off my property, Erica. Now!"

I jumped as a golf ball smacked into my barricade. *Clang!*

"I just wanted to talk to you! Knock it off!" I peeked back over the drum to the leaner version of Grady. Same dark hair. Same blue eyes. But where Grady always looked healthy and robust, there was something wiry about Tommy these days. Almost foxlike. In happier times he had even had the same hint of a smirk. Today, he just had a big ol' shiner. I hadn't noticed Tommy's black eye at first what with all the deadly flying projectiles crowding my vision.

"I said get off my property!" Another golf ball came shooting toward me. Luckily it hit the drum, making another deafening *clang!* "I fricking hate you!"

"You hate me? Since when?" I shouted, trying to get even lower to the ground.

"Since you ruined my life!"

When would people realize that I was far too busy messing up my own life to put any thought into ruining anyone else's? "What are you talking about?"

"Things were perfect before you came back to town!"

Clang!

"Then you come home, and Dickie dies—"

Clang!

"MRG hangs me out to dry—"

Clang!

"And Shelley dumps me!"

Clang! Clang! Clang!

Wow, that was loud.

"Tommy, that is totally unfair! I was not the one who killed Dickie. I did not make you get involved with MRG. And Shelley—"

Clang! Clang! Clang!

"You know what?" I shouted, grabbing a golf ball that had landed at my feet. "Let's see how you like it." I popped up and whipped the ball back at Tommy.

Crash!

"And now you broke my freaking window!"

I dropped back to the ground. Well . . . crap. In fairness I had been too scared to take the time to aim.

"I hate you so much!"

"I'm sorry!" I shouted back. "But you started it!"

"You started it when you came back to town!"

Clang! Clang! Clang! Man, his aim was like dead-on.

"Why do you have so many golf balls?!" Not really one of the questions I had come to his place to ask, but it seemed pretty important right now.

"It's one of the things I do now, Erica," Tommy

shouted back. "Clean up the lost balls around the course in Honey Harbor then sell them back to golfers on the side of the road. That's where I'm at now. All thanks to you!"

I shook my head. Not that he could see me. "Look, Tommy, you really want me to go?"

That resulted in a barrage of fire. I clutched my head until he was through. I was guessing that was a yes.

"I just want to ask you a couple of questions about the woman you were hanging out with the other night. At the bachelorette party?"

Everything went very quiet.

"Tommy?"

"I know she drowned," he said in a much more somber voice.

"So the police have been by?"

"Your boyfriend hasn't been if that's what you mean."

"No, I know. He's pretty busy these days."

I peeked over the drum. Tommy was looking out toward the lake. He looked kind of dejected actually. "You probably think I did it."

"No, I . . ." I was surprised by how upset I was seeing Tommy like this. Again, Tommy had always been a bit of a douchebag, but at least he had been a happy douchebag. Not this gaunt, miserable-looking creature. "Look, I'm just trying to help out Candace. She needs to know what happened to Lyssa. The town needs to know. People don't feel safe."

"She's a sweet girl," Tommy said, his expression losing more of its edge. "Candace, I mean."

I knew Candace had helped out with getting Tommy's charges reduced to misdemeanors.

"So maybe you could tell me what happened that night?"

He shook his head. "Not much to tell."

"I was under impression that you two might have hooked up?"

He didn't say anything.

"At the town gazebo?"

"Yeah," he said with a huff that was too pathetic sounding to be a laugh. "I'm a romantic like that."

"What happened afterward?"

"I left."

"What about Lyssa?"

"Don't know. She was on her phone. Still at the gazebo."

"So you left her there? Alone?"

"What do you want me to say, Erica?" Tommy asked, balling his fists. "Yeah, I did. She told me to go because her boyfriend was coming to find her. So I left. I leave and people die."

I put my hands up. "I didn't mean it that way." I never really gave a lot of thought to how Tommy had taken Dickie's death, but they had been close since kindergarten. It made sense he had guilt over what had happened even though it wasn't his fault. "I just meant . . . nobody was around? Were there any cars you didn't recognize?"

"No. Nothing like that. But what business is it of yours?"

"I told you. I'm just trying to help C—"

"Oh come off it. Like I'm supposed to believe that. You don't help anyone. You're not a helper. You're a ruiner!"

"Tommy, I never meant to ruin your l—"

Whoa. Another golf ball.

"Tommy, I—" I had to hit the ground again.

"Just get out of here, Erica. I don't want to talk to you anymore."

I couldn't leave yet though. I still needed to ask him about his eye.

"Tommy, if you'd just hear me o—"

A golf ball whizzed right by my ear.

"Okay! Message received." I started army-crawling my way back to the dock. "No more questions. Sheesh."

"So is it just me?" I grabbed another handful of chips resting on the car floor near Rhonda's feet. "Or has this entire town gone crazy?

"Golf balls. Wow."

I leaned back against the sun-warmed car seat. Even with the window rolled down, it was still pretty hot. But I'd rather be on a stakeout with Rhonda than dodging golf balls from Tommy. At least here I had junk food. Plus I didn't have any more leads to follow at the moment.

"And I don't know what I'm supposed to do about Freddie. I tried to apologize. I know I behaved badly, and I don't want a *friend break,* but we don't keep secrets from each other," I said, shaking my head. "Why wouldn't he just tell me about breaking up with Sean in the first place? It's like I'm the one who's getting dumped as Freddie's best friend, and I don't even know what I did."

"I hear you."

"And with my mom and Grady acting all weird on top of that . . ." I shook my head. "I just don't know how much more I can take."

"Sure."

"But you want to know what the worst part of all this is?"

I thought I heard Rhonda mumble something like, *Can't wait to hear this one.*

"We should all be coming together for Candace."

Rhonda had just put a chip in her mouth, but stopped mid-chomp to look at me. She studied my face a moment before chewing again. "You're right."

"And actually it's not just for Candace," I said. "It's for the town."

Rhonda nodded. "Yeah, people are pretty upset. Mr. Coulter thinks we should start up a neighborhood watch. He wanted to know if OLS would participate."

I shook my head. "I mean I'd participate in something like that, but I don't know if it will help. I don't think people are going to feel better until the killer is behind bars."

She nodded.

"What's your theory?" Rhonda was an ex-cop. She had to have some thoughts on the subject. I had already told her everything I had learned from Candace and Tommy. "I mean, I know you're busy with this insurance thing, but what do you think happened to Lyssa? What should my next move be?"

"Well," she said, leaning back in her seat. "I do have one idea."

"What is it?"

"If you really want to solve this murder—like right away—there's only one way I can think of to do it."

"What is it?"

"You've gotta find out what was in that bag."

Chapter Thirteen

"Lyssa's bag, you mean?"

"Think about it," Rhonda said, grabbing another chip. "The night Lyssa is murdered she is carrying an oversized bag around that she won't let out of her sight? Sounds pretty suspicious to me." She shrugged. "Who knows what could have been in there. Drugs? Money? Priceless jewels?"

I frowned at her. "I doubt it was priceless jewels."

"The point is," Rhonda said with a *point* of her finger . . . to really drive the *point* home I guess. "Whatever it was, I'm thinking it was the motive for her murder."

"Well, yeah," I said, leaning back in my seat. "That thought had occurred to me too, but how am I supposed to find out what was in the bag? I doubt Amos is going to tell me. And I don't think breaking into the evidence locker at the sheriff's department right now is a good idea."

"Well, I don't know," Rhonda said. "I can't come up

with everything. I'm just trying to point you in the right direction."

"I know," I said. "Thanks."

"Now about this whole thing with Freddie . . ."

I looked sideways at her.

"I think . . ." she said, before biting her lip, "you do need to give him some space."

I flopped my hands onto my thighs. "But he needs me, Rhonda. I can tell. If he and Sean really did break up, then I should be there for him, bringing him ice cream, listening to him complain about the ice cream I was bringing him, about how I never choose the right bowl for the ice cream, and—"

"I know. I know," she said, holding up a hand. "Be that as it may, he has a right to his space."

"But . . . but we've never had space in our relationship before."

She nodded, her supercurly red hair shuddering around her face. "But relationships change over time. They evolve. You need to evolve with them. And maybe it would be good for the both of you to let other people into your lives like . . ." She fake-coughed Grady's name.

"Um, I wasn't the one who didn't want Grady in my life. That was Grady." I sighed. "Besides, he's being all weird now. Like he's launching Grady 2.0 . . . which probably has anti-Erica software. And . . . I don't like all these changes! I feel like I should have been consulted first."

"Freddie will come back," she said, patting my leg. "You know he can't quit you."

I sighed again. "I guess I'll have to take your word for it." I leaned back in my seat and propped my feet up on the dash. Rhonda whacked them off pretty quick. "Thanks for talking to me about all this, Rhonda."

"No problem. Any time."

"Are you sure about that?" I asked, shooting her a look. "Because when I first got here I kind of got the impression that you weren't happy to see m— Oh my God!" I suddenly yelled. "I forgot to bring you lunch yesterday! I totally forgot!"

Rhonda smiled.

"I am so sorry! Why didn't you call me?"

"I think I was too dazed from the lack of food and— Oh! Crap! There he is," Rhonda said, lifting her camera from her lap and raising it to her eye. "Frick. There's grease on the lens."

My gaze snapped over to the clearing in the distance. Now, it was hard to tell given the distance—I didn't have a big lens to look through like Rhonda—but from what I could see . . .

"Whoa, is that him?"

"That's him," Rhonda said, clicking furiously.

"Where are your—" I remembered Rhonda had binoculars. I grabbed them from the glove compartment.

Our target was a large, large man, mid to late thirties, with reddish-blond hair that fell to his shoulders. He was wearing low-slung jeans . . . and nothing else. Well, I mean, I'm sure he had shoes or boots on, but I wasn't looking at his feet. He also had a small tree resting on his shoulder. Lucky tree.

We both watched in silence another few moments.

"He . . . does not look hurt," I said.

"No, he does not," Rhonda replied.

"He's also very . . . sweaty."

"Uh-huh."

"And dirty."

"Just the way I like them," Rhonda muttered.

I gave her a once-over, but she had no attention to give me, so I turned back to take in the view. "It feels kind of wrong to be getting paid for this."

"Don't worry," Rhonda said while furiously clicking her camera. "You'd be amazed how much easier it gets in a short period of time."

I walked back into town after leaving Rhonda to her photography session.

Man, I was getting tired of all the walking I was doing lately. But that's what happens when you get used to your best friend driving you everywhere and then you go on a friend break.

It was probably for the best though. I needed time to think of a way to find out what had happened to Lyssa's bag without getting Amos fired. But how? I guess I could get Candace to ask the sheriff's department, but I doubted they'd give the information to her either.

I needed more ideas.

By the time I made it back to Main Street I was still stuck . . . and hungry from all that walking and thinking.

I shot a look over to Vivienne's Pastry Shoppe. I couldn't help but wonder if Freddie had remembered that he had to reorder the cake, now that he was on the wedding and I was on the murder.

I trotted a few steps over.

It probably wouldn't hurt if I just popped in to make sure . . . and maybe get a cupcake.

Bells jingled as I opened the door.

I loved Vivienne's place. It always smelled like

sugar, vanilla, cinnamon, and other sunshiny happy things. But it wasn't just the atmosphere that made it so special, it was Vivienne herself. She was one of a kind. She had this lust for life that was infectious. She was always laughing . . . and eating . . . and laughing some more. She was a hedonist in the best kind of way.

Strangely, though, even though the place was usually a bit of a hot spot . . . today, it was empty. Huh. I looked around at the cozy little tables with nobody sitting at them, before swinging back around to make sure that Vivienne's was in fact open.

"Erica," a voice called out. "I thought I heard someone come in."

I smiled at the older woman sweeping in from the back room, rubbing her hands on a dish towel.

"Hi, Vivienne," I said. "Are you open or . . . ?"

"I'm always open. I just have an icing class going on in the back, so you'll have to bear with me. What can I do for you?"

"I promise I won't take up too much of your time. I just wanted to ask if Freddie had been in to talk to you about Candace's wedding cake."

"Don't you worry, honey. It's all taken care of. Freddie was in this morning actually to sample cakes. He's already made a decision, so we're all ready to go."

I frowned. "Hadn't Candace already chosen what she wanted?"

"Well, yes," Vivienne said, making a face. "But it was carrot. Joey's sister . . . what's her name?"

"Antonia."

"That's it," she said, snapping her fingers. "Anyway Candace chose carrot because it was Antonia's favorite. But Freddie insisted that that was an act of sabotage because carrot cake is nobody's favorite. We decided red velvet would be best."

"Oh. Okay." Hopefully he had checked that out with the bride first. "Well, I should get going, but while I'm here . . ."

"Yes?" Vivienne asked, flashing me a knowing smile. She knew I loved her cupcakes.

"You wouldn't happen to have any—"

"Grady's icing a fresh batch as we speak."

I froze. "I'm sorry. I must have misheard you. Did you say . . . ?"

"Grady," she said with a knowing smile. "Sheriff Forrester. He's my private lesson." She waved her towel in the air toward the door that led to the back. "Why don't you come and say hello?"

Chapter Fourteen

"Oh, no, no, no," I said, waving my hands in front of me. "But . . . I'm sorry, are you sure we are talking about the same Grady?"

She waved me toward the swinging door with the window. "Come. See for yourself."

I walked ever so carefully toward the door and peeked in the window. Well, I'll be a monkey's girl-friend—or uncle!—however that went. Didn't matter. I needed to focus on the sight before me.

Yes, yes, it was indeed Grady . . . my Grady—or everyone's Grady—Sheriff Forrester! It was indeed Sheriff Grady Forrester in an apron putting the last swirl of vanilla icing on a cupcake.

"Quite the sight, isn't it?" Vivienne said, coming to stand beside me.

I swallowed. I couldn't quite answer, so I just nodded.

"He's got quite a talent for it," Vivienne said, lean-ing in closer. "Frosting, I mean."

"Oh yeah?" I said, struggling to find my voice.

"Yeah, he's got those big, big hands, you know."

I shot her a look. Oh, she was loving this.

"But they're real steady."

Just then Grady brought his finger toward his mouth. It had a dab of icing on the tip. I held my breath as it touched his lips.

Vivienne jabbed me in the ribs. "What I wouldn't give to be that frosting, eh?"

I swallowed again.

"Do you want to go in and say hi?" she asked, raising an eyebrow.

"You know what? I think I'm just going to go."

"Really?" Vivienne asked.

I took a couple of steps away from the door. "Yeah, yeah, I have a lot to do." Like try to figure out what the hell was going on with Grady and somehow find a way to get that vision of him . . . and the icing out of my mind.

"You sure you don't want to go back there," Vivienne said with a jerk of her head. "And sample the merchandise?"

I wagged a finger at her. "You . . . you are bad."

She let out a big, loud laugh. "Don't I know it, honey."

"Nope. Nope. I'm really going to go."

"Well, okay," she said. "But you just keep in mind life is too short not to enjoy a good cupcake every once in a while."

Chapter Fifteen

"What now?" I groaned to myself as I rolled over in bed to get at my phone. The calendar notification was dinging for some strange reason, but I didn't have anything going on today.

I looked at the screen.

Well . . . crap.

Yes I did. I did have something going on today.

I had forgotten that I had scheduled a time to meet Mrs. Roy at her place to discuss the flowers first thing this morning.

After Vivienne's, I had gone back to the retreat to apologize to my mother and see how she wanted me to handle apologizing to everyone else, but I couldn't find an opportunity to get her alone. She was always either talking to the guests or Zaki. I thought it was best to lay low. A lot of people had paid good money to come to this retreat, I didn't want to cause any more problems. That being said, I knew I had to handle it today. My behavior was inexcusable. And I would handle it today, and get the investigation going again . . . somehow . . . once I handled this.

I mean, sure I could always text Freddie to get him to take the meeting with Mrs. Roy, but he might see that as a thinly veiled excuse to initiate contact. And I was all about respecting his space these days.

I could always cancel the meeting . . . but every wedding needed flowers.

That only left me with the option of taking the meeting. On the one hand it probably meant I would lose another hour of my life to a merry-go-round conversation with Mrs. Roy, but on the other hand, I had promised Candace that the wedding would be great. And it would be. Regardless of what was happening between Freddie and me.

And . . . wait a minute, Mrs. Roy's place was pretty close to the gazebo.

I wasn't thrilled about visiting the spot where Lyssa had been found, but that's what investigators did, right? I needed to get into the headspace of the killer . . . see what the killer saw. It was worth a shot. I didn't have any better ideas.

Half an hour later I was across the lake and at the Dawg asking Big Don if I could borrow the bike his nephew used for deliveries. I really needed to think about buying my own—especially if Freddie and I were going to keep fighting like this. I would have taken the boat, but Mrs. Roy's was on a shallow part of the lake. There were lots of rocks.

It didn't take long to cycle over. Once I got there, I laid the bike on her front lawn. I really liked this side of the lake. It was peaceful. The wind always seemed to be in the trees. Which was weird because they had actually cleared a good deal of the trees for Mrs. Roy's gardens. . . . which currently didn't have a single flower blooming in them. It was late spring, how could there be no flowers? This was bad. Who ever heard of a bride with a bouquet of tree branches? That wasn't romantic. That was pokey. Somebody could lose an eye.

I walked up to the cottage and knocked on the door.

It was immediately answered by a loud woof and then a howl from the backyard. A second later, Carmen showed up in the fenced-in strip of yard beside the house.

"It's okay, Carmen. I was invited."

That just made her howl louder.

"Wow. Tell me how you really feel."

I waited as Carmen howled for someone to answer the door. After a minute, I knocked again. Not entirely sure why. Carmen's howling could have woken the dead. Oh . . . bad thought. Too soon.

Still no answer.

She wasn't home.

Well, this had been a complete waste of time.

"You looking for Mrs. Roy?"

I whipped around. It was a boy, maybe ten, on a bike. I think his name might be Cole? I was pretty sure I went to high school with his mom, Carrie. Hey, there was another side-by-side comparison I could ponder later.

"Have you seen her?"

"She's not home. She went out about ten minutes ago. Grocery shopping."

"But she was supposed to meet me here now."

He nodded with a "I totally get it" look on his face.

I seriously doubted that he had been stood up that many times in his life to warrant that level of understanding, but either way I appreciated the commiseration. "She's like that," he said. "You're Erica Bloom, aren't you?"

Uh-oh, I was known for many things in this town. Most of them inappropriate for ten-year-old boys.

I nodded.

"You want to know about that woman who—" He made a slicing motion with his finger across his neck and made a gargling sound.

"No! I mean . . . no." What was Carrie letting this kid watch on TV? "I just wanted to talk to Mrs. Roy about some flowers."

"It happened over there," he said, pointing to the gazebo in the distance.

Apparently he knew quite a bit.

"I live right over there," he said, pointing to a cottage. Closest one to the gazebo.

Yup, that was Carrie's place. At least it was back in high school. I probably should have thought about canvassing the neighborhood before now.

I nodded at the kid again. I had no idea what I was supposed to say. I'd point to my place—well, my mom's—but you couldn't see it from here. "Cool."

"I know you and your friend like to solve all the murders in town."

I shot him a sideways look. "I wouldn't say *like,* and—"

"My mom says you're going to get arrested one of these days for sticking your nose where it shouldn't be."

I shrugged. Hard to disagree with that.

"But she says you'd probably like that because you're hot for Sheriff Forr—"

"All right. All right," I said, holding up my hands. "You just know all sorts of things, don't you? But shouldn't you be in school?"

"Summer break started last week."

"Right, well—"

"I know what happened that night. Want me to tell you?"

Chapter Sixteen

I stared at the creepy kid before me, jaw dropped. Well, I didn't know for sure he was creepy, but he was far more comfortable with death than I was comfortable with. And that mixed with the fact that his eyes were still all big and little-kid-like—well, he was a bit creepy.

This was also a bit of a predicament. While I was still pretty new to the private investigation business and knew next to nothing about child-rearing, I did have a sneaking suspicion that questioning a kid about a murder—without a parent present—was a big no-no.

"I don't think you should—"

"My mom heard the whole fight. She told her friend Sandy all about it when she thought I was playing video games."

I nodded. I remembered Sandy from school too. She always went around telling people that she thought their makeup was *a little much.* Kind of like Freddie telling people they needed their bangs cut. "You probably shouldn't eavesdrop on other people's conversations."

"Do you eavesdrop?"

"What? Do I eavesdrop?" I put my hand to my chest. I suppose I should have seen that coming. But I wasn't really an eavesdropper per se. The conversation between Joey and his sister notwithstanding.

"I know you're lying. There's this detective on TV who says when people answer a question by repeating the question, they're lying."

I don't know why this kid was bothering to ask me any questions at all. He already had all the answers. "I was going to say not often . . . and usually not on purpose."

He nodded. "So you want to know about the fight?"

I did. And he knew it. But I did not need to add the title of Erica Bloom, inappropriate child questioner, to my already infamous reputation. "I don't think your mother would appreciate me talking about . . . this . . . with you."

"That's not a no."

I threw my hands up. "I gotta go. You're going to get me in trouble." Not to mention the fact that he was really freaking me out with all his valid observations. I hustled down the front door steps.

"So you're not investigating the murder?"

I didn't answer. Just kept walking. He'd know I was lying anyway.

"And you don't want to hear about the catfight?" he called after me.

I stopped, but I didn't turn to look at him. "Do you even know what *catfight* means?"

"It's when chicks fight."

I turned. "You will not refer to females as chicks, and . . . are you saying your mom heard two women fighting that night?"

The kid smiled. "I knew you wanted to know. When I grow up, I want to be a private investigator too."

I frowned. Hopefully not in Otter Lake. I had a feeling he might put us out of business.

"Did she say anything else?"

"She—"

Suddenly the kid stopped talking.

"What? What happened?" I asked.

But the kid just swallowed. He was looking at something behind me.

Something or someone.

I peeked a look over my shoulder.

Uh-oh.

Chapter Seventeen

"And you must be Erica Bloom."

I turned to face the older woman standing behind me in the sheriff's uniform. She was a little heavy, had lots of graying hair swirled back into a bun, and had an almost grandmotherly way about her . . . you know, if it weren't for the gun at her hip.

I flashed her my winningest smile. "Sheriff Bigly? I thought you were a—" I don't know why I thought she was a man. What was wrong with me? I rebrightened my smile. The look on her face told me I would get nothing for my efforts. Not even an honorable mention.

She nodded. "Cole, you go on home. I'm done talking with your mom."

He looked over at me and said lowly, "Hit me up later." He then darted a quick look at Sheriff Bigly and added, "Good luck with the po-po."

I shot my hands in the air and shook my head as he sped off on his bike. "Kids. What are you gonna do?"

She nodded. "I'm glad we ran into each other, Ms. Bloom."

"You can call me Erica," I said. "Otter Lake is kind of a first-name—"

"I'd like us to get to know one another," she said.

"Okay," I said carefully.

"Why don't I go first," she said with a nod. "Tell you a little about me."

I swallowed hard and waited.

She squinted and looked up at the sky. "Okay, well, let's start with the important stuff," she said with another nod. "I'm a widower. I have three kids. Seven grandkids. And one more on the way."

"Congrat—"

"Thank you. We're all pretty excited about it." She scratched her cheek. "Let's see, what else?" The finger scratching her cheek popped into the air. "I've been lucky to have a long career in law enforcement."

"That's nic—"

"I say lucky because I like people. I really do. And I think they like me. For the most part." She looped her thumbs around her belt. "I'd like to think I'm a pretty nice lady. I especially like helping people. That's why I offered to cover for Grady Forrester. You see, I'm retiring. Otter Lake will be my last stint before I hang up the badge. But Grady, he's a good guy. And from what I've heard, you think so too, so we've got that in common."

"Uh-huh." For the life of me, I couldn't figure out why I was beginning to find this conversation so terrifying. But I was finding it terrifying. She was one intimidating grandma.

"You know what else I like, Erica?" she said, peering at me from under her hat. "Can I call you, Erica?"

"Sure?" Hadn't I just said she could call me that? Uh-oh, she was making me doubt myself already. Look alive, Erica.

"I like sleep. Like it a lot. Always have." She nodded some more and looked out toward the lake. "You know those deep long sleeps in a cool room under a warm blanket? Nothing better." She wagged a finger in the air. "When I get that kind of sleep, well, I wake up wanting to spread sunshine to everyone I meet. When I don't . . ." She chuckled. "I can be a bit of a bear."

I just nodded. Seemed safest.

"Here's the thing though, and you wouldn't know this yet, but as you get older, it gets harder and harder to get a really good night's sleep."

"It does?"

"Oh yeah. You know for women I think it starts when you have your first baby. There's all those night-time feedings and diaper changes. Now, of course, if you have a supportive partner that can be a big help, but I'm convinced something happens to a woman's brain when she becomes a mother. It changes. Senses are heightened, you know?"

I had no idea what she was talking about, but I was still nodding.

"I swear to you, I never needed a baby monitor. If one of my babies so much as sneezed—didn't matter if they were two floors away and six rooms over—I would hear it." She tapped her ear.

"Wow. That's really—"

"Horrible."

Huh, I was going to go with cool.

"You know why, Erica?"

"Sleep?" I guessed.

She snapped and pointed at me. "Bingo."

I smiled.

She was smiling too, but somehow her smile made mine wither on my face.

"It's not babies though that keep me awake these days."

I tried to say *No?* but my voice cracked. I had to clear my throat. "No?"

"No." She shook her head sadly. "Lots of things keep me awake these days. I have trouble turning my mind off. Ever have that problem, Erica?"

"Sure, I—"

"In fact, I haven't had a good night's sleep in days now."

"Really?"

"It's funny though, what happened to that poor girl," she said, looking back at the gazebo, "that doesn't keep me up at night."

"It doesn't?"

She turned back to meet my eye. "No, because I know I'm going to find the person who did that, and see that justice is done."

I nodded. Well, that was good.

"So you know what does keep me up at night now that I'm here in Otter Lake?"

I suddenly had a bad feeling about where all this was headed.

"It's you, Erica. You and Freddie Ng."

Yup, that's where I thought we were going.

"I can tell by the look on your face that you already know where I'm going with this."

And she was psychic. Great.

Sheriff Bigly rocked on her heels. "But let me say, Ms. Bloom, I'm not one to put much stock in rumors."

"Rumors?"

"Erica Bloom and Freddie Ng. Amateur sleuths? Town security officers? Your hijinks are legendary."

I smiled. "I wouldn't say I—"

"I don't like hijinks."

"Of course not." Probably didn't help her sleep.

"But as I mentioned, I don't put much stock in rumors."

I sensed a *but* coming.

"So I looked you up in the files at the Otter Lake Sheriff's Department."

So's were so much worse than *but*s. I pinched my lips and nodded.

"You have quite the—I won't say record, because you have yet to be convicted of anything—but you have quite the long list of investigations filed away under your name."

I shook my head.

"I've seen a lot in my day, Ms. Bloom. But never have I seen a file like yours. Trespassing. Break and enters. Indecent exposure. I believe there was even something about grave-digging in there?"

This time I nodded. Really didn't see the point in arguing. That would probably end up with me getting arrested.

"And now I find you . . . what exactly were you doing just now, Ms. Bloom?" she asked with a smile that said she couldn't quite believe what she had to say next. "Were you questioning a nine-year-old boy? Without a parent present?"

My hands went up again. "I thought he was ten." She didn't look impressed. "And really, I wasn't questioning him. It was more like he was badgering me into accepting information."

She sniffed and nodded. "So, am I to take that to mean you are not looking into the death of Alyssa Norton?"

"No," I said, shaking my head quickly. "Well, at least not in any official capacity. It's just that Candace is my friend, and she's really upset with what has been happening. Obviously. And she was all crying and telling us that she couldn't get married without knowing what happened to Lys—"

She held up her hand, and I stopped talking. It looked like every word out of my mouth was making her just a little more tired. I couldn't decide if that was worse than Amos wanting to throw up every time he saw Freddie and me. Speaking of Freddie, he was going to want to hear all about the new sheriff in t—

—except I wasn't talking to Freddie.

"I want to make this really clear for you, Ms. Bloom," Sheriff Bigly said, taking a step toward me. "You are going to stay far, far away from this investigation."

An insane little part of my consciousness wanted to say, *Or what?* But I was pretty sure that *or what?* involved me eating dirt and getting cuffed.

"I hope we understand each other."

I nodded. "It's just—"

She stopped me short with a look.

"Well, it's just that Otter Lake is a special kind of place. It's a close-knit community. Sometimes locals would prefer to talk—"

"Ms. Bloom, I'm not playing. You take one step over

the line," she said, pointing at the dirt. I took a quick look down. There wasn't a line, but part of me wouldn't have been surprised if there was. The dirt might have done it to itself out of fear. "I will take you down. You've already ruined one sheriff's reputation. I won't let you near mine."

I biked my way back into town without stopping at the gazebo. I was shocked by my first conversation with Sheriff Bigly . . . and then that shock turned to anger as I pedaled in the growing heat of the morning. I think it showed too. People were crossing the street when they saw me coming. I probably looked like the Wicked Witch stealing Toto.

And why was I thinking so much about *The Wizard of Oz*?

Oh yeah, that's right. Freddie and I had watched it a couple of weeks ago when we *weren't* on a friend break.

I mean, I did not ruin Grady's reputation as sheriff. Everybody respected Grady. And what did Sheriff Bigly expect? Was I not supposed to talk to my neighbors? That's not how Otter Lake worked. Everyone was affected by what happened to everyone else, and in this case, everyone was upset about what had happened to Lyssa. There was no way I could not talk about it.

I dropped off the bike back at the Dawg and headed to the marina on foot. I needed to get back to the retreat. Maybe I could catch my mother during a break to apologize. Sheriff Bigly had made me so mad, I wanted to get this apology over with then find a way to break this case wide open. I'd show that sheriff I was more than

put her hand to her chest. "I didn't say it. *You*
."

owered my voice. "I'm just saying it's your hand.
might have nerve damage or—"

Nah, it's just a flesh wound." Joey wiggled his fin-
in the air.

cringed as the nail had bounced around. "Please.
ase don't do that."

"Really, it's fine, Erica," Joey said. "I need to get
ck to Candace. I don't like her being alone right
ow."

I studied his face. Something about the way he had
aid that made my antennae perk up. "You mean
because she's so upset?"

"Well, there's that, but . . ." He shook his head.
"Weren't you the one who told Candace you thought
ou saw somebody suspicious looking at the cottage
he other day?"

"Well, I don't know if they were suspicious or not,
ut . . . yeah."

"I don't know if we're just paranoid after what hap-
ened to Lyssa," he said, "but I thought I heard some-
e walking around last night. By the time I got out
ere . . ." He shook his head.

"What did Amos and Sheriff Bigly have to say
out all this?"

He shrugged. "That we're supposed to call if any-
ng happens. That they're keeping a close eye on
rything. That they're doing everything they can to
d Lyssa's killer. That kind of thing."

"Not exactly reassuring."

"Nope."

an indecent-exposuring, vandalizing, grave-digging
detective. I was a detective who kept her town safe.
I'd show her . . . and Freddie. I'd show them all!

As I walked, my anger calmed down a bit, and I
couldn't help but notice that the town somehow felt different today.

I mean, it was a lovely spring day, but . . . nobody
seemed too happy about it. Nope, Mrs. Carter normally had a big smile, but, right now, it was nowhere
to be seen. There she was just hurrying down the street
with her jacket clutched to her chest. She wasn't even
waving at anyone as she went by. Oh, and I had seen
Katie Myers with her four kids when I had walked by
the park earlier. She looked more stressed than usual
too. And she always looked stressed. Or . . . maybe it
was worry I was seeing. Even Big Don had been different. I mean, the man barely said anything on a good
day, but today he just seemed troubled.

It made sense. What had happened to Lyssa—in our
very small town—was shocking. Yes, we'd experi-
enced murders before. But this was different. The
way it happened . . . outside, like that . . . possibly
randomly . . .

Somehow Otter Lake just didn't feel as safe as it
used to.

Not safe at all.

It especially didn't help that a large werewolf of a
man was going into Dr. Robertson's office . . . with a
bloody rag wrapped around his hand.

Chapter Eighteen

I hurried across the street and peeked my head in the door of Dr. Robertson's office. Joey was seated in the waiting area.

"Erica, you don't have an appointment."

I turned to the woman sitting behind the half wall in the little reception area. It used to have a glass partition separating it from the rest of the room, but it caused everyone to shout their information and was considered to be generally unfriendly. "I know, Flo. I'm just visiting."

"Well, you'll have to skedaddle if someone needs a chair."

I looked around. Nobody was there but Joey trying to flip through the paper one-handed. There were at least ten seats open. "Got it."

Joey smiled as I sat down beside him. It wasn't a happy smile, though. Not that he should be happy-smiling given that the cloth covering his hand was covered in blood.

"Joey," I said, looking at his hand. to you?"

"I'm fine. It's nothing," Joey said. hand and took the cloth from it.

Holy frickin' crapfish!

Nail!

Big rusty nail sticking out of the webb tween his thumb and forefinger.

"It was a birdhouse."

"A birdhouse did this to you?"

"Candace has been wanting one for a wh thought now might be a good time with eve going on." He shot me an embarrassed smile. traction, you know?"

I nodded.

"But I was trying to put it up and . . ."

"I think maybe I should take you to the hospi

"Nah, Dr. R said he'd take a look at it first."

It was cute the way Joey had called him Dr. had settled into Otter Lake quite nicely. I mea had kind of introduced himself to the entire tov a bang on New Year's Eve, so everybody knev thing about him almost instantly. Got rid of awkwardness of people finding out he had beer little bit at a time. Plus, he was good with his h least he used to be—so he had been pickin of handyman work.

"I'm still thinking the hospital might b idea. You know, Dr. Robertson just loves office surgery, so he has new war stories to town."

Flo huffed a laugh from behind the cou

We both looked at her.

I lowered myself into the seat beside him. "Well, it's really sweet the way you keep trying to cheer Candace up."

He shook his head. "I know it's not going to change anything. I just want her to know that . . ." He sighed. "I don't know what I'm trying to say."

"No, I get it. You can't make it better, but you want her to know that you *want* to make it better."

He nodded.

"You could probably just tell her that instead of . . ." I looked down at his hand, and instantly regretted it.

"I can't really get her to talk about much of anything right now."

I searched his face for what he meant by that, but he didn't meet my eye.

"She's just so sweet about everything." He shook his head. "I mean, I know my sister's being a—" He cut himself off. "I love my sister to death, but she's being awful. If I try to talk to Candace about it, she just acts like Toni's a complete angel."

"Candace does try to see the best in everyone."

"Yeah, but she can be honest with me," he said, bringing his good hand to his chest. "I think she might be worried that I'll take my sister's side."

"Or maybe she just doesn't want to deepen any divide between the two of you. She loves you so much, Joey." I remembered what she had told me about Joey being her *home*. "She probably doesn't want to put you in a bad position."

He nodded. "I just hated seeing her bend over backward to make Toni happy when Toni's not going to be happy."

"Why does Toni—" I cut myself off. I was going to say *hate*, but that seemed like a bomb of a word. "Why does Toni feel the way she does about Candace?"

Joey leaned back in his chair and looked up at the ceiling. "Ever since I got out of prison, my sister's been treating me like I'm made of glass."

I nodded. In fairness, he had fallen off a roof and put a nail through his hand in the space of just a couple of days, so I could see how she might feel this way, but it didn't seem like the right time to point that out. "Is it because of the way you went to prison?"

"She won't say it, but I know she feels guilty. It's not her fault though. I made my own choices. And now she's somehow got it into her head that I need a woman who can take care of me. And she thinks Candace is this . . . weak person, who can't take care of herself."

"And I'm guessing you can't convince her otherwise?"

"Nope. Not at all," Joey said. "I love my sister so much. I can't imagine her not being at my wedding, but she's making this impossible." He sighed. "Maybe Candace and I should just get married at the courthouse."

"Whoa. Whoa. Whoa. That is not going to happen." I was thinking that Joey maybe didn't appreciate the amount of hours that had already gone into this shindig . . . and the friendships that had been lost. "Let's not get crazy. And what about Nonna? She wants to see her grandson married in a traditional ceremony, right?"

He nodded his head. Man, he was looking so glum.

"Listen. Maybe I could talk to Antonia."

Joey frowned and shot me a sideways look. "Are you sure you want to do that? Toni can be a little . . . well, she's tough."

"Sure, but I'm—" I was about to say *good with people* but then my mind flashed back to Tommy and the golf balls. So many golf balls. "I can always just give it a try." And it's not like my to-do list was that . . . well, best not to think about that either.

"You can try," Joey said. "Thanks, Erica."

I nodded and patted his arm.

Just then Dr. Robertson walked out from the back. "So who's next, Flo?" She pointed at Joey. Joey waved . . . with his bad hand.

Dr. Robertson smiled. "You did the right thing coming to me first."

Joey turned to me with very wide eyes and just a hint of a smile. "If anything should happen to me in there . . ."

I patted his arm. "I'll tell Candace you love her."

"Mom?" I closed the front door of the lodge behind me.

By the time I had got back to the retreat, it was getting pretty late in the day. I was hoping I might be able to catch my mom just before dinner.

I walked to the kitchen that was bustling with caterers. "Has anyone seen my mother?"

"She was here a minute ago," one person, with avocado smeared down the front of her apron, said.

I nodded my thanks and headed to the hallway just as I heard a noise come from the back.

Oh, she had to be in her bedroom.

"Mom," I called out again, walking down the hall. "I know you are probably really upset with me and you have every right to be." I turned the doorknob to her bedroom. "I just wanted to say that—"

I swung the door open and . . .

It hit the wall.

I couldn't stop it . . . what with . . .

"Mom? Zaki!"

My mother and Zaki sat huddled in her bed looking as horrified as I felt . . . with the sheets clutched to their naked, naked chests.

"What are you doing?!"

Chapter Nineteen

"Don't answer that!" I shouted. "Please don't answer that."

I lunged for the door handle.

"Erica? Darling?" my mom called out as I slammed it shut. "Don't go. We should talk about this."

"Don't have to!" I shouted. "I'm good. It's fine. I'm just going to . . . go." I almost patted the wood face of the door, but my hand didn't seem to want to touch anything. "Oh! And, uh, sorry about the other night." I spun away.

Well, that was one thing off my to-do list.

And it had only cost me the soul of my inner child.

I hurried down the hall and back out the front door of the lodge.

It was all fine though.

My mother was an adult. I was adult.

This was fine.

I just needed a bit of fresh air. I sat in one of the

Adirondack chairs and pinned my hands between my knees.

And . . . and . . . besides, I had liked Zaki when I had met him that one brief, brief time. So, you know, maybe this was a good thing. And it was probably a really good thing I hadn't shouted *Get off my mother!* like I had wanted to. That might have made future encounters even more awkward.

I rocked a little in the chair.

This must have been what the twins were talking about earlier when they said my mother should really tell me something. And hadn't one of them said, *Erica's not an idiot. She's going to figure it out*? Well, ha. Joke was on them. I hadn't.

I mean, of course I hadn't. My mother didn't date! If that's what we were calling it. She was married to her work and to . . . well, me.

But this was cool too.

Rhonda said relationships changed . . . evolved. Well, this one was evolving with a bang.

"Erica?" my mother said, sweeping out of the lodge. "Are you all right?"

"I'm fine. So fine. Everything's great. You can go away now," I said, shooing with my hand without looking directly at her. I was worried the sight of her might cause flashbacks. And I didn't really think this was something we needed to talk about.

"I brought you a carob muffin and lemonade."

Dammit. My mother made a really good carob muffin. She passed me a plate and a glass then sat in the chair beside me. I guess we were talking after all. I broke off a corner of the muffin and shoved it in my mouth.

An awkward moment of silence passed while I chewed.

My mom and I often had trouble jumping right into conversations. So I guess it wasn't surprising that this occasion was no exception given that I had walked in on her afternoon deligh— Oh God, and now I needed to bleach my brain.

"So . . ." my mother began.

"So," I said.

"Sorry I was so busy yesterday," she said. "I could tell you wanted to talk but—"

"It's fine. I just wanted to say sorry for the . . ." What was I sorry for? I seemed to be suffering from short-term memory loss.

"I understand. Well, maybe not understand. I'm sorry you and Freddie are going through something," she said. "But don't worry. The retreat's going well."

"Good," I said. "Good. I'm glad."

"You . . ." she began, seemingly like she was now going for the elephant on the porch, "haven't noticed any of the canoes missing lately, have you?" *And* she bailed.

"No. No. I don't think so." Not that I would have noticed something like that.

"I thought one was missing yesterday. I hope the ladies aren't taking them without letting me know. There's so many women. It's hard to keep track of everybody."

I nodded.

Another moment passed.

Okay, this was ridiculous. "You know . . ." I began. "You could have just told me."

"I know, darling. I'm so sorry," she said quickly. "I was just waiting for the perfect time and—"

"Well, that back there," I said, jerking a thumb in the direction of her bedroom, "was not it."

Her eyes went very wide and she shook her head in a shudder. "You're telling me."

We looked at each other and burst out laughing.

It was that hysterical kind of laughter. Like the kind that makes tears stream down your face. And it went on for a really long time. I guess we both had a lot of nervous energy to kill.

Once we had calmed down enough to talk, I wiped my eyes and said, "So how long has this been going on?"

"About six months."

"Six months!"

"I met him at that yoga meditation retreat I attended in Tuscon."

"Why didn't you tell me sooner?"

"Well, I wasn't sure where it was going at first, and all the experts say don't bring a new partner in to meet your child if you're not sure it's going to last."

"Mom, I'm not a child."

She smiled sweetly. "You'll always be my baby."

I frowned at her. "So, it's serious then?"

She shrugged, but it was one of those happy, totally infatuated shrugs.

"He treats you well?"

"So well."

"Wow." This was . . . strange. As bizarre as it sounds, I never pictured my mother being in a long-term relationship.

"So, what do you think of him?" she asked.

"Well, I only met him one time really—oh God, and

then at the campfire! He thinks I'm insane, doesn't he?"

"No," she said, shaking her head. "No."

The second *no* somehow really cast doubt on the first one.

I dropped my head into my hands. "That was why you didn't want me at the retreat. You were afraid I was going to embarrass you, weren't you?"

"Of course not. I just wanted you two to meet in a less formal setting, and . . ."

"And what?"

She shook her head and suddenly looked kind of sad. "I was afraid of you attending this particular retreat because . . ."

"Because?"

"It's me, isn't it?" she said with a nod. "I'm the reason you're still single."

"You are?" I mean, I may have laid some blame at her feet once or twice for my inability to sustain a lasting relationship. I hadn't exactly had a traditional childhood not knowing who my father was, and she had always bucked the idea of traditional forms of—

"I put too much pressure on you."

Wait a minute . . .

"To carry the mantle of Earth, Moon, and Stars. You feel the pull, but you're worried you can't answer the call and have a relationship—"

"Mom, believe me. That's not it," I said, leaning my head back against the chair to look up at the sky. My eyes were drawn back down though to the sight of Caesar ambling his way down the porch. He must have heard the siren song of my mother.

"Well, if I'm not the reason you're still single—"

We certainly glossed over that rather quickly.

"Then there's only one other explanation."

I gave her another suspicious side-eye. "There is?"

My mother stooped over to lift Caesar to her lap. I grimaced in pain for her. She was going to pop a disk lifting that kind of weight. "It's Freddie."

I stared at her. "Now Freddie is the reason I am still single?"

"And you are the reason he is still single."

"What?"

"Well, maybe not the entire reason," she said, nuzzling faces with my fur brother.

Gross. She'd be single again soon if Zaki saw her doing that . . . *and* my mother wasn't single. That still felt weird in my head.

"Actually," she went on. "It's more like you insulate and protect each other so that neither one of you has to dig any deeper to figure out what your issues really are."

"What?" I asked again in a super high-pitched voice.

"You both really want a significant other, right?"

"Right."

"But you both are each other's significant other. There is no room for anyone else."

"That is so not . . ." I shook my head. My knee-jerk reaction to most of her observation was that she was crazy . . . but . . . Freddie was the person I spent the most time with . . . and I had been miserable when I felt like he was freezing me out. "Say . . . say, you're not totally wrong, then—"

"Why, thank you, darling. That's high praise coming from you."

I frowned.

She shrugged.

"What I was going to say is that current fight aside, Freddie is really important to me. I don't want us to not be friends."

"Of course not," she said. "That's not what I'm suggesting at all."

"Okay . . ."

"You two have to stop being codependent. And you have to help each other make room for other people."

"Freddie and I are not codependent," I said. "He eats way more pizza than I do and—"

"You stop each other from facing uncomfortable truths."

Suddenly I was squinting and looking around. Probably looking a bit like Robert De Niro. Maybe not *my* best look. "What truth am I protecting Freddie from exactly?"

"Probably from answering *the question*."

I sighed and flopped back in my chair. "And we're back to the question." I'd only known about my mother's relationship for like two minutes, and her new boyfriend was already starting to annoy me.

"Well," my mother said, tilting her head side to side, "you two did put on quite a show that ensured neither one of you would have to answer *the question*."

"No, we didn—"

She shot me a look that seemed to say for the first time ever she was truly concerned she might have given birth to an idiot.

"We may have done that a little bit," I said, swatting at a black fly. I hated those little suckers.

"Did you ever ask Freddie if he was nervous about

bringing Sean to town for the wedding? That maybe that was the reason he didn't invite him?"

I frowned at her. How did she know all of this? Who was she talking to? Everybody . . . she was probably talking to everybody. Otter Lake was like that. "No. Why would I do that? It's a nonissue, everybody knows Freddie is gay."

A chipmunk suddenly popped up onto the porch. My mom's arms tightened around Caesar. The twins like to feed the little critters peanuts, so they were pretty bold these days.

"I know that everybody knows that Freddie is gay," she said with a grunt as Caesar squirmed. "But he has never brought anyone around before, and everyone is going to be there."

"But nobody would have said anything."

"I don't think so either, but you never know." Caesar was pushing himself up on his hind legs on my mother's lap to break her grip as she tried to talk around his head. "Mrs. Jones used to throw holy water on me when she thought I wasn't looking. She meant well. It took me a long time to figure out why I was always damp."

"I know but—"

"Or maybe it's not that," she said, spitting fur from her mouth. "Maybe he's nervous about how to act with a boyfriend in front of everyone he's ever known. He's never done it before."

I frowned. "I guess it's possible."

The chipmunk was creeping closer toward us on the porch.

"Seriously?" my mother said, beads of sweat popping up on her forehead. Caesar wriggled harder in her arms.

I stuck out my foot, and the chipmunk scurried away with a squeak.

"Thank you," my mother said with a sigh, and Caesar settled back down. He shot a look at me that spoke of plots for my death though.

"Yeah, right back at you," I grumbled.

"The deeper question here for the both of you," my mother said, meeting my eye with a scolding look, "is why haven't you talked about it? You are best friends."

"I . . . don't know." I frowned and sank back in my chair. "Where is all this coming from?"

"Zaki and I . . . have spoken on the topic. He helped give me an outside perspective."

I shot her a side-eye. "So that's going be how it is from now on, huh? Now there'll be two of you psycho-analyzing me?"

If I was not mistaken, she looked to be blushing. Or maybe her color was just from wrestling a sumo-sized cat. We sat in silence a good long while. Finally she said, "I may not have invited you to the retreat, but I did invite Grady."

"You did what?" Okay, that was overstepping. That was a big ol' boundary cross. That was—

Just then my phone rang. I looked down at the screen. "It's Candace."

My mother nodded.

"Hey, how are you doing?"

"Erica, did I catch you at a bad time?" Something about her voice didn't sound quite right. Granted, she'd been through a lot, but she sounded almost scared. "Not at all, what's up?"

"Well, this may sound crazy, but I need to ask you something."

"Go for it."

"You haven't been in the shed behind my place, have you? Or Freddie?"

"What? The shed behind your place? Why?"

She sighed, but her breath sounded shaky. "I guess that's a no."

"What's going on?"

"Nothing. I'm just crazy," she said. "I haven't slept much since . . ."

"Candace, was someone in your shed?"

At that point, my mother jumped to her feet, dropping Caesar somewhat unceremoniously onto the porch, and went inside.

"Nothing's been taken, but I swear things have been moved around."

"Where's Joey? Did you call the sheriff's department?"

"He's . . . I don't know where he is exactly. He said he had to run an errand, but I can't get a hold of him."

Oh crap, he might have had to go to the hospital after all. I jumped to my feet.

"What about Antonia and Nonna?"

"They left. Joey doesn't even know they're gone. Things were getting a little . . . tense, so Antonia took Nonna to a hotel."

"I get it," I said quickly. "Doesn't matter. Did you call the police?"

"I did call over to the department, but Sheriff Bigly said . . ."

I could feel myself getting angry already.

". . . just keep an eye on things and give her a call if anything else happens."

"What? Seriously?" I pulled my hair back from my face.

"Well, I did tell her that it was probably my imagination."

And Sheriff Bigly wouldn't know that Candace hated to cause trouble for anyone even when she really needed help. And why didn't she know that? Because she wasn't from Otter Lake. "Okay, I'm coming over."

"You don't have to do that."

"We don't know who killed Lyssa or why, and now someone is snooping around your property? I'm coming over."

"I really don't know that for sure. Like I said, I'm tired, and—"

"Already on my way."

Just then my mother came back out and she tossed me her boat keys. "Bring her back here."

Chapter Twenty

Some clouds had rolled in and it was getting dark fast. I really didn't love boating at night, but I made it without incident to Candace's. I tied the boat off and headed up the path to her place. Turned out, I also really didn't love walking up to a cottage in the dark not being able to see what might be hiding in the woods. Stupid Freddie. Again, this was another one of those things we were supposed to do together. My mother's words were still rattling around in my brain though. Maybe I was being too hard on him. Maybe he really was freaked out by the idea of bringing Sean to Otter Lake, and I was like some sort of security blanket slash punching bag for all of his upset feelings. Maybe I was freaked out by the wedding too, and—

Just then a tree branch snapped in the distance.

And maybe I was about to die because I was distracted with too much introspection.

I hurried up the cottage steps and rapped on the

door. Enthusiastically. I heard Candace scream on the other side.

"It's just me," I said loudly, but, you know, not too loudly. Not sure why. I guess I didn't want the person spying on me from the woods overhearing our conversation. "Let me in."

The door whipped open, and there stood doe-eyed Candace clutching a double-pronged marshmallow skewer.

"Hey," she said, reddening and putting the skewer down on the table by the door. "Sorry. I don't even know why I was holding . . . that."

We both looked at the metal rod.

"My imagination is totally running away from me."

"I get it," I said, closing the door.

Man, Candace looked even more tired. She had dark circles around her eyes and she had gone back to the "obviously unwashed hair loosely piled on her head" look. Not for the first time in my life, I wished I was a hugger. She looked like she could use a hug.

We stared at each other for a moment before I raised my arms. Oh what the hell.

She fell into my arms so hard, I fell back against the door.

"Thank you so much for coming, Erica."

"There, there," I said, patting her back. Her shoulder had somehow jabbed itself under my chin, pinning the back of my head against the door. And here I was worried a hug would be uncomfortable. "You seemed a little more freaked out now than you were when I spoke to you on the phone. Has anything happened?"

"I keep hearing things outside," she said, stepping back and shooting a look over her shoulder.

"What kind of things?"

"I don't know," she said, fiddling with her hands. "But . . . but, okay, so I was just in the kitchen getting a glass of water and, well, the window's stuck, so I'm hearing all the bugs and frogs and then . . ."

"And then what?"

"They all went quiet," she said. "Like that." She snapped her fingers. "Then right after I heard this twig snap—" Her eyes darted over my face. "You probably think I'm crazy."

"Are you kidding me?" I squeaked. "That's really freaking creepy. It's like when my mother and I are at the retreat, like in the living room or something, and everything's cool, then all of a sudden, out of a dead sleep Caesar whips his head up and looks at the window."

"Exactly!"

"And you know he can hear something that we can't, and . . . and it's probably not good."

Candace nodded.

"Okay," I said, nibbling my lip. "I'm not doing a good job of calming you down here, am I?"

She waved what I was guessing was supposed to be a dismissive hand in the air, but it came off a little frantic. "I haven't heard anything like that though in like twenty minutes. I think if anyone was going to do something, they would have done it by now."

"Okay, whatever, I'm taking you back to my mom's," I said, grabbing her elbow. "You can text Joey and tell him to meet you there. Did you call the sheriff again?"

"No, I felt . . . silly, I guess, after the last time I spoke to her."

I clenched my fist. *Bigly.* "She does that to people."

"Are you sure your mother won't mind if . . ."

"You know, the only thing bothersome about you is that you're always worried you're bothering other people. Now come on."

She grabbed her keys off the table by the door and moved to head out. I didn't follow though.

"What?" she asked, looking at me.

"Aren't you forgetting something?" I said, looking at the table.

"The skewer?"

"Um, yeah," I said. "It's a long sixty-second walk to the boat. Do you need anything before we go?"

"Not really," she said, but then a strange look came over her face. "But . . ."

"But what?"

"I know it sounds silly, but . . ."

"Candace." I swear, people trying not to be annoying were very annoying.

"My dress," she said, placing her hands on either side of her head.

"What about your dress?"

"My dress is actually in this wardrobe container in the shed. We didn't have any room because this place is so small and—"

"Your dress is out there?" I pointed at the back window.

"It was fine when I checked earlier, but now with the whole frog-blackout . . ."

"You want to make sure it's okay."

She nodded. "I know it's just a dress, but what if it's an animal or something that got into the shed and—"

"It's not just a dress," I said. "It's your wedding dress." I was really trying hard to think like a bride.

"We'll just check it out real quick and then we'll get out of here."

"You know what? I'm sure it's fine." The hand she had waving in the air said it was fine, but the look of her face told a whole other story.

I dropped my chin and looked at her from underneath my brow. "I have a question you might want to ask yourself."

She waited.

"Do you want Freddie procuring you a new wedding gown?"

"Let's go," Candace said, walking out the door. "Quick."

Chapter Twenty-one

"It's not that I think Freddie has bad taste," Candace whispered.

I nodded.

"It's just . . . he can be very rigid about the way he feels things should be done."

"You don't have to tell me that."

"And for the most part, I really like his choices, but for my dress—" An animal scurried under a bush like two feet away from us and Candace nearly snapped my forearm like a twig.

"It's okay. It's okay," I whispered, trying to pry her fingers from their death grip. "Just an animal. Maybe even a toad."

"Sorry."

"No problem."

We continued clutching each other's arms as we crept around the side of the cottage. I was holding a lantern. I didn't exactly like the way it was lighting us up, but it was really dark, so we didn't have much choice. Besides, it was probably just a raccoon causing problems back here. Or maybe a skunk.

Probably wasn't a killer on the loose.

Probably.

Candace's dress had better be really nice.

As we passed the chairs Candace had placed around the fire pit, a strange noise sounded from the distance . . . like the shed distance. It was maybe something . . . falling?

"What was that?" Candace hissed.

"I don't know," I said quickly. "But pass me that," I said, waving at a chair. I spotted another marshmallow skewer resting on one of the arms. Candace gave me her skewer and reached for the other.

"Do you think that was a raccoon?" Candace whispered.

"A big raccoon."

She nodded.

"Like a bear-sized raccoon."

We froze.

"You don't think it's a bear, do you?" Candace asked.

"You didn't leave any food in there, did you? Like candy for the wedding or something?"

She shook her head no.

"Well, then, I doubt it's a bear. But a raccoon could make a real mess of your wedding stuff." I believed that too. I also believed that if the murderer was hiding out in Candace's shed waiting to kill her, he or she could have done it three times over by now. Hopefully. But then again, maybe he or she wasn't in a rush.

"Erica, listen. I know you're like really brave and stuff—"

"Do I look brave to you?" I was pretty sure my eyes were widened to three times their normal size.

"Maybe we shouldn't—"

"Did I ever tell you about Freddie and the bat?" I asked, taking a hard swallow. We still hadn't moved. Both of us had our eyes glued to the shed.

"Freddie and the . . . what?" Candace whispered. "No."

"Yeah, yeah," I said, taking a step forward and pulling Candace with me. "So this one time we were sitting on his back porch and he's all like, *Do you hear that?* And I swear I couldn't hear anything." We crept closer to the shed. "But he keeps saying he hears something—like a rustling under the cover of the barbecue. And I'm thinking, You're crazy, Freddie. I don't hear anything. But he won't let it go. So I say to him, *Then take the cover off and see what's there.* But he's looking kind of spooked, and he starts going on about rabid skunks and raccoons, so he picks up this broom, turns it around, and pokes the handle under the cover of the barbecue." We took another step forward. "But nothing happens. No sound. No nothing. There's nothing under there. And I'm thinking I knew I hadn't heard anything. Then just as he says, *I guess you were right—BAM!* this bat comes flapping out from under the barbecue right at Freddie's face. It's all blind from the sunlight and crazy. Freddie starts screaming like someone is stabbing him, and I'm screaming too. He throws the broom in the air, and my beer goes flying." I took a quick breath. "It was pretty funny."

"Erica, why are you telling me this story right now?" Candace whispered. "Do you think an animal is going to come flying out at us?"

"Just the opposite," I said, shaking my head. "I mean, what are the odds of something like that happening twice?"

"That's not very good logic."

"No, it isn't, is it?" I said quickly. "You know, I'm sure your dress is fine. Maybe we should get out of her—"

Just then the shed door banged open and a blur came tearing toward us.

Chapter Twenty-two

"Bat!" I shouted.

It wasn't a bat though.

"Erica!"

Candace and I stumbled back clutching each other, before falling to the ground.

"Who is it?"

"I don't know!" I fumbled for the lantern and raised it toward the trees.

Man! Definitely man! Running for the woods!

"Hey! Who are you? What are you doing here?"

Shockingly, he didn't answer. Didn't even stop.

Candace and I stayed clutching each other, listening to him crash away through the trees.

A moment later, we were still clutching each other, but in silence.

The only sound was our breathing.

Candace and I helped each other get to our feet. Luckily neither one of us impaled ourselves on our marshmallow sticks.

"Are you okay?" I asked.

She looked at me with big eyes. "I think . . . I think maybe I recognized that guy."

"Really?"

"Well, Lyssa only showed me one picture on her phone. But that . . . that could have been Justin, her boyfriend."

I dropped Candace off at the sheriff's department, and told her I'd be back to pick her up in a bit. I didn't exactly want to waste any time talking to Sheriff Bigly at the moment. One because she would probably see my helping a friend out as investigation interference, and two, I had another sheriff that I wanted to have a word with.

Enough was enough already.

Yup, I was feeling pretty righteous and wound up by the time I got back into my mom's boat. Somebody needed to tell Sheriff Grady Forrester that it was time to get back to work, and if nobody else was going to do it, I guess it had to be me.

I started out across the water feeling like I totally had right on my side. The cool night air brushing back my hair as I headed on my mission seemed to prove it.

Sadly, in the short, short time it took me to get to Grady's part of the lake though, I had decided that seeing him was the worst idea I had ever had, and I was really praying he wasn't home.

I'm mean, seriously, for all I knew that lady who made sampler plates was back . . . or he was baking more cupcakes.

One never knew with Grady these days.

Unfortunately for my failing nerves, as I pulled alongside his dock it became clear that he was home. His boat was there and a yellow glow filled the front window of the cabin, so, yup, he was home.

It would have been a pretty cozy sight, if, you know, this didn't severely suck.

I took a deep breath. I could do this.

This town was in crisis, and it needed its sheriff back. I knew with all my heart that Grady would have gone over to Candace's to check things out when she first called, and maybe this whole tragic chapter in Otter Lake history could have been finished. I mean, it wasn't like I was asking him to cut his vacation short because some kids were running wild with spray paint. This was murder.

Worse yet, a part of me was wondering if maybe Sheriff Bigly hadn't been a little bit on to something when she accused me of ruining Grady's reputation. Not that I believe his reputation as sheriff was ruined, but maybe it was partially my fault that Grady thought this town didn't need him. Freddie and I had undermined his authority more than once the last couple of years. Maybe he thought people didn't care if he was heading up this investigation or not.

But they did.

At least I knew that I did.

And he didn't just get to bail on everything.

I trudged my way up the path that led to Grady's door, checking my phone quickly to make sure I hadn't missed a text from Candace.

Nope, no text.

Okay, well, no problem. As I had told myself many times now, *I could do this.*

No matter how difficult.

I took a deep breath.

Hard to deny that seeing Grady, though, always stirred up all sorts of feelings—longing, regret, sadness, anger . . .

. . . lust.

I stopped walking. My eyes were glued on the front window of the cabin.

What the . . . ?

Grady was sitting on his couch, wearing earphones . . . and not much else. In fact, I couldn't quite be sure, but he might not be wearing anything at all. It was hard to tell because he was . . . knitting . . . and the yarn was draping over all the right—or wrong, depending upon how you looked at it—places.

This too . . . was new. I swallowed hard. Grady had never been into the yarn arts when we were together.

I tried to get my feet moving again, but . . . my God, the muscles in his forearms danced beautifully with the rhythm of his needles. It was mesmerizing. And all those muscles with the yarn? The contrast was just . . . overwhelming. It was kind of like seeing a fireman holding a kitten. Or a Viking holding a lamb. Not that I had ever seen a Viking holding a lamb. But if it looked anything like Grady holding yarn then—

Oh my God! What was I doing? This was wrong! I had only meant to come up and knock on Grady's door, and now . . . now I was an exhibitionist! No, wait, that wasn't right. It was the other one. A voyeur! A Peeping Tom! Like I had been at the cake shop . . . oh no, it was a pattern!

Just then my phone buzzed in my hands. I yelped and flung it in the air.

I bent quickly to pick it up.

Maybe Grady hadn't seen that. It was dark out here, and he had been really focused on his stitches. I knew you had to be careful with knitting. It wasn't like crocheting. You drop a stitch and—

I knew that wasn't the case.

Nope, something had already changed in the air.

It was that strange prickly feeling you get when you know someone is looking at you.

I slowly rose to my feet and looked back at the window.

Grady's face was still tilted down toward his knitting, but his eyes were targeted directly at me.

I waved a hesitant hand of greeting in the air. It withered and sank back down pretty quick.

He waved back.

Well, that was a good sign . . . unless he waved at all the Peeping Toms in his yard.

Chapter Twenty-three

"Hi . . . Grady."

"Erica."

Turned out he wasn't naked after all. He had his swim shorts on. "I, uh, didn't know you were a knitter." He was standing in the frame of his door, but I was keeping my distance on the lawn.

"Just taken it up recently."

I looked down at my phone quickly. Spam text. Of course it was a spam text.

"My mother still runs that knitting group at the library."

"Right," I said. "I always thought I should maybe . . ." There wasn't any point to finishing that thought.

"So," he began, "you want to tell me why you were staring at me through my living room window?"

"I wasn't . . . doing that," I scoffed.

Grady held his stern sheriff's expression.

"Fine, I was, but it was a total accident. I saw you knitting naked, well, not naked, and totally by acci-

dent, and I thought, *Oh, I wonder if Grady is okay?*"
I said, nodding. "Because not a lot of sheriffs knit.
Naked or otherwise."

Nothing. Just the stare-down.

"I thought maybe something had happened."

Grady raised his eyebrows. "Something had happened? Like what?"

"Like . . ." I flung a hand in the air. "Like maybe
someone had died and you were knitting them . . .
something. And then I thought maybe now's not the
right time to inter—"

Suddenly the strangest thing happened. A smile
broke out across Grady's face. Then he laughed. Hard.
Like we're talking almost guffaw territory.

"Um . . . Grady?"

He shook his head. "I haven't seen you this embarrassed since . . ." He shook his head again. "Doesn't
matter. It's okay. I'm sure it did look weird to see me
knitting. Naked." He smiled again at me, but this time it
was no regular smile. Oh no. It was that smirk he always had on his face back in high school. That stupid
smirk that always . . . made me want to jump him. Gah.

"Now what were you worried that this was a bad
time for?"

I blinked. Suddenly I had no idea what it was I was
doing here. It was a little like rehearsing a play for
months—years—only to have the other character flip
the script at the last minute . . . *which* was probably
where that expression came from.

"I was just . . ."

He planted his hand on the frame of the door and
twisted his shoulders side to side.

"What are you doing?" I asked.

"Stretching. I think I pulled a muscle wakeboarding the other day." He twisted his shoulders again. "Lower back."

My eyes darted down, got stuck there for a second, then jumped back up. "Well, stop it."

"Stop stretching?"

"Yes," I practically shouted.

He smirked again. "But I thought you liked to . . . watch?"

My jaw dropped. It dropped so hard I wasn't sure I'd ever be able to get it back up.

Grady laughed. "Sorry. Sorry. Just kidding. Now, you were going to tell me what brought you over here tonight?" He then chewed at the side of his thumbnail, which should have been gross but really just brought a lot of attention to his mouth, and a lot of my body parts were taking notice.

"Stop it!"

He dropped his hand. "I already stopped stretching."

"Not the just the stretching, the chewing, and . . . all this," I said, waving a hand out to him, mainly at his pectoral area. "You need to stop all of it." I mean, it kind of seemed like he was flirting with me right now, and I wasn't entirely sure why that was making me so angry, but it was.

Angry . . . and very, very confused.

Grady looked down at his chest. "I'm not really sure how to—"

"Hey, Grady!" a voice called out from behind me.

I jumped.

You have got to be kidding me.

I felt my shoulders tense. That had better not be who I thought that was.

"Hey, Freddie," Grady called out. "Come on in."

Come on . . .

Freddie brushed by me and up the steps to Grady's house.

. . . in?

"What's Erica doing here?" Freddie asked Grady.

He shrugged. "I've been trying to figure that out."

"Me?" I asked, looking at Freddie. "What are you doing here?"

"I was invited. I called Grady to ask his advice about some permits for the wedding, and he invited me over for a beer to discuss it."

My eyes snapped back to Grady's. "You invited Freddie over?"

"I did," he said with a nod. "Did you want to come in and join us for a—"

"No!"

"You don't have to yell," Freddie said. "She's always yelling . . . and chasing people."

I yelled some more in my head—gibberish-type sounds. My brain was broken. I could no longer form words.

"Well, if you don't want to come in," Grady said. "What can I do for you?"

"What the hell does that mean?"

This time there was no smirk, just Grady's eyes darting side to side. "It doesn't mean anything, I was just asking you again—"

"You know what?" I said, backing away from the steps. "I'm just going to go."

"Are you sure?" Grady asked.

"And you," I said with a point, "you need to get back to work."

"I do?"

"Call Bigly."

"Are you sure you don't want—"

"She's fine," Freddie said, moving to close the door. "What do you have by way of a microbrew?"

Chapter Twenty-four

"And then Freddie said, *What do you have by way of a microbrew?*"

Rhonda laughed—then caught my expression and stopped. "You're right. It's not funny. But this is good news, right? You always wanted Freddie and Grady to get along."

"Not without me!"

"These are strange times," Rhonda said. "But on a more serious note, how is Candace doing?"

I thought my stuff was pretty serious, but not by comparison, I guess.

Once again Sheriff Bigly had promised Candace that they would look into it.

At least she had dropped Candace back to the retreat—hoping to have a word with me—but we had thankfully not crossed paths. She had also shown Candace the picture of Justin on Lyssa's phone again. Candace was pretty sure that was the guy who had come crashing out of the shed. He had a distinctive spiky haircut.

I filled Rhonda in on all this then added, "Candace is staying at the retreat today because Joey's finishing up some work on Mr. Garrett's back porch."

"That's good," Rhonda said. "So you made any headway on finding out what was in Lyssa's bag?"

"Nope. I can't think of a way to get that information that doesn't involve me getting arrested." I sighed. "You know, I'm starting to think it might have been a bit unrealistic for us to promise Candace we'd find Lyssa's killer before the wedding."

"What?" Rhonda snapped. "What kind of attitude is that?"

"A realistic one," I said pretty miserably. "I mean, it's not like I didn't want to crack this case. For a whole bunch of reasons." Candace. The town. Lyssa . . . especially for Lyssa. "But I just don't think it's going to happen." I held my hand out. "Pass me the gummies."

She pulled the candy bag away. "No way. These gummies aren't for quitters."

"But I bought them." They were a peace offering for the missed lunch. "And I'm not saying I'm quitting. I'm just saying I may not be able to solve this in time for the wedding." I waved my hand out some more. "Come on. It's an emergency."

"You have a gummy emergency?"

"I have licorice stuck in my teeth, and I was hoping if I ate some gummies, I could dislodge it."

"Forget it. No gummies for you."

"Rhonda . . ."

"You need to get hungry . . . for justice."

I blinked at her.

"No, you listen to me," she said, straightening herself up in her seat. "This situation doesn't call for 'sad sack Erica.' It calls for 'crazy, who knows what she'll do next Erica.'"

I let my head loll to my side, so I could look out the window.

Rhonda whacked me on the thigh. Hard.

"Ow!"

"You need to stop feeling sorry for yourself this instant."

I rubbed my thigh. "I'm not really feeling sorry for myself. I'm feeling sorry for Candace and—"

"Well, then it's a good thing she's got you on her side, isn't it?"

I shot Rhonda a very skeptical look.

"Come on, you're no mere mortal."

That earned her an eyebrow raise.

"You're Erica *Doom*," she said, adding some serious gravity to the *doom*. "How many murderers have you helped bring to justice?"

"A handful."

"A handful," Rhonda repeated, mimicking my pouty voice. "That's awesome! Where's the Erica who somehow feels it's her job to solve each and every crime that happens in Otter Lake?"

I sighed. "Maybe she's on vacay with Grady." I hoped they were having a good time. Maybe drinking maitais by the lake. Playing volleyball. Eating—

"Well, you get her back here and get her back out there!" Rhonda pointed out the window.

"Get her back out where?" I asked with a frown. I was getting confused referring to myself in the third person. "That's the problem. I don't know what to do.

Lyssa's not from Otter Lake. She has little to no social media pres—"

"So?" Rhonda asked, looking like she was close to smacking my leg again. "Follow up on all your leads. Go back and see Tommy. Ask about the shiner—you know, if you can get close enough to ask. Talk to Candace again. See if there's anything else she remembers. Canvass the neighborhood. Nobody ever said investigating was easy."

We sat in silence for a moment. I prodded at the piece of licorice stuck in my teeth until it gave way. "You know what? You're right."

"I know am right."

"I'm going to do it," I said with a nod. "There's still time. I'm not giving up. I have to at least try." No, I wasn't about to sit back and do nothing while someone I cared about suffered. Maybe I wouldn't be able to figure out what happened to Lyssa in time for the wedding, but trying was better than doing nothing.

"That's the spirit. Oh! Here we go." Rhonda tossed the gummy bag into my lap and whipped up her camera. Our target was walking across the lawn with another tree resting on his shoulder.

Now that "fix Erica time" was over, I was thinking it was time to address another situation. A Rhonda situation.

"Um . . . Rhonda?"

"What?" she asked, camera clicking furiously.

"I need to ask you something."

"What is it? I'm trying to concentrate here." I could tell. Rhonda always stuck her tongue out just a little bit at the corner of her mouth when she was really focused on something.

"Um . . ." I just needed to say it. "Why . . . why are you still here?"

"What do you mean?" She never took her eye from the target.

"You have enough photos," I said. "*We* have enough photos. You have photos of him lifting trees. You have photos of him digging in the dirt. You even said you've got a couple of photos of him moving a boulder. You've built a case for the insurance company. He's not hurt. I think it's time to send those photos off and call it a day."

Rhonda took a few more snaps then rested the camera on her lap. "I can't. Not yet."

"Why not?" I asked, studying the side of her face. She was refusing to make eye contact with me.

"It's hard to explain," she said, suddenly looking pained. "But something's just not right about this whole situation. And I can't leave until I figure out what it is."

I frowned. "What do mean, something's not right?"

She threw a hand out. "Like what is somebody with that much potential doing committing insurance fraud?"

I cocked my head at her. "Um, correct me if I'm wrong, but isn't that all you know about him? That he's committing insurance fraud?"

She leaned back into her seat. "Oh no, you learn a lot about a person watching them hour after hour. He's . . . he's a good guy."

"Really. And what is it exactly that leads you to believe he is a good guy?"

"Well, for one," she said, straightening up and looking at me, "he tosses bits of food from his lunch to birds."

"That's it?"

"No, that's not it," she said with a frown. "But it is pretty adorable."

"Maybe, but it doesn't cancel out insurance fraud. And it is possible he was just littering and the birds were there."

"Nope." She pointed out the windshield. "Look at how he is handling that tree."

I took a quick look out the window. "I'm not sure I want to see how he handles . . . wood."

She snatched her gummy bag back from my hands. "Don't be disgusting."

I chuckled. "I'm sorry. Can I have the bag back?"

"No."

"Fine," I said, throwing my head back against the seat. "Tell me how he handles the trees."

"Look for yourself."

I did. I did look for myself. I had no idea what I was supposed to be seeing though. "It's a half-naked guy carrying a tree across the lawn. Why does he always have his shirt off?" For that matter, why did Grady always have his shirt off? It was very annoying.

"No, look at how careful he is with them. He never breaks a branch. He always digs the hole to just the right depth. Then he really gives them a good watering." She let out a long, slow breath. "I'm willing to bet every one of them survives its first winter."

"You're starting to scare me."

"What?" she asked, looking at me wide-eyed.

"Rhonda, he's a target."

"So . . . ?"

"So?" I fired back. "I'm starting to think you're falling for the target."

She looked back out the front. "I am not."

I dipped my chin into my chest and stared at her.

"I just . . . kind of want to talk to him before we turn him in."

"What?" I said, swiveling against the passenger door so I could fully face her. "You can't be serious. Freddie will lose his—"

"I know. I know," she said, closing her eyes. "I won't actually do it." She sighed. "I was just thinking it would be nice if I could."

I kept staring at her. "But you won't."

"I won't."

"Because you'd mess up any chance we'd ever have of working with an insurance company again."

"I know," she said miserably. "And I won't, but I can't let this go yet. I just know there is something more going on here, and I can't leave until I know what it is. Besides, we want to impress the insurance company, so we need to be thorough."

"I don't know, Rhonda," I said. "I'm not sure I'm comfortable with—"

"And why is it you and Freddie always get to be the idiots when it comes to love?"

I sighed and slouched back in my seat. "Just lucky, I guess."

Again, Rhonda was right. Not about our insurance scammer being a good guy, but about the fact that I needed to get back out there. And I knew just where to start.

The gazebo.

I still hadn't checked out the crime scene since Bigly had scared me off, but it was about time I did. I doubted that I'd find anything there given that the police would have combed through it by now, but that wasn't the point. I needed to follow every lead. Look under every rock. Explore every avenue . . . or dirt road that led to the gazebo, as the case may be, on Big Don's nephew's bike.

One never knew what surprises might lie around the bend.

What the . . . ?

I skidded to a stop and leaned back onto the bicycle seat, my feet balancing me on either side.

This . . . this *was* a surprise.

I brought a hand to my brow in a vain attempt to deflect some of the sun bouncing off the lake. The gazebo was actually a beautiful sight. Someone had strewn white gauze all around the structure and it was rising and falling gently in the breeze. It must have been hung the day before the wedding—in fact, I could see one side of it sagging where it had lost its pinning—but that wasn't the problem. The problem was, why was it still up? And why were all the plastic bins still there? And the chairs? It looked like the crime scene hadn't been touched. In fact if it weren't for the police tape fluttering around the gazebo railings, it would look like the sheriff's department had never been there at all.

Huh.

Okay, well, yes, I had figured that Bigly would have to bring in a specialized crime scene investigation team, but shouldn't they have come and gone already? What the heck was going on?

I glided down the bumpy walking path that led to the lake.

This made no sense. While my first impression of Bigly hadn't exactly been a warm one, I didn't get the feeling that she was incompetent.

There was something off about all this.

I stopped again right at the entrance to the gazebo. I couldn't go down to the dock because the police tape clearly said DO NOT CROSS, but I didn't need to, to see the supplies all neatly stacked and pushed to one side.

Freddie must be going nuts, not being able to get his hands on that stuff.

Yup, this was all very odd.

I scanned the shoreline on either side of the gazebo then turned to do a full three sixty. It was a beautiful spot and the trees blocked most of the view of the neighboring cottages, but—

Just then I caught sight of movement in the woods to my side.

I scanned the trees to pinpoint it.

There.

Somebody was there. They weren't moving now. But they were definitely there.

And . . .

They were wearing a windbreaker. It was the same person I had seen outside of Candace's!

"Hey, you!"

The figure jolted then started up the hill deeper into the forest.

Frick!

I really needed to stop doing that. Calling out never worked. I could catch them though. The bike trail led up the hill and they weren't moving that fast.

I pumped my legs trying to get up enough speed on

the flat section of the trail to make it up the incline. It wasn't easy with the uneven dirt, but I wasn't about to give up. That windbreaker was not getting away this time. I just needed to catch up then I'd ditch the bike and—

"Bloom!"

Sheriff!

Sheriff Bigly jumping out of nowhere right into my path!

The back wheel of the bike skidded away from me and the next thing I knew I was sliding across the dirt.

Ow! Ow! Ow!

Okay, I lost some skin on my knee . . . but there was no time for that!

I jumped to my feet. I could still catch windbreaker. I just needed to—

Bigly grabbed my arm. "Where do you think you're going?"

"I have to catch windbreaker! She's getting away." I still couldn't say for absolute certain it was a woman, but the shape and the way she moved—it was my best guess.

"What are you talking about . . . windbreaker?"

"There's no time for that," I yelled. "She's getting away!"

She retightened her grip on my arm. "Who's getting away?"

I pointed up the hill. "The person in the windbreaker."

The person who I could no longer see . . .

"I don't see anybody," Bigly said.

I huffed in frustration. "I'm telling you there is a

person in those woods wearing a beige windbreaker that knows something about Lyssa's death."

Sheriff Bigly studied me a moment then said, "Stay." She walked a couple of feet away but I could see she was talking into the radio at her shoulder.

"If you just let me go, I can catch up to the person and—"

"And what?" she shouted back at me. "Make a citizen's arrest of a . . . windbreaker? I don't think so." A crackle sounded at her shoulder and she walked away a little farther so I couldn't hear.

"By the time you get Amos out here," I shouted after her, "the person will gone. Just let me go. I'll keep a distance and—"

"That's not happening, Bloom," she said, walking back over. "Besides, you've got other plans."

"I do?"

"You're coming with me."

Chapter Twenty-five

"You hurt?"

I mumbled something. I wasn't really hurt. I mean, yes, my knee hurt—in that hissing kind of way skinned knees do—but I doubted she wanted to hear about that.

Bigly didn't arrest me. She didn't even take me to the sheriff's department.

She took me to the Dawg.

That's right, the Dawg. I had finally made a breakthrough in this investigation, but instead of chasing it down, we were contemplating menu items. Well, Bigly was. I was too busy being frustrated and trying to ignore the pain in my knee.

"You still take your coffee black, Judy?" Big Don asked, coming up to the table, pot in hand.

"I do."

He huffed a laugh, poured the coffee, then walked away . . . without asking me if I wanted one.

I stared after him. I guess Bigly caught the look on

my face because she said, "That's probably my fault. He'll be back."

I shot her a questioning look.

"We used to date."

I blinked at her. "You and Big Don used to date?"

She picked up her mug and nodded. "Forty-some years ago." She studied my expression. "Surprised, aren't you?"

"I . . ."

"You didn't think I knew the first thing about Otter Lake." She smiled. "But I used to be quite the regular."

Actually I was more surprised that Big Don had ever dated. I couldn't see it. He was just too . . . burly.

"We were both pretty fiery back then. Couldn't stop fighting long enough to make it work," Bigly said, taking a sip of her coffee and looking at me over the rim. "So why don't you tell me all about this windbreaker of yours."

I had to give my head a little shake to get back to the topic at hand. "I thought Candace already told you about the first time I spotted the person at her pl—"

She cut me off with a wave of the hand. "She did. But I want to hear it from you."

I sighed then told Bigly everything. When I was through, she asked, "Could it have been the same man you and Candace found rummaging in her shed?"

"I don't know. Maybe. The man wasn't very tall. He was slender too. But I still think that person in the windbreaker was a woman. I can't say why exactly, but I do."

She nodded.

I waited for her to say something, but she didn't. "Well?"

"Well what?" she asked before taking another sip of coffee.

"Well, don't you think that's suspicious? That the person in the windbreaker was at both Candace's place and the crime scene?"

She squinted. "Hard to say."

"What you mean is that you won't say," I said, leaning back in my chair. "At least not to me."

She smiled and tapped the side of her nose. "I had you pegged for a quick one, Bloom. Right from the start." She looked over to the bar. "Hey, Don! You got any of that pecan pie you used to make?"

He planted his hands on the bar and nodded.

"Get a piece for Erica here. I think she needs it. My treat."

I folded my arms over my chest. "I don't want your pie."

"It's not my pie," she said, lifting her coffee cup to me. "It's Don's pie."

"I don't care whose pie it is. I don't want pie."

She took another long sip before saying, "It's the least I can do seeing as I caused that spill you had on your bike."

I huffed. "It's not my bike either."

"Then whose bike is it?"

"It's Don's. I mean it's his neph—it doesn't matter! I want answers, not pecan . . ." The thought trailed away at the sight of Don coming toward me with a plate of pie and a really generous scoop of vanilla ice cream. He placed it in front of me and walked away.

"Go ahead," Bigly said.

I picked up the fork, but before I dug in I asked, "Why are you being so nice to me?" I pointed the fork at her. "And don't give me that crap about it being because of the tumble I took on the bike. I'm pretty sure you meant to do that."

She smiled. "Well, I tried being the bad cop with you. That didn't work. And I can't arrest you for riding a bike past a crime scene. So now I'm trying the good cop approach."

I waited. Well, actually it was more like I couldn't answer because buttery pecan filling was melting in my mouth.

She watched me for a moment then said, "I know you think that the sheriff's department isn't equipped to handle this investigation."

"You're right, I don't," I mumbled. "Not when you've got the crime scene—"

She held up her hand again. It was a very intimidating hand. "You need to accept that there may be more going on here than you are aware of."

"But I don't get it. Why haven't you cleared the scene? Why were you even at—"

Again with the hand. "I've already been through this with your partner, Freddie. And if he wasn't able to annoy any information out of me, you certainly won't."

"Freddie came to see you?"

"Threatened me with teams of imaginary lawyers if I didn't let him at those wedding supplies."

I sighed. She was right. There was no way I was going to be able to annoy answers out of her if Freddie couldn't. Freddie was very annoying when he wanted to be. Just ask my poor bangs.

"Listen. I get that you are friends of the bride. And I get that your . . . Otter Lake Security team cares about this town." She leaned toward me and put her hand over her heart. "But you need to leave this one alone and trust that we can handle it."

We met eyes for a moment before she pushed back her chair and got to her feet. "Now you finish your pie, Bloom, and think about what I said." She dropped some money on the table. "Or the next time I run into you anywhere near this investigation, I will lock you up."

I didn't say anything as she walked away, but I was totally muttering in my head, *I thought you couldn't arrest someone for just biking around a crime scene.*

"I'll find a reason."

My eyes snapped up to hers.

She winked.

I was so ready for this day to be over.

I glided over the lake enjoying the feel of the cool wind rushing over me. I didn't know what to think about anything anymore. I mean, part of me was wondering if maybe Bigly was right. Maybe I should just let the sheriff's department handle this. But on the other hand, private investigators looked into murder investigations all the time. It was part of the job. And while I didn't officially have my license, I was working under someone who did—Rhonda—and I *had* brought murderers to justice before. Of course, I usually was working with Freddie in those circumstances, but the point still stood. And, again, I had a bit of a problem sitting back and doing nothing when someone I cared about needed help. Maybe my mother should do a retreat on that.

When I pulled up to the retreat's dock, I found Candace waiting for me.

"You do not look happy," Candace said when I cut the engine. "Beer?" She lifted a bottle. Organic. Gluten-free. My mother's stash. "I heard the boat coming. Thought you might want this."

I smiled at her then jumped out to tie off the boat. "Have you tried one yet?"

"No," she said with a frown. "Are they that bad?"

"They're not good." I laughed, but it came out sounding as tired as I felt. "Joey's not back yet?" I asked, taking one of the beers from her.

"He didn't actually get to work today. His sister called. She said that Nonna wasn't well and . . ."

I nodded. "She needed him to come right away."

"I insisted he go. It's not like . . ." She shook her head. "He should be here soon." She then tilted up her bottle and took a sip of the rice beer. "Oh . . . oh wow. That really is terrible."

"Told you," I said, taking my own sip. I had to swallow pretty hard to get it down. "Let's sit." I walked down to the end of the dock, slipped off my sandals, and dipped my toes in the water. Candace did the same.

"You look kind of tired," Candace said. "Is everything okay?"

"I ran into Bigly today." I launched into the story of my day, recapping all that had happened.

"Erica," Candace said when I was through, "you know you don't have to do this. When you guys came to see me the day of . . . the day the wedding was supposed to be, I said I needed to know what happened to Lyssa—and I still feel that way, but—"

"Don't start," I said, pointing my beer bottle at her. "Your constant consideration is really . . . aggravating."

I looked over at her and we both smiled as the twilight sounds washed over us.

A little while later, Candace flicked her toe in the water and said, "You know, I don't think there's a spot in Otter Lake that isn't beautiful." She had obviously not seen Tommy's front lawn. "But I think your mom's island is my favorite spot."

"Oh yeah?"

"It's just so quiet . . . and peaceful. And safe. I've been hiding out inside at my place, but here, everything feels okay." She tilted her head back. "I wanted to show it to Lyssa but sightseeing wasn't really her thing."

I nodded.

"Erica," Candace said a moment later, "do you believe in bad luck? Or like curses?"

I put my beer down and rested my hands behind me on the dock, so I could look up at the first stars dotting the sky. "I don't know. I mean I'm sure I felt like I've had bad luck before. But it probably wasn't." Suddenly I looked at her. "You're not thinking—"

"That my wedding is cursed?" she asked. "Yeah, I kind of am."

"No, don't think that. What happened to Lyssa was tragic, but it doesn't have anything to do with—"

"Nobody wants this wedding to happen," she went on, looking back out at the water. "You know, except for Joey and me. And maybe you, Freddie, and Rhonda."

"Come on, that's not true. There's lots of people who—"

"His sister hates me," she said quickly. "My parents hate him. Maybe all that bad energy . . ."

I sighed. I wanted to argue with that, but Antonia had made her position pretty clear, and I didn't want Candace thinking she was crazy for feeling what she was feeling. "If Antonia doesn't love you yet, it's because she doesn't know you. And I'm sure the same is true for Joey and your parents."

Candace shot me a pained smile. "I don't even know if they are going to show up. My parents, I mean. They said something about it maybe not being possible to change their flight."

"I'm sorry. Is it really all because—"

"Joey's an ex-con? Pretty much. That and they don't think we've known each other long enough. I wish Bethanny was coming. We've gotten so much closer since New Year's, and she could always get through to them." She sighed. "But we either wait for Bethanny to be able to afford to come home, and then Nonna can't be there. Or vice versa."

"Hey, what about Joey's nonna? She wants to see you get married."

Candace shot me look. "She's got dementia, Erica. I could be the queen of England and she wouldn't know the difference." A strange look came over her face. "Unless I was a squirrel. Then she'd notice for sure. She really hates the tree rats." Suddenly her eyes widened. "That sounded awful, didn't it?"

I laughed a little. I couldn't help it. "Kind of."

"I don't know what's wrong with me?" She put her hands over her face. "And am I a bad person because I still want to marry Joey? Like right away. Even after what happened to Lyssa?"

I nodded sympathetically. "Probably."

Candace's hands dropped and her eyes went crazy wide.

"I'm kidding!" I near shouted. "Of course you're not a bad person. You're in love. You've found your person. It's not selfish to enjoy that."

"Are you sure?"

"Completely."

"Seriously, though, you haven't heard all of it." Candace suddenly looked sad again. "I've just got all this . . . guilt."

"Candace, it's not your fault that Lyssa—"

"No, that's not it. Do you want to know just how bad a person I am?"

"Absolutely," I said. "It might make me like you more."

She tried to smile, but the sadness was too strong. "When it first happened—I mean, before I found out she was gone and I just saw Amos walking up to our place—I thought to myself, *What's Lyssa done now?*"

I met her eye.

"Horrible, right?" She looked back out at the water. "It's just she always had to be the center of attention. And I was fine with that back in college. I didn't want the spotlight. But my wedding day?" She let out a shuddering breath. "Then I found out she was dead.

And now . . . I'm just so sad. Yes, Lyssa had her faults, but we all do. And it was like . . . she had this big emptiness in her that all the attention in the world couldn't fill up." She quickly swiped a tear from her cheek. "It's got to be horrible feeling that way."

I nodded some more. That was sad especially because any chance Lyssa had of finding another way through life had been taken from her.

"And"—she shook her head—"as much as I do love Joey, and as much as I want to marry him . . . it's just, well, not that the wedding doesn't matter . . ."

I looked at her.

"But it's not right what happened to Lyssa."

I nodded.

"And the wedding's just a day. It's our life together that's important. Because at any moment it could all be taken away." She looked up to the sky filling up with stars. "I'm sorry. I'm all over the place tonight. I know I'm not making any sense."

"Of course you're all over the place. You're human. If Freddie were here he'd say—" My brain caught up to my words and they died in my mouth.

"You okay?"

I took a deep breath and looked back up at the stars too. "I'm fine. It's just Freddie and I have never had a fight like this before."

She nodded. "I saw Freddie today about the location for the wedding. He wanted to have it at Hemlock Estates, but I guess Matthew's still doing renovations, so I think we're going to have the reception, at least, in the upstairs of the community center."

I frowned. "Where they have the bingo nights?"

She nodded. "Freddie's not happy, but there's enough room and . . . well, there's enough room."

I tried to hide everything I was thinking—cracked linoleum, wood paneling, sweat smells rising up from the hockey arena below. It was pretty hard.

"And if it makes you feel any better," she went on. "I think he's pretty upset too."

"It does," I said. "It really does. Thank you."

She laughed.

"What? You're not the only bad person around here." I looked at her. "But Freddie's and my problems are nothing compared to what you're going through."

She squeezed her eyes shut. "I'm so tired of thinking about my problems. Tell me how you're doing."

"Well," I said, curling my feet up into a cross-legged position, "you know what the worst part of this whole fight is?"

She looked at me.

"I don't even know what started it all." I brushed a pebble from the dock into the water. "I mean, obviously something happened between Freddie and Sean, but—"

"Oh Erica . . ."

Candace looked back to the water as my eyes bored into her.

"You know something."

She shook her head. "I . . . I'm not supposed to say anything."

"Oh my God, is Freddie dying? Was the whole breakup thing a lie? Is he sick and he didn't want me to kn—"

She frowned at me. "Freddie's not dying."

I let go of the breath I was holding. Okay, that might

have been a bit of a leap. "Please just tell me what is going on. I'm going nuts here."

Candace looked at me for a long, hard moment. "Okay." She threw a hand in the air. "He's going to kill me, but . . . okay."

Chapter Twenty-six

"So why did Freddie and Sean break up?"

A pained look crossed Candace's face, and it wasn't just because she had another sip of the gluten-free beer. "They had a big fight."

"Okay, about what?"

She grimaced.

I felt my cheeks go hot. "Was it . . . about me?"

She didn't answer. She didn't need to. The look on her face said it all. "How is that possible? I like Sean. I liked him the moment I met him."

She smiled sympathetically. "That's not the problem."

"Okay."

"Well," she said, before taking a breath, "you know how Freddie didn't invite Sean to the wedding?"

"Yeah, he said Sean was busy with school," I said quickly, "but my mother thinks he may be worried about bringing a boyfriend to town for the first time."

"Yeah, Sean's not busy with school," Candace said,

shaking her head. "And Freddie's not worried about bringing him to town. At least I don't think he is."

"So what's the problem?"

"From what Freddie told me, the whole thing really just got blown out of proportion. Freddie told Sean that maybe this wasn't the best time for him to come down. He knew I had invited Grady to the wedding, and he didn't want you to be alone."

"What?" I suddenly felt ten degrees colder. "Are you serious?"

"Sean, I guess, was a little upset by this and said something to the effect that *you* were Freddie's priority. Freddie said that wasn't true, that you're both priorities to him. And then he said to Sean that it wasn't fair to make him choose between him and his best friend. Sean said he wasn't doing that, but that you always came first, and—well, I think you get the idea."

"Oh my . . ." The words trailed away as an overwhelming mix of emotions fell over me. Freddie and Sean had been doing so well, and . . . I had ruined it. But I never asked Freddie to be my emotional chaperone! But on the other hand, that was so sweet that Freddie was so worried about me. But who asked him to? And how did all this end up with Freddie being supermean to me? I didn't do anything! "I don't believe it. This is terrible."

"I know," Candace said. "I told Freddie he should just talk to you."

"Yeah, that would have been better than just being angry at me because—"

"He values your friendship so much."

I dropped my head into my hands. "The whole thing

is ridiculous though. I would have been fine at the wedding."

"I said that too."

"I need to fix this. I can't believe . . ." I was shaking my head again. "What did Freddie think was going to happen?" Actually I knew what he thought. He probably had some vision of dancing with Sean under a tent while I sat all alone at a white linen-covered table drinking champagne. Meanwhile, I wasn't picturing that at all. I was picturing myself dancing obnoxiously with Rhonda to like Beyoncé or something.

Suddenly I caught my hands waving in the air.

"What's wrong? Did a fish bite your toe?"

"Did a fish bite my toe? You are adorable," I said with a smile. "No, I was just picturing the wedding, and—screw the community center—I know where it should be!"

"You do? Where?"

"The retreat! What about having the wedding at the retreat?"

"Oh . . ." I could see the excitement in her eyes. "You don't think your mother would mind? I mean, we don't have a lot of money. And she's already—"

"Money! What are you talking about money?" I pushed her on the arm—I meant for it to just be one of those playful pushes to get across the point of how ridiculous what she was saying was, but suddenly Candace was in the water.

"Candace! I am so sorry!" I mean, you couldn't tell by all the laughing I was doing, but, "I totally didn't mean to do that."

Candace splashed around in the water then found the edge of the dock with one hand and dragged the hair out of her face with the other. "Do you think it would really be okay?"

"One hundred percent. A thousand percent. I mean, she thinks marriage is an outdated patriarchal institution—"

Candace's eyes widened. "Really? That doesn't sound like your mom especially given that—"

"Whatever," I said, waving my hands out. "Doesn't matter. She likes you. It will be fine."

A beautiful smile stretched across Candace's face. A smile I hadn't seen in a long time. A deep-dimple smile.

"If you think your mother wouldn't mind . . ." She shook her head. "Thank you, Erica."

"You are so welcome!" I pushed myself off the dock to join her.

"Hey," she said, treading water. "I know weddings aren't really your thing, but there's something else I wanted to ask you."

"Shoot," I said, putting a hand on the dock.

"You don't think . . . you would consider . . ."

"Consider what?"

She winced. "Being my maid of honor?"

"Um, yeah," I said, rolling my eyes. "I don't know what took you so long to ask."

"Really," she said rather sarcastically. And for Candace that was supersarcastic.

I splashed water in her face. But it was cool because she splashed me back.

I was so happy all of a sudden. I mean, sure, everything was still so very messed up . . . but I finally knew what was wrong with Freddie. And if I knew what was wrong I could fix it. Just like I fixed the wedding location, I could fix it all! "Or my name isn't Honorable Erica ever-powerful ruler."

"Did you say something?"

Oh crap, that last part wasn't supposed to be out loud. "Nope."

Chapter Twenty-seven

"Freddie!" I shouted, banging my fist against the door. "Open up!"

Still no answer. I had been banging for at least five minutes.

I banged some more. "Seriously, get up!" I took a couple of steps back to look up at his bedroom. Yup, the window was open. He could totally hear me. Fine, if he wanted to play it that way. I whipped out my phone and called him. It went to voice mail. Okay, I would try texting.

Answer your phone.

I called again a moment later.

It rang twice then I heard, "Why are you calling me at *I hate you* o'clock? Don't you have a murder to be solving?"

"Get down here and open your door."

"It's like two in the morning. Go home."

"I'm not going home until you talk to me." I originally thought I could wait until morning to talk to

Freddie, but after a couple of hours of tossing and turn-ing in bed, I couldn't stand it anymore. This had to be settled now. "Come down."

"No."

"Freddie."

"No."

"Come down now."

"No."

"If you don't come down now, I'm going to start singing."

"You wouldn't."

"And I'm starting with Aretha."

I saw the light come on upstairs. I knew that would work. Freddie hated my singing voice. He especially hated it when I went for the big voices.

A minute later, the door opened. "What do you want?" he asked, looking very grumpy in his bathrobe and slippers.

"Okay, you need to explain to me why you did what you did," I said, crossing my arms over my chest.

He frowned. "What did I do?"

"Not invite Sean to the wedding. Because of me?"

"Who told you?" he snapped. "It was Candace, wasn't it? I knew it was a mistake to talk to that well-intentioned, troublemaking bride."

"It's not important who told me," I said, arms still crossed. "The question is, why would you do that in the first place?"

He let out a disgusted-sounding sigh. "I just knew how difficult this wedding was going to be for you. Given the side-by-side comparison of you and—"

"Gah!" I threw my hands in the air. "There is no side-by-side comparison between me and Candace."

He frowned. "I meant you and me." He moved a hand back and forth between us. "Like you've been trying to get a relationship going with Grady for years now, and Sean and I just fell into one like the first night we met."

Huh. Wow. Hadn't thought of that comparison either.

"I didn't want to rub that in at a wedding of all places, so I thought it would be good if I could devote my complete attention to your needs. And then Sean went and blew it completely out of proportion—"

"And you took it out on me," I said, making sure the sentence finished exactly where I wanted it to.

"Oh," Freddie said, tightening his bathrobe. "I'm so sorry that being a good friend to you puts me in a bad mood."

We blinked at each other a moment then I gave my head a shake. "Freddie, I don't want you putting your relationship at risk out of some misguided belief that I need you to take care of me. And why didn't you just tell me what was going on?"

"'Cause then you would have blamed yourself," he said with a sigh, "and it would have been *Wah, wah, wah, I'm Erica, relationship destroyer.*"

"I would not have been— Wait a minute." I wagged a finger in the air. "Wait, just one minute."

Freddie straightened up. "What?"

"You said you didn't invite Sean to the wedding because you wanted to devote your attention to my needs." I shook my head. "But that . . . that doesn't make any sense."

"I'm sorry. Again, what?"

"First," I said, popping up a finger, "*devoting your*

complete attention to my emotional needs? That doesn't sound like you, and—"

"You are very rude at two in the morning. I do not like two A.M., Erica."

"And two, I think there just might be another reason for why you didn't invite Sean to the wedding. A deeper reason," I said, pointing directly at his chest. Freddie brought his hand up to cover the spot. "A reason that you are probably too afraid to even admit to yourself."

"Are you doing a Poirot thing right now. Is that what this is?" Freddie drawled. "What are you even talking about?"

I jabbed another point at him. He took a step back. "The reason you didn't invite Sean to the wedding is because you're . . . chicken!"

"Chicken? That's it." He moved to shut the door. "I'm going back to bed."

"Oh no, no," I said, pushing it back open. "You weren't worried about me falling apart at the wedding."

"I'm always worried about you falling apart in public places."

"No. No. No. That was just the cover-up. This is about you."

"Seriously, what are you talking about?"

I moved my pointing finger to the air. "My mom hinted at it . . . but I didn't listen. You're afraid to bring Sean to town as your boyfriend."

Freddie frowned. "No I'm not."

"Yes, yes you are. It makes complete sense."

"You're crazy. This—"

"Give me your phone," I said, holding out my hand. "No."

"Give me your phone."

"No," he said, taking his phone from his pocket and clutching it to his chest. "Don't you remember how this ended the last time?" He backed up farther into the house.

I followed him in. "Just do it."

He rolled his eyes and tossed it to me. "Take it. I don't want you tackling me again. Besides, you're not going to find anything. I haven't called—"

My thumbs flew furiously over the screen.

"What are you doing?" he asked, a tinge of nervousness coming to his voice.

I didn't answer.

"Are you texting someone?"

I quickly walked past him and hustled a few steps away, making sure there was a good distance between us before I started reading out loud what I was texting. " *'Hey Sean, I know it's late, but . . .'* "

Chapter Twenty-eight

"Erica," Freddie warned in a low scary voice. "What are you doing? You didn't send that, did you?"

"I did now," I said, pressing send.

"He has an exam tomorrow! It's two o'clock in the morning!"

Just then Freddie's phone buzzed.

I smiled. "Don't worry, he's awake. He says *hey*."

"Give it!" Freddie said, taking a few quick steps toward me.

I jumped away and scurried into the living room. "Nope. Nope. My mother said we needed to stop protecting each other from the things that scare us, and I will not be the answer to the question of why Freddie Ng is still single."

"What?! Have you been drinking?"

"Of course not." I knew I was supposed to be respecting Freddie's space and all that, but doubling down seemed like a much better idea. I probably did get that from my mother. "Now where was I, *I'm sorry*

I woke you,' I said, dictating to myself again. " *'But I need to tell you something.'* "

Freddie's eyes widened to the size of coasters. "Erica . . ."

"What? I'm helping you face your fears. Become a better person. You know, like you did getting me on that bull," I said.

"The bull . . . ? You mean the bachelorette party? Sean and I had just broken up. I was upset!"

"Yeah, at me. For absolutely no good reason." I looked back at the phone. " *'I am so sorry for everything. You were right. Erica can take care of herself. And I should have made you the priority.'* "

"Erica!"

He rushed toward me, but I jumped up onto the couch then over to the other side.

"Shush." I held up a finger. "He's writing something back."

"Since when can you not read and listen to me yell at you at the same time?"

A second later, the phone buzzed again.

"What does it say?"

My eyes darted over the message. " *'I really appreciate you saying that,'* " I said with a nod. " *'And I'm sorry too. I was too harsh.'* "

Freddie started to say something, but I waved him off. "He's writing something else." Just then it popped up on the screen. " *'I didn't mean what I said about . . .'* Erica?" I looked up. "What did he say about me?"

"Given how you're behaving right now, nothing that wasn't totally justified."

I looked back down at the phone. "Wait, he's writing

something else. '*I really do like her. And I would never want to do anything to affect your relationship.*'"

"Aww." I put my hand to my chest. "I knew I liked Sean." I dropped my hand back to the phone to reply.

"What are you writing now?" Freddie asked.

" '*I know you're really busy with school,*' " I said with my dictation voice, " '*but I would love it if you could come for the wedding.*' Send."

"What?" Freddie clutched his hair. Like honest to goodness clutched his hair. "I can't believe you just did that!"

"Freddie, the town knows you're gay."

He stared at me with some crazy, crazy eyes. Lots of white. "Of course the town knows I'm gay. That's not the problem."

"Then what is the problem?"

Freddie dropped his hands from his hair then fell heavily onto the couch. It was like that last text had just sucked all the air right out of him. "Sean coming to town . . . as my date?" He shook his head. "That's a really big deal. Coming to the wedding . . . it's like he's meeting my family."

"So?" I asked, walking back around and dropping down beside him. "That's a good thing. You're taking it to the next level."

"I don't know. I don't know if I'm ready for that."

"Of course you are. You guys are great together."

Freddie looked up to meet my eye. "But what if we're not? What if it doesn't work out? What if he finds out who I really am . . . and he breaks up with me?"

I searched Freddie's eyes. He really was scared. I needed to handle this sensitively. Say just the right thing. I patted his hand. "If he does, then . . . I know just where we can hide his body."

The tiniest hint of smile came to his mouth just as his phone buzzed again.

"What did he say?"

I read the message then met Freddie's eye again. "It says he'd love to come."

"He'd love to?"

"Says it right there." I pointed at the screen.

Freddie's face twitched to a smile. "Not just *like* to come?"

"No, he'd *love* to come."

"Now quick, end it," Freddie said. "Before you screw it up."

I quickly typed a good night to Sean then leaned back against the couch.

We were quiet for a few moments.

"I really *was* worried about you too, though," Freddie eventually said.

"I know."

He slouched to the side a bit so he could look at me. "But I think maybe I just didn't realize how easy it is to default to our relationship when other ones get tricky."

"Same," I said with a nod. "Maybe . . . maybe we do have to rethink things."

"What do you mean?"

I looked at him. "Like maybe we do need more boundaries between us."

Freddie dropped his chin to his chest. "You do realize you're saying this after you just texted my boyfriend pretending to be me."

"Exactly," I said, throwing my hands in the air. "I'm way out of control. That campfire?"

"That was awesome," Freddie said with a snicker. "You're going to be hearing about that for years."

I backhanded him lightly on the arm. "Stop it. I'm being serious. I mean, we can't just go back to the way things were bef—" Just then I jerked up. Something caught my eye. "Is that the packaging for a new cappuccino machine?"

"Oh my God, yes," Freddie said, jumping up. "It cost as much as a small car, but wait until you taste the hot chocolate."

"Well, why are we just sitting here talking about our relationship like weirdos?"

"I know, right? Let's go!"

Freddie and I were too excited and hopped up on hot chocolate to go back to sleep after that. Besides, we needed to get an early start to our day. Now that we were back together and had all of our neurons firing, it was time to get to work. We still had a week. We could do this.

Just like I had been checking in on the wedding preparations while Freddie and I were on the outs, he too had been doing a bit of investigating on his own. On our third cup of hot chocolate gold, he informed me that he had found out just the day before through the Otter Lake gossip mill who had first found Lyssa and called it in. Thankfully we were being supernice to one another, so Freddie didn't point out that I really should have been on that sooner.

Freddie drove us into town right at the first glow of

sunrise. It was actually a good thing we were up with the birds given who it was we needed to talk to.

Ned and Bob, the town's most dedicated anglers, were right where we expected to find them. A little ways down from the gazebo, hooks already in the water.

"I think maybe you should take the lead on this," Freddie said as we walked down the bike trail toward the men. He had parked his old, beat-up Jimmy at the top. It was so good to be rolling on four wheels again. "I mean, you have been on this case since the beginning."

"But questioning is your speciality," I said. "I really could have used you over at Tommy's."

"Well, aren't you sweet." Freddie smiled, adjusting the sling around his shoulder, and checking on Stanley who was asleep in the pouch at his hip. The sling was designed especially for dogs, but it did look a lot like the ones mothers of newborns used. The pouch had insect shield technology because according to Freddie you can't be too careful when it comes to West Nile. "Would you look at us? We are like best-friend newlyweds again."

I smiled back.

"Okay, so I'll take the lead," he said, pulling ahead.

Yup, things were pretty much back to normal.

"Ned. Bob," Freddie called out, raising a hand.

"Told ya they'd be by," I heard Bob say.

"Surprised it took you so long," Ned called back. "What kind of investigation are you two running?"

Freddie chuckled. "We've been experiencing a few hiccups organizationally speaking, but we're on the case now."

The men nodded. Bob said, "We heard Erica chased you round a fire. Glad you're both okay."

Freddie smiled as I ran a hand over my face.

"Well, you know Erica," Freddie replied. "So down to business."

"You want to know about that poor girl, God rest her soul."

We both nodded.

"'Fraid there's not a whole lot we can tell you," Bob said. "We just spotted her and called over to the sheriff's department. First time I've actually used this damn phone my wife got me." He patted one of the chest pockets of his fishing vest.

I sighed. "Are you sure that's—"

"Except"—Ned exchanged looks with his fishing buddy—"there was that one other thing, Bob."

Bob nodded. "Yup. There was that one other thing."

Chapter Twenty-nine

Well, that was easy.

"What one thing are we talking about here?" Freddie turned his face away from the men to shoot me a superexcited look. He loved it when people said stuff like that.

Ned tipped his chin over to the gazebo. "Well, when we first saw her . . ."

"God rest her soul," Bob added.

"God rest her soul. We weren't exactly sure what it was we were seeing."

"That's right," Bob said, scratching his chin. "We just saw something strange-looking floating in the water."

"And . . . ?" Freddie prodded.

"So we walked up to get a better look."

"It was a little tricky because we had to get past all the boxes for the wedding, but if you see—there at the part that looks out to the water," Bob said, pointing at the gazebo. "That part is all clear."

I frowned. I was trying to anticipate where they were going with this, but I was coming up blank.

"Anyway when we walked up into the main part of the gazebo, we realized we needed to stop moving around."

"Why's that?" Freddie asked.

"Well, we could see clear as day that it was a body in the water," Ned said, stroking his salt-and-pepper beard.

"And there were all sorts of footprints on the floor."

"Footprints?" Freddie asked.

"That's right." Bob nodded. "If you recall, it was pretty muddy that day."

Ned rested the end of his pole on the ground and turned to completely face us. He jerked a thumb at Bob. "We both know enough not to go walking around in a crime scene."

I frowned. "But . . . did you think it was a crime scene right away?"

"We suspected," Ned answered.

"How come?"

"Because a couple of the bins had been knocked over," Bob said, shaking his head.

Ned pointed back over to the gazebo. "And the banister of the railing was cracked. It looked like there had been some sort of fight."

I whipped my head around. I hadn't noticed any cracks, but then I was looking from a distance. I should get a pair of my own binoculars.

"Looked like maybe someone had been pushed into the water."

Now it was Freddie's and my turn to exchange glances. Freddie seemed a little disappointed. I was too. It was good to have this information, but it didn't really move us any further ahead. We knew the police suspected foul play, and I guess now we knew some of the reasons why, but that still left us with Tommy, Lyssa's boyfriend, Justin, and a windbreaker as suspects.

"What kind of footprints were they?" Freddie suddenly asked.

I mentally high-fived him. Good question.

"Well, that was the really interesting part," Bob said with a smile.

"You see, we waited there a while for Amos to show up," Ned went on, "so we got a real good look."

Bob leaned his pole toward us. "But what we saw . . . it's all a lot of speculation on our part."

"We're fine with speculation," I said. "Freddie?"

"Always."

"Well," Ned said, scratching at his brow just underneath his fishing cap, "from what we could tell, there were at least three separate prints."

"One looked like a pair of men's work boots."

I nodded. Those were probably Tommy's . . . or Justin's.

"Another had one of those really tiny heels," Ned said, pinching his fingers together.

"Like a stiletto," I offered.

He snapped his fingers. "That's it."

Okay, good chance those were Lyssa's. I remember thinking I'd be crippled if I attempted to walk around in the heels she was wearing that night.

"But it's the third . . ." Bob said, shaking his head. "That got us to thinking."

"Thinking?" Freddie asked. "What were you thinking?"

"Well, it was weird because they were heels too," Ned began. "Or at least a woman's shoe."

"The heel was bigger, though," Bob said, picking up the thread. "Sensible."

I chewed my lip. Okay, I didn't know what to make of that.

"And it was kind of . . ." The struggle to find the word played out on Ned's face. "Creepy."

"I still don't like to think about it," Bob said with a bit of a shudder.

"What? Think about what?" Freddie was going to lose it if they didn't get to the point soon.

"Well, most of the floor was a mess," Bob said.

I nodded. "Right. You said it looked like there had been a fight."

"But those shoes made a really distinct print. Like the person who was wearing them was standing in one spot for a while."

I frowned. "I don't get it."

Ned sighed as a troubled expression came over his face. "Well, it's the way the shoes were facing."

"Like the person who was wearing them was standing by the railing," Bob said, looking equally disturbed, "facing the water, watching . . . something."

Chills raced over my body. "Oh."

"Oh," said Freddie.

"Oh," the men said in unison.

So someone, a woman—not Lyssa—was standing by the railing looking out at the water watching something.

Something?

Or maybe someone.

Maybe someone drowning to death.

Chapter Thirty

"Okay, we need to hurry if we want to catch Tommy while he's still groggy."

In an effort to keep the momentum going, Freddie and I decided it best to head right over to Tommy's. Bob and Ned's story had been disturbing to say the least, but it also left us more determined than ever to find out what had happened that night. It was time Tommy told us everything.

"Him being groggy didn't help me much last time I was over there."

"Yeah, but there's a difference between first-thing-in-the-morning groggy and mid-morning groggy," Freddie said. "He might give us the answers we need before he even registers that he's awake."

We had to drive through town to get to Tommy's side of the lake. It was a beautiful morning. Calm and peaceful. The spring air fragrant with . . . well, spring. No one was really up and about yet, except . . .

"Slow down for a second," I said, whacking Freddie's arm.

"What?" he asked. "What's going on?"

"Just slow down."

Freddie slowed the Jimmy to a crawl and followed my gaze to the public park by the water. "Is that Grady?" he asked, way too much amusement in his voice. "Doing yoga?"

It was. It was Grady doing yoga. Warrior pose to be specific.

And he wasn't alone.

There were five women in warrior pose too. It was the yoga-in-the-park crew. My mother was cofounder. She went whenever she could.

I shook my head. But it made no sense that Grady would . . . actually, who was I kidding? It made perfect sense. This is exactly something that Grady 2.0 would do.

Just then Grady stretched back to reverse warrior and—

"Oh crap!" I hissed. "Duck!"

"Why would I do that?" Freddie asked, stepping on the brake. He then waved at Grady before doing a double take as he caught me trying to stuff myself onto the truck's floor.

"Because I can't let him catch me watching him again."

Freddie smiled. "Yeah, I heard about the knitting the other night, you little perv."

"I am not a little . . . perv. Grady just keeps catching me off guard and—"

"Why are you whispering?" Freddie asked. "He

can't hear you, and I'm pretty sure he knows you're in the truck with me."

"You can't be pretty sure of that."

"Who else would be hiding on the floor of my truck? He can see me talking to someone."

"Stanley."

"Oh, Erica, he knows I use a crate. I never put Stanley's safety at risk."

I reluctantly pushed myself up in my seat. Yup, he was still in reverse warrior . . . and waving.

I raised a weak hand in the air before saying through my teeth, "Drive on."

"Sure. Sure," Freddie said. He eased off the brake and we started driving again . . . at maybe two miles per hour.

"A little faster," I said.

"Whatever you say, buttercup," Freddie answered cheerily. He then sped up . . . but only for a second . . . before parking at the side of the road.

"What are you doing?!"

"I just thought of something." Freddie jumped out of the truck and went round back to get Stanley.

He wasn't seriously thinking of—

Oh thank God. He wasn't headed for the park. He was crossing the street. "Come on!" he shouted at me.

I got out of the truck. Where was he going? The hardware store?

I trotted after Freddie. "What are you doing? The hardware store isn't going to be open yet."

"Then we'll wake Doug up," Freddie called back. "This is life-and-death stuff."

I sped up to a jog to catch up to Freddie. "What are you—"

Freddie stopped at the sidewalk and cocked his head. "Do you hear that?"

I frowned. I did hear something. Music. Coming from the workshop behind the hardware store?

"I think Doug is already awake," Freddie said. "Come on."

I hustled after Freddie feeling very uncomfortable. It was early. Freddie thought "2 A.M. Erica" was rude, but "6:30 A.M. Erica" felt just as bad.

We slowed our pace as we approached the small building. At least the door was open and . . .

Nope, that made it worse.

Because it allowed us to see Doug—respected owner of the hardware store, generally a stoic man—with his back to us, hips jerking side to side to the song "Stayin' Alive."

Freddie cleared his throat . . .

. . . and Doug threw a wrench into the air.

He spun around with his hand clutched to his chest. When he saw it was us, he chuckled. "You two startled me. I didn't know anyone was there."

"Sorry," I said.

Freddie wasn't feeling the least bit uncomfortable though. He walked right in. "I've never been back here before." He looked at Doug. "This place is awesome."

Doug chuckled. "My version of a man cave, I guess."

I couldn't quite get where Freddie's excitement was coming from. There was lots of equipment and tools back here, and the place had the smell of old varnish and gasoline. There were also stacks of records and an old turntable.

"Would you look at all these records?" Freddie said, thumbing through one of the stacks. "This place is retro-tastic. Where did you get all of these?"

Doug shot an amused look to me then back to Freddie. "I bought them."

"You're a collector?" Freddie asked.

"I used to DJ," Doug said. "Long time ago."

"You used to . . . DJ?" Freddie asked.

Uh-oh.

I grabbed Freddie's arm. "Will you excuse us one second?" I asked Doug.

He nodded, looking bewildered.

I walked Freddie to the far corner of the workroom. "Freddie, I know what you're thinking, but—"

"Would you look at this hair?" He held up an album cover. "It's glorious."

The three men on the cover did have impressive hair. Especially the one in the middle. His was parted down the center and feathered at the sides.

"Do you think I could pull off this hair?" Freddie asked.

"I'm . . . having trouble seeing it." I waved a hand in the air. He was distracting me again. "I know what you're thinking, but I'm not sure Candace wants a seventies-theme reception."

"I'll text her," Freddie said, pulling out his phone.

I threw my hands up. "Well, you're just going to make sure all of Otter Lake is awake, aren't you?"

" *'Found a DJ. Doug at hardware store. Leans heavily to seventies music though. What do you think.'* " Freddie looked up at me. "There."

"We don't even know if Doug wants to DJ though and—"

Freddie's phone buzzed. His eyes darted over the screen. "She thinks it's cute and then she goes on to thank me obsessively. Doug?" Freddie called out as he walked back over to the unsuspecting hardware man. "How would you feel about wiping the dust off some of the records and DJing at what promises to be the wedding of the year?"

"I . . ."

"I'll take that as a yes," Freddie said, snapping his fingers. "Now we need you to open up the shop. We're going to need some equipment."

"Ready?"

"Ready."

It did take a little more convincing to get Doug to agree to handle the music for the wedding. We offered to pay him, but once Doug had gotten his mind around the idea, he flat-out turned us down. The only thing he wanted from us was to find out what had happened to Lyssa. Once that was taken care of, we got down to the business of why Freddie wanted to stop by the hardware store in the first place. We needed to suit up for our meeting with Tommy. And a babysitter for Stanley. Doug was kind enough to supply us with both. Afterward we made one more pit stop then headed back to Freddie's to get his boat. We wanted to approach Tommy's the same way I had, so we knew what to expect.

"Okay, masks down," Freddie said.

We flipped down the visors to our hockey masks.

"Shields up," I added.

We held up our garbage can lids.

"Okay, go time," Freddie said, striding up Tommy's

lawn. Well, as much as one can stride over lots and lots of junk. "Tommy!" he shouted, banging on his lid with a stick. Unfortunately it wasn't one of those old-fashioned, metal garbage can lids—so that would have made a nice sound—it was plastic, so—

Wait a minute. I picked up my own stick—actually it was half a hockey stick—and banged on the rusted-out steel drum I had hidden behind last time I was here.

Freddie smiled at me. "Nice."

"Tommy!" I shouted.

"Get your dirty boxers out here!" Freddie yelled.

"Ew."

Freddie shrugged.

A moment later, Tommy stumbled through the door onto his porch. Wow, that was quite the bedhead he had going on.

He squinted against the sun and scratched his head. "What the h— Oh goddammit, Erica. You brought Freddie? I hate him too."

"Yeah, she brought me," Freddie said. "We need to have a word with you, Tommy boy."

Tommy looked at us a moment, then—it was hard to tell but I think he muttered something along the lines of "No, you need to eat some golf balls."

"He's going for the bucket!" I shouted.

"Not this time!" Freddie charged across the lawn and up the porch.

Just as Tommy was reaching down to get some ammo, Freddie toe-punted the bucket as hard as he could.

Golf balls flew everywhere.

"What are you doing?" Tommy shouted, charging

toward Freddie. "First, Erica breaks my window. Now you're making a m—"

And he stepped on a golf ball and flipped into the air.

He hit the porch with a *thump!*

Freddie looked back at me laughing—

—then he stepped on one too and—

I hissed some air through my teeth.

Freddie's *thump* was even louder.

"My hip!" Freddie yelled. He shouted a bunch more after that but it was garbled and . . . obscene.

I picked my way over to the porch, so I could get a better look at both the men rolling around on its floor.

"So . . . Tommy," I said. "We brought coffee and muffins." I jerked a thumb back at the boat. "Do you think we could talk now?"

Tommy just groaned.

"Cool." I looked over at the other mass on the floor. "Freddie? You okay?"

He rolled over to face me, hand clutching his back. "I've missed this so much."

Chapter Thirty-one

"There are more muffins if anyone wants them."

Ten minutes later we were all sitting on Tommy's porch drinking coffee and eating muffins. He had some pretty rough lawn chairs leftover from . . . the eighties maybe? They did the job though.

"Nah, I'm good," Freddie said.

Tommy just stared at me a moment then looked away.

We didn't say anything for a good long while. Just drank coffee and ate. Finally Freddie said, "Tommy, dude, don't take this the wrong way, but . . . your place is a mess."

He exhaled roughly. "Whatever."

"No . . . no whatever," Freddie went on. "It's bad. Like your lawn is a cry for help."

Tommy balled up the tinfoil his muffin had been wrapped in and tossed it at Freddie. "Shut up, man."

"Look, I know you don't want to hear this from us," I said, getting ready to run if he made any sudden movements. "But . . . I think maybe it's time for you to pull up. Dickie, he wouldn't want you living like this."

He didn't throw anything at me, just said, "What the hell do you know about what Dickie would want?"

"Good point." I nodded. "Fair enough."

"Why are you guys here anyway?" he asked, looking out to the water. "I told you everything I know the other day, Erica."

"You didn't tell her who gave you that black eye," Freddie said, looking at him over his cup.

Tommy shook his head. "I told the cops. I don't have to tell you anything."

"Come on, man," I said. "We're just trying to help Candace."

He shook his head. "You know what's funny?" Tommy asked, not looking very funny at all. "Candace was the only person who kept talking to me after everybody found out what we did. She barely knew me, but . . . whatever. This town sucks."

"Well," Freddie said, "in fairness, you were kind of a douchebag to the town, so now you're even."

I shot Freddie a look. I mean, he was right, but we needed to focus on the task at hand. "Tommy, help us help Candace."

He took another rough breath. "Fine. You know what? It makes no difference to me. Sheriff Bigly can suck it. It was Lyssa's boyfriend. He punched me."

"When?"

"After I was with . . . after the gazebo, I went home." He stopped to take a sip of coffee. Then wiped his mouth with the back of his hand. "Walked the whole way. I was kind of wasted. Then right when I'm about to go inside, this frickin' kid with spiky hair comes out of nowhere screaming about me scaring his girlfriend. He had followed me, I guess. Like stalked me all the way home. I don't know what he saw or what she had said to him, but he was nuts. Like he was on something." He shook his head. "At first, I tried to tell him that his girlfriend was the one who had come on to me, but the guy just kept going on and on about her being an angel. I couldn't . . . I didn't want to burst the kid's bubble, so I let him hit me." Tommy shrugged. "He left after that."

Now I didn't know what Lyssa's exact time of death was, but it was hard to imagine her just waiting by herself at the gazebo for upward of forty minutes for her boyfriend to follow Tommy home, confront him, and then come back.

"There," Tommy said, tossing his paper cup on the lawn. "Now you know everything. So you can be on your way."

Freddie groaned and pushed himself to his feet. "Yeah, we got stuff to do, but . . ." He looked around the yard again. "Do you need help cleaning this stuff up?"

Tommy frowned at him like he was crazy.

"I'm thinking Sunday." Freddie looked at me. "That work for you?"

"Um . . . sure?"

"Sean will be in town. I know he'll want to help."

"Yeah, the retreat will be over by then," I said. "I can definitely help. My mom would probably come, but I'm not sure if—"

"Why would you do that?" Tommy asked, still looking angry. "I hate you guys."

"Yeah, but you're bringing everybody's property values down," Freddie said. "Besides, Erica's right, it's time for you to pull up."

Tommy didn't say anything just looked out at the water.

"Okay, Sunday," Freddie said, getting to his feet. "And try not to throw any more crap on it before then."

I followed Freddie down the lawn toward the boat. "That was really sweet of you." It really was. I mean, yeah, we had never been close with Tommy. Quite the opposite actually. But it didn't seem right to just watch a neighbor flail and not throw him a rope. "I should have thought of it."

"It's okay," Freddie said happily. "You're not me. And, I mean, Sean thought he liked me before—wait, you're not all mad that I volunteered you for something, like Candace's wedding, without asking you first?"

"Not this time."

He resumed walking. "That's because you have wedding issues."

I snatched a golf ball off the ground and whipped it at Freddie. Hit him right in the thigh.

"Ow!" he said, rubbing the spot. "You have violence issues too."

Chapter Thirty-two

"Hey Mom!" I called out, waving a hand in the air. "Can I talk to you a second?"

After Tommy's place, Freddie and I decided to head back to the Dawg for lunch to go over everything. And there was a lot to go over. Our lunch ended up turning into an all-afternoon meeting. We were making lots of headway on the wedding, but, as had often been the case, the investigation had hit another standstill. So from what Tommy had told us, we did know for sure that Lyssa's boyfriend, Justin, was in town the night of the murder, but that was all we knew. And it seemed that Sheriff Bigly wasn't faring much better. The fact that the sheriff's department still hadn't arrested anyone had the town on edge. Otter Lake citizen after Otter Lake citizen came up to our table at the Dawg expressing concern. And some of that concern was taking on a bit of a hysterical edge. Mrs. White had found a dead garter snake on her doorstep just this morning. While she was fairly certain her cat had left it there as a present, she couldn't rule out the possibility that it was a threat of some sort.

All of our excitement from the morning had gone by the time we left the Dawg. Maybe we were just tired, but it also felt like we were failing Candace . . . and Lyssa.

We also weren't totally in the clear for the wedding either. I still hadn't actually asked my mother if we could use the retreat as the location. I was pretty sure she'd be okay with it, but it was presumptuous of me. Freddie really liked the idea of having the wedding at the retreat, but you could tell he was mad he didn't think of it first. Kind of like I was upset that I didn't look into who had found Lyssa. We worked better as a team.

Freddie had come back with me to the retreat and was now mingling with the other guests. He wasn't at all concerned about running into anyone who had seen our campfire fiasco. Then again, I guess he was the one being chased.

I watched my mother make her way through the crowd. It looked like they were just about to get another campfire under way.

"Where have you been, darling?" my mother asked. "I heard you leave late last night."

"Sorry about that," I said, rubbing my eyes. It had been a very long day. "I needed to . . . Freddie and I made up."

She clutched her hands together. "That's wonderful."

"Yeah, it is," I said with a smile. "Um . . . I need to talk to you about something." I nodded and scratched my brow. It had all seemed like such a good idea to offer the retreat to Candace last night, but maybe I should have asked my mother first. I mean, the retreat was teeming with people, and she had never been a traditional-marriage type of person, and well . . . it was her retreat.

"Mom," I said, squinting at her in the sun. "I, um, kind of did something last night that involved you."

My mother's eyes widened. "What it is?"

"I kind of told Candace she could have the wedding here." I pointed to the ground. "At the retreat."

She didn't say anything for a moment, but then she flung her arms around me.

I smiled even though my face was covered with hair. That was pretty much the reaction I thought I would get.

"That's a wonderful idea!" my mom said, leaning back to look at me. "I mean why not? I'm already performing the ceremony. Why didn't we think of this sooner?"

"Wait," I said, stopping to spit some of my mother's hair out my mouth. "You're doing what now?"

"The ceremony." She rocked me back and forth in her arms, which was not pleasant on my sleep-deprived brain. "Didn't Freddie tell you?"

"No."

"Oh, maybe he thought you already knew."

"You're doing the ceremony. But . . . I thought you weren't a big fan of traditional marriage?"

My mother pushed me back to look at me. "What are you talking about?"

"You know, you always used to say it was society's way of enslaving women?"

"What?" She swatted my hand. "I did not."

"Sure you did."

"When?"

"I don't know when. I was a kid."

My mother chewed her lip. "Hmm, that must have been during one of those phases where I was experimenting with making my own homeopathic remedies, because I don't remember that at all. It was a strange time. I love weddings! I've officiated enough of them."

I was suddenly rapidly blinking.

"Here at the retreat." She put a hand to her chest. "For a while there I was ranked New Hampshire's number one choice of marriage officials for atheists, agnostics, and the LGBTQ community. I love love in all its forms."

I was still blinking.

"I was even in a magazine. Freddie didn't tell you any of this?"

"No."

A look came over her face. "Oh well, he knows how uncomfortable you are with—"

"Why haven't I seen you"—I flung my hand around—"officiate any marriages at the retreat?"

"Well, there just isn't the demand there used to be, now that gay marriage is legal throughout the country, and I haven't really tried to drum up more business, because I'm so busy with the retreats, and, well, I know how much weddings bother you."

"Weddings don't bother me. Who told you weddings bother me? Why does everybody keep thinking weddings bother me?"

My mother sighed. "Okay, maybe they don't bother you. You're just not a wedding person."

For some reason, I didn't like the way that sounded

when it came out of her mouth. "Okay, well, good. I'm glad that's settled."

"Oh! But I'm going to need you to do one small favor for me. We were hoping you'd show up."

I took a step back and waved my hands in front of me. "Nope. You already said yes. No takebacks."

She took a step toward me. "From both you and Freddie."

"I can't speak for Fred—"

"To make up for how you two behaved at the last campfire."

I felt my shoulders drop in defeat. "You just had to go there."

She put her arm around my shoulder. "Come on, we're just about to get started."

My mother led me over to the fire. I waved a hand for Freddie to join us.

"Erica, Freddie, welcome," Guru Zaki said. "You are just in time."

We smiled and nodded at everyone as we made our way to the only free log seat by the fire. This was the second week of the retreat, so at least most of the original participants who had seen our campfire dance had left, but I recognized just enough who had stayed on for another week to feel pretty ridiculous.

"Tonight we have a very important exercise," Zaki said. "You will be assigned a partner, and your partner will have a question provided to them by us that they will in turn ask you."

My mother leaned to my ear and whispered, "We don't want friends teaming up. You and Freddie can help us split up some pairs. Zaki and I were going to do it, but it's better if it's not someone who's actually running the workshop."

"Now, we won't be asking you *the* question," Zaki said, making the group titter, "but rather it is meant to be a personal question that will help guide you toward all the answers you seek."

My mother walked toward him. "We're hoping the experience—"

Freddie slapped my arm.

What? I mouthed.

"We're?" he whispered. "That is too cute. It's like they're already married."

I frowned.

"And your new stepdad is kind of hot."

"Shut it."

Freddie pinned his lips together, but I could so see the smile in his eyes.

"Now," my mother went on, "as mentioned, we've already picked your partners for you—most of you already know who that is—because we felt it might make it easier to share some of your more vulnerable secrets with an empathetic stranger."

"Wait," Freddie said. "Does that mean we can't be partners?"

"My mom said—"

"Yoo-hoo! Freddie!"

His panicked eyes flashed over to the voice. "Old Yeller is still here?"

Now, it was my turn to smile. "I told you a couple of last week's guests opted to stay another week."

"But I already have a bit of tinnitus in my ear from talking to her last week."

Old Yeller was still waving.

"Off you go," I said. "Don't leave her waiting."

Freddie sighed and got to his feet. "If her question isn't *Have you ever been diagnosed with hearing problems?* then I am going to have a real problem with this exercise." He ambled away.

Suddenly Zaki appeared in front of me holding a stack of envelopes. "I am glad that you have come, Erica. I am afraid that some of our earlier encounters have been . . ."

"Messed up?"

He laughed. "You are funny."

Glad someone thought so. "I'm sorry for how Freddie and I behaved the other night," I said superfast, before adding, "Is one of those envelopes for me?" Huh, apologizing wasn't so bad if you said it superquickly then changed the subject. I needed to keep that in mind for next time.

He sorted through the stack, than passed me an envelope with my name on it. "Do not open it yet," he said with his perpetual smile. "Give it to your partner. They will read it to you."

"Who is my partner?"

"Mary. She's sitting over by the picnic table." I looked over to where he was pointing. Oh, it was Eeyore. I didn't know she was still here. Okay, well, that was fine, I could do sad. It was better than being partnered with the woman with hypochondriac tendencies. But then again, I think she had gone home. All the nature was trying to kill her. The doctor had left too. Couldn't take all her questions. I guess that's what you get for going around telling everyone you're a doctor.

I stepped over the picnic table bench to sit opposite

Eeyore, I mean Mary. She looked like she wanted to do this exercise even less than I did. She met my eye, but didn't smile. Didn't do anything. Oh wow, and if I wasn't mistaken she was still wearing the same T-shirt and khakis. Maybe she didn't know we had laundry facilities. Or maybe Freddie was right. She was too sad for love.

"Do you want to go first?" I asked. "Or do you want me to?"

She made the barest of shrugs.

"Right," I said with a sharp inhale. "Well, I guess I'll go first. Here's my envelope."

She opened the flap and looked at the card inside. A flicker of interest—or was it confusion?—crossed her face.

"What does it say?"

She cleared her throat. "It doesn't say anything." She took the paper out and turned it around for me to see. "It's blank."

Chapter Thirty-three

"Blank?" I whipped my head around to find Zaki, but he was chatting with my mother by the fire. "That's weird."

She nodded.

"Oh . . . my mother didn't know I was coming." Of course, that made sense. But why go to all the trouble of giving me a blank envelope? I drummed my fingers on the table. "Huh. Okay. Well, maybe we should read your question."

Mary shrugged in a halfhearted way and passed me her envelope. I ripped it open and pulled out the card. "Okay, yours says, *Why are you so sad?*" I blinked before looking up at her. "Wow. They really didn't mess around with yours, did they?" She was probably wishing she had gotten the blank one right about now.

"You know," I said, throwing the envelope on the table. "I get that I'm Summer's daughter and I should probably be toeing the company line, but if you don't want to answer . . ."

"No, I think maybe I should talk about it," she said, nodding slightly.

I straightened up in my seat. I kind of felt like I needed to brace myself for some reason.

She took a slow, deep breath. "Do you believe that a person has one true love? A soul mate?"

I frowned. That . . . was unexpected. "I don't know if I believe we have just one, but . . ." I was trying to find a way to finish that thought, but it was hard to think with the voice in my head repeating Grady's name over and over. "What do you believe?"

"I believe . . ." she said with a hard swallow, "that the love of my life died three and a half weeks ago."

I froze. "Oh wow . . . wow . . . I am so sorry to hear that." I stiffened. I definitely hadn't seen that coming. I had no idea what to say. Or if I should say anything at all. I mean, she had said she wanted to talk about it, but . . . three and a half weeks? "Were . . . were you together long?"

She folded her hands on the table. "We weren't together at all." Mary fiddled with her hands. "We worked together."

"Oh."

She looked up at me. "For twenty-three years we worked together. Side-by-side cubicles." She smiled a little at the thought.

I wrapped my sweater more tightly around my body. "That's a long time."

"Nobody knew me as well as Frank did." She shook her head. "Vice versa too."

"How . . . how did he die, if you don't mind me asking?"

"Sudden heart attack," she said with a swallow. "At the office. I was there."

"I can't imagine what that must have been like for you." And just like that Grady popped into my mind again. If something like that ever happened to him—

"I'm glad I got to be with him at the end," she said, nodding and gripping her hands together.

"Can I ask why you two . . . ?"

She closed her eyes and nodded. "He did ask me out a couple of times when we first started working together. But I didn't think it was a good idea." She huffed a small laugh at that. "We were working together, you know? But I think really I was just too afraid. My parents went through a really nasty split when I was a child, and my dad left." Suddenly she looked up at me and smiled. "Maybe that's my answer," she said with air quotes.

I smiled back at her. I doubt it had much life though.

"I think I was too afraid of losing him," she said with a pained nod, "so I never really got to have him."

"I . . . I think I know a little bit about what that's like." Yup, suddenly this was all hitting a little too close to home.

"He meant so much to me. I was afraid if we started dating, if he really got to know me, he wouldn't like me anymore. And I couldn't bear the thought of losing him as a friend. I wasn't ready. I thought I needed more time."

"So as the years passed you never once told him how you felt?" I cringed a little. It had just come out before I could stop it.

"He started dating other people—had a daughter with one—and as the years passed we were just so far down that friendship road, I didn't know how to go back." She looked off at the fire. "He called me his work sister. I was too late. That's how he saw me."

"But . . . are you sure? Maybe he was just too afraid to be rejected again." And that was just as bad. What was wrong with me?

She nodded. Tears suddenly fell down her cheeks. "When he collapsed in our office kitchen . . . I was holding his hand trying to reassure him that the ambulance was on its way, and you know what he said to me?"

I shook my head.

She took a shuddering breath. "He looked at me and said *I wish it could've been me.*"

My breath caught, and I had to blink my own tears away.

"I know. I tried to tell him that it was him. That it was always him. But I don't know if he heard me. He was gone so quickly after that."

I grabbed her hand and gave it a squeeze.

"I think *that* more than anything else is what makes me so sad," she said with a nod. "I don't know if he died thinking I didn't love him."

I gulped down a breath and blinked my eyes again. "I am so sorry."

"It was all just such a waste, you know? I didn't think that that could happen. That twenty-three years could pass and neither one of us would . . . bend. How does that happen?"

I shook my head, but I knew. I knew exactly how that could happen.

"I am so sorry, Mary."

She nodded. "And that's it. That is why I'm so sad."

"I think you should tell my mother this. Maybe even tell the group. Your story . . . it could help other people, and maybe that could help with some of your . . . pain."

She frowned. "You think my story could help people?"

"It's already helped me."

She just stared at me, confused.

I pushed myself to my feet. "You have no idea how much you've helped me. I am so sorry for everything you have suffered, and I hope you can forgive me . . . but I've got to go."

Mary looked up at me. "Is something wrong?"

"Yes," I said with a nod. "There is."

"Well then, of course, go."

I turned to the fire. "Mom!" I shouted. "You're needed over here."

"Erica?" Freddie called out as I raced toward him and his partner. "What are you doing?"

"I need your boat."

"But—"

I snatched the keys from his breast pocket. "I'll be right back . . . or not if I'm lucky."

Chapter Thirty-four

Grady. I had to see Grady. I didn't know what I was going to say . . . but I had to say something. No way was I losing the love of my life to a heart attack thirty years from now in an office cubicle. Metaphorically speaking. And yes, I also realized that we'd have to figure out a way to do things differently—I mean, he was already a whole new person—but I needed him to know that I wanted to try. I'd do anything. Frick, I'd go to all of my mother's retreats to get another chance if that's what it took. I just wanted to hear him say that he wanted that too.

We were wasting so much time.

The more I thought about it, the faster I drove *Lightning*—which wasn't smart given how dark it was.

I didn't want to hit anything. Oh God, or worse yet, I could flip the boat and die and Grady would never know that I wished it could've been me . . . or him . . . or however that went.

I slowed the boat and took a deep breath.

I needed to calm down. I looked over at the lights twinkling from the shoreline.

I slowed the boat even more.

Besides . . . maybe it was a good idea not to just rush right over there anyway.

I could take my time. I needed to think about what I wanted to say. Maybe just do a drive-by of the marina. Just one. I didn't want to give myself too much time to back out. Then I'd head right over to Grady's. I didn't want to get over there shouting gibberish . . . like . . . like Ebneezer Scrooge from *A Christmas Carol*. That wasn't romantic. That was weird.

Okay, one drive by the marina and then I would go over.

I turned the boat and as I circled back around, the headlight swept across the town gazebo. What the . . . ?

The light was only on it for a second, but . . . I could have sworn I saw someone.

Okay, that was strange.

Why would someone be hanging out on the gazebo with bins of wedding decorations?

I swung the boat around again for another look.

Crap! That was definitely a man.

What was he doing?

I think he saw me spot him—I guess a boat shining its headlight on you twice in quick succession was a tip-off. He ducked down behind a stack of bins. A stack of bins that was now toppling to the floor. Son of a—

"Easy on the bins!" I shouted, wondering just for a second when the wedding had become more important than catching a potential murder suspect.

I tried to bring the boat in closer, but I didn't want

to ground it. If I could just get the headlight of the boat on him. Just then I remembered that Freddie had one of those expensive beams that swiveled. I killed the boat's engine and grabbed the handle for the light and focused the beam on the spot where the man had disappeared. At first I could just see the tangled mess of bins, but then a man jumped up. A man with spiky hair! Lyssa's boyfriend! Frick! He was running down the planks that bridged the gazebo to the shoreline. "Hey! Stop! I need to talk to you!" Even though that was potentially a really bad idea seeing as he was our prime suspect for murder. I almost yelled *Actually, never mind!* but he never stopped running. Again the calling-out thing never worked.

I hit the steering wheel hard with the heel of my hand. There was no way I could tie off the boat and get there in time to be sure it was him.

But I had to do something!

I pulled my phone out from my back pocket.

"Freddie, you need to borrow my mother's boat and get over to the gazebo."

"What? Why? I'm making real progress here. My question was—"

"I think I spotted Lyssa's boyfriend rummaging through all the wedding stuff."

"Seriously?"

"I'm going to call over to the sheriff's department—"

"What? You will do no such thing! She's going to arrest you. She told you that."

"I know she did, but . . ." I chewed the corner of my thumbnail. "She probably didn't mean it."

"Let's just check it out first. We'll call if—"

"Check it out? We are a legitimate business now. The police tape is still up. You know we cannot cross that line to see what he was after."

"Fine, we won't cross the line! But don't call yet either. We need to find out what it is he's looking for. Then if it's important, we'll call. Anonymously. There's an app for that."

"I don't know—"

"Just hold on. I'm coming." He chuckled. "Hey, it's just like that song—"

"We don't have time for songs, Freddie!"

"Right. Right. Just don't do anything till I get there."

Freddie ended the call. I rested my phone at my chin and looked over the still water. Okay, what was Freddie thinking? If we weren't going to cross the police tape, how were we going to find out what Lyssa's boyfriend was looking for—

Oh . . . no.

I knew what Freddie was thinking.

We were going swimming.

Chapter Thirty-five

"It's cold," I said, stretching my toe down into the water. "Very, very cold."

"Don't be such a baby," Freddie said, rummaging in the compartment under one of the boat's seats.

"I'm not being a baby. It's really cold." And dark. And kind of creepy.

Normally I liked swimming at night, but somehow this was different. It was quiet, and the sight of the gauze floating around the gazebo seemed . . . lonely.

I stuck my toe in the water again. Man, my shorts and tank top were going to get all wet, and I was already cold. But I wasn't taking them off. I'd had a bad experience with skinny-dipping in the past. "Okay, I'm just going to do it."

"Then do it."

"I don't see you doing it," I called back over my shoulder.

"I'm going to. I just need to find the waterproof flashlights, and—" He grunted. "This boat is a mess.

"All right. I'm just going to do it. I'm just going to—wah!"

And I was in the water. Freddie had pushed me in.

"Cold. Cold. Cold."

"You're welcome," he said. "And I'm sure it's not that bad."

"It is that bad. And hurry up. I don't know how I'm going to explain the delay of seeing the guy and calling Sheriff Bigly, even anonymou— What are you doing?"

"Putting on my life jacket," Freddie said, snapping some buckles into place.

"Why?"

"I don't like night swimming," Freddie said, coming over to the edge. "If a fish touches my leg, I might start freaking out or something, and I don't want to drown."

I grabbed the edge of the boat. This treading water was getting tiring. "Okay, but what does any of that have to do with night swimming? The fish don't only come out at night."

Freddie rolled his eyes. "Someone died here. I won't be able to see the fish and, you know," he said with a little shrug, "my imagination might get the better of me."

"How?"

He threw his hands up in the air. "Well, I might think it's like a lake zombie grabbing my ankle."

"Wow."

"I know. It's ridiculous. But an active imagination is the sign of high intelligence and—"

"That's not what I was going say," I said, shaking my head.

"What were you going to say?"

"Pass me one too."

Freddie stared down at me. "But you like night swimming."

"I used to like night swimming!" I near shouted, opening and shutting my fist in the universal gimme-gimme gesture. "Now pass me one. Like right now. It feels like a million things are touching me. I'm freaking out."

"Here!" Freddie shouted. It landed on my head. I had to flail around to get it on, but things did feel much better once it was secured. Good luck dragging me under now, lake zombies.

A minute or two later, Freddie was in the water with me and we were dog-paddling our way over to the gazebo, both of us clutching waterproof flashlights. Funny how life jackets really slow things down.

"Now, be careful as we get closer," I said. "There's lots of . . ."

"Ow! Frick! For the love of—my toe! I think I broke my toe," Freddie wheezed.

". . . rocks. There's lots of rocks around the gazebo," I said. I gingerly put my toe down to find the bottom. Ew. Slimy. I then reached my hands down so I could half swim, half crawl my way to the floor of the gazebo. "Hurry up," I said, turning back to Freddie. "What are you doing?"

"Bleeding out."

"Just come on." I pointed the flashlight at the gazebo.

Freddie scoffed when he made it to my side and saw the mess of bins on the gazebo floor. "Even if he's not the murderer, I'm totally going to kill this guy. Look at the mess he made."

I couldn't help but agree. The guy had managed to knock over a stack of chairs, and all the bins that had been so neatly packed were dumped on their sides.

I swept the flashlight slowly across the floor. "Do you see anything? I mean, anything that he could have been looking for?"

"No, this is all just wedding crap," Freddie said. "And not even the good stuff. I've already made a new seating chart."

I looked around. He was right. There were some linens maybe. Napkin rings. Oh no! Was that the cake topper? It looked like the groom was missed a leg. I suddenly had the urge to call Joey and make sure he didn't have any more home-improvement plans. "What's that over there? It looks like . . . a present?" I settled the flashlight on a large box wrapped with ribbon, half propped up on some linens.

"Why would a present be in one of the bins?"

"Maybe I can . . ." I stretched my arm under the railing of the gazebo as I pushed myself up on a slimy rock. This could end really badly, but I just wanted to turn the box a little to see if there was a label. Unfortunately I tipped it over and . . .

"What the . . . ?" Freddie gasped.

Whoa. I met Freddie's eye. "It's not a present . . . was that the money box?"

"If it is, somebody was overly generous."

We turned back to look at what had to be thousands of dollars spilling out of a bag hidden in the box.

I looked at Freddie . . . whose cheeks were suddenly lit up . . . with blue light. Then red. Then blue.

Oh crap.

"I think we've got company," Freddie said, looking over to the police cruiser pulling over by the gazebo.

This was bad, bad, bad.

"Should we make a swim for it?" Freddie asked.

Footsteps pounded down the wooden planks.

"Erica Bloom and Freddie Ng, you stay right where you are."

"No," I said, shaking my head. "She's knows where we live."

Sheriff Bigly was suddenly looming over us. She did not look happy.

I cleared my throat. "Sheriff, shouldn't you be in bed?"

"Yes. Yes, I should."

"We are in so much trouble."

Chapter Thirty-six

"We were going to call you."

"Right after we got out of the water," Freddie said. "Calling you was our next move."

"Please don't get cute." Sheriff Bigly waved a hand at us. The other hand was covering her eyes and clutching her temples.

We were seated in Grady's office on the sofa wrapped in blankets.

After what seemed like an eternity, she took a deep breath then let her hand fall. "I thought we had all come to an understanding."

Freddie and I exchanged glances.

"What did she get you?"

I frowned. "Pie. You?"

"Ice cream."

Sheriff Bigly slapped her desk. "Forget the pie. Forget the . . . what is the matter with you two?!"

Hard to tell if that was rhetorical or not.

"No, really. I want to know."

I shrugged. "I—"

"'Cause I can't figure it out." I guess it was rhetorical after all. "I really can't." She planted both hands on Grady's desk. "Are your lives really so boring?" I could feel Freddie stiffen beside me at that, but he was having the good sense to keep his mouth shut. "Do you think I *want* to arrest you? Do you care at all about your friend Candace? Because I'm pretty sure she wants to find out what happened to her maid of honor."

"Whoa," I said, holding my hands out, but that dropped the blanket off my shoulder and I was still really cold, so I hiked it up real quick. "We are trying to help Candace."

"By making my job harder."

Freddie cleared his throat. "I—"

Bigly pointed at him. "You think you're pretty funny don't you, Ng?"

"I didn't even . . . what did I say?" Freddie asked.

"You two have no idea what you screwed up tonight."

Screwed up? I hated it when we screwed things up. I told Freddie we should have called her!

"We left everything in the gazebo for a reason," Sheriff Bigly said, still leaning on the desk. "We were there tonight. We've been waiting for Lyssa's boyfriend to show himself. Waiting for days. That's why he was rummaging about Candace's shed. That told us we were on the right track. We knew he'd eventually figure out what he was looking for had to be at the gazebo, not Candace's. Then he finally shows up and somebody shines a big ol' light on him, and he takes off. Amos tried to catch him, but that boy is fast. Amazing, really, given what we know about him."

I suddenly felt like I would be sick. That was why she just so happened to be at the gazebo the other day. "I swear to God, Sheriff Bigly, if I had known—"

"Known what? Are you honestly going to sit there and try to tell me that you wouldn't have interfered?"

"I wouldn't have. We all want the same thing here." I meant that too. In those other stories she was thinking of, I was either trying to prove someone I love innocent—like myself—or I was fighting for my life. "And what do you mean the condition he was in?"

"Lyssa's boyfriend Justin is a very unstable young man. That is all you need to know."

"But . . . if you were there, why didn't you show yourself right away?"

"She wanted to see what we'd do," Freddie said. "Probably building a case for when she arrests us."

"No. No. Let's back up a moment," Bigly said. "Erica, you said we all want the same thing, and I want to know if that's true. Do you really want this all settled for Candace? Or is this all about Otter Lake Security making the sheriff's department look stupid once again?"

"We really don't want that," I said whereas Freddie asked, "Do you know where the money came from? I'm assuming Lyssa. Am I r—"

"Stop talking!" Sheriff Bigly said, hitting the desk. "What makes you think I would tell you anything about this case?"

"Professional courtesy?" Freddie mumbled.

"Professional . . . professional courtesy?" She chewed her lip. I think to stop herself from saying all the words that were really going through her mind. Most of them four-lettered. "I should put you in a cell for trying to make a sheriff insane. That's what I should do."

"So . . . does this mean we can get the wedding stuff from the gazebo now?"

I slapped his leg.

"Take it. Justin's not coming back there." Sheriff Bigly's jaw flexed. "But I need you two to hear me on something."

I nodded quickly and slapped Freddie's leg some more until he was nodding too.

"If you want to help your friend, you will tell no one what you saw at the gazebo." She jabbed a finger on her desk. "Do you understand? The money is not public knowledge, and I would like it to stay that way."

We both nodded again.

"Now get out of my office."

We popped up to our feet.

As we were heading out, we spotted Amos with rubber gloves counting the money at his desk. His lips were moving. It looked like he was almost done.

Freddie slowed down. "What's that, Amos?"

"Thirty-nine thousand, nine hundred," he said, eyes still on the money.

"Thirty-nine thousand?" Freddie asked.

"Forty," Amos said with a smile. "It's all there."

"Dammit, Amos!" A shout came from Grady's office.

I pushed Freddie toward the door. "Let's go! Let's go! Let's go!"

Chapter Thirty-seven

"Order. Order!" Freddie shouted. "I am calling this meeting to order."

"Stop banging that spoon on the table, Freddie."

The next morning, Freddie, me, and Rhonda were all gathered in the war room for a brainstorming session. Okay, yes, we had promised Sheriff Bigly we wouldn't tell anyone about the money, but we knew Rhonda wouldn't tell anyone. She was an ex-cop. She knew exactly how much trouble we could get in. And the war room was really just Freddie's kitchen—although he did have a big whiteboard on wheels in it for brainstorming.

"Well, we need to get started, and you two won't stop talking."

I shot Rhonda a look. We were talking—whispering actually—about why she was still taking pictures of shirtless insurance guy. She was sticking by her whole "something isn't right about this situation" excuse, but I could see the lovesick look in her eye.

"Seriously, ladies, we need to keep in mind the reason why we're doing this."

"For Lyssa," Rhonda said.

"For Lyssa," I repeated. "And for Candace."

"Of course for Candace and—"

"That's enough. Gold star for you both. Let's start with what we know," he said, still in pajama pants and a Hooters T-shirt. He was holding a wooden spoon in one hand and an erasable marker in the other. "Lyssa hid a bag with forty thousand dollars in the wedding's money box."

Freddie wrote Lyssa on the board, drew an arrow from her name to a box, then put a dollar sign above the arrow.

"We also know that her boyfriend slash ex-boyfriend, *it's complicated*"—he put air quotes around that—"knew about the money." He wrote the name Justin on the board then underlined it. "Now, we need to focus on what we don't know."

"Why did she hide the money in the first place?" Rhonda asked.

Freddie began scribbling Rhonda's question on the board in point form.

"Where did she get it?" Rhonda went on. "Why didn't she put it in the bank? Was it ill-gotten gains? How did her boyfriend, ex-boyfriend know about the money? Was he—"

"Rhonda!" Freddie snapped.

"What?"

"I can't write that fast." He looked at me and held out the marker. "You do it. You're the court reporter."

"My skills don't translate to whiteboards."

Freddie glared at me.

"Besides, you don't have to write it all down yet," I said. "Let's just talk." These types of arguments happened every time we tried to have a meeting. "I think we have to assume there is something shady about how Lyssa got the money, or, yeah, she wouldn't have had that much in cash," I said. "As for why she hid it . . . well, the only person we know for sure who knows about it is Justin, so maybe she was hiding it from him?"

"He obviously feels he has some sort of claim to it," Rhonda said, "and he's hiding from the police, so . . ."

"So Lyssa's boyfriend knows about the money, and he wants it bad," Freddie said, tapping his chin with the marker. Suddenly he threw his hands in the air. "So then we have our trap." He beamed at us.

"Freddie," Rhonda said, "did you buy new aftershave?"

"That is your response? No *Great plan, Freddie*? No *Go Team!*" He gave the air a little punch.

"It's just I'm really sensitive to smells." She backslapped me lightly on the arm. "You're HR. I think we should adopt a no-scents policy."

"Why? We already have one," Freddie snapped.

I cleared my throat. "She said *scents* not *sense*, Freddie."

"*Tomayto, tomahto.*"

Okay, someone needed to take control here. "Rhonda, your motion is seconded and passed. Freddie, let's hear more about your plan."

"What? That is so unfair. What am I supposed to put on my face after I shave?"

"Motion passed," I repeated. "Now back to your

plan. I don't see how it would work. We don't have the money," I said. "Sheriff Bigly has—"

"Erica. Erica. Erica," Freddie said with a sigh. "Please try to keep up."

"I'm sorry. I'm having some trouble thinking this morning. Maybe if someone had made the cappuccino." My eyes slid over to Rhonda. It was *so* her turn.

"Turnabout is fair play, Miss 'I'm sorry I forgot your lunch.' "

"I made up for that with the gummies," I said, shooting her a look. "Oh, I get it," I said, suddenly turning back to Freddie and wagging a finger at him. "You want us to pretend to have the money."

He put a hand over his face and nodded.

"See? I just needed a minute."

"He's taken so many crazy risks to get to that money and Sheriff Bigly said he was unstable. I'm willing to bet he's hoping the police haven't found the money," Freddie said. "I don't think he's going to stop now. We can't all be great thinkers."

"But how are we going to trick him into thinking we have the money?" Rhonda asked.

"We move all the wedding supplies from the gazebo and Candace's house to a location of our choosing," Freddie said, moving his hands that were paralleling each other from left to right. "We wait for this Justin character to show up. Then *pow!* We nab him."

"It sounds so straightforward. I wonder what could possibly go wrong?" I reached for my cappuccino only to realize, *That's right, I don't have one.* I shot Rhonda another filthy look.

"What did I do this time?"

"Nothing. Nothing."

Rhonda looked back to Freddie. "So what's the location of our choosing?"

"My garage of course," Freddie said.

"Your garage?" I asked. "Why would we—"

"Rhonda," Freddie said. "For the sake of the business, you really need to make the cappuccino when it's your turn. Erica's killing me here."

"Oh, never mind, I got it," I said. Freddie had his entire house wired up with surveillance equipment like a museum filled with priceless artifacts. He had contacted a number of surveillance companies saying that he was in the security business and wanted to try their products before he recommended them to anyone else. A few businesses were quite accommodating—even though we had yet to recommend a single security system to anyone. But Freddie was quite the salesman. So, yeah, some he got for free . . . and some he asked for as birthday and Christmas presents from his family.

"It's perfect," Freddie said. "I'm the wedding planner, so it makes sense I would store supplies at my house."

"Well, co-wedding planner," I said.

"I can't even . . ." Freddie said with a shake of his head.

"But say this works and we do get Lyssa's boyfriend to break into your garage," I said. "What do we do then? Throw a blanket on him and wait for the police to arrive?"

Freddie blinked at me like I was an idiot—which was not fair because that was a totally legitimate question . . . unlike some of my earlier questions.

"I'm serious. What if he has a weapon?"

"I wouldn't break into somebody's home without a

weapon," Rhonda said once again, folding her arms across her chest.

"We are not going to throw a blanket over him. That's ridiculous," Freddie said.

"Then what are we going to do? Call Sheriff Bigly and hope the guy waits around long enough for her to arrive?" I was saying it like it was the stupidest idea ever, but I did kind of like the thought of delivering Bigly a suspect all wrapped up with a bow. I don't know what it was about the woman, but deep down I kind of wanted her to respect me . . . or at least not think I was a complete idiot.

"You two have no imagination," Freddie said. "No vision. No—"

"We're not going to physically restrain him with, like, our bodies, are we?" Rhonda asked. "Because there's some legalities that might be involved in that."

"No, we're not going to restrain him with our . . . *bodies*," Freddie said. "That sounds weird."

"Then what are we going to do?" I asked.

He double-popped his eyebrows. "Well, let's just say we're not calling it a trap for nothing."

Rhonda and I waited for more information.

"All right," Freddie said. "Good meeting. Super-efficient." He drew a happy face on the board and left.

Chapter Thirty-eight

"It's been three, no, four days," I moaned.

"I know."

"I don't think it's going to happen. Not before the wedding. Probably not at all."

Freddie sighed.

One of us—Freddie, Rhonda, and me—had been watching Freddie's computer screen nonstop now for three days. That on top of the wedding planning was making life really unpleasant.

At first Freddie had terrified me with his whole "they don't call it a trap for nothing" declaration. I was imagining him rigging up one of those rope traps where the person steps on the trigger, then before they even realize what was happening, they're swinging in the air upside down by their ankle. I really didn't think Freddie's garage had the clearance for that kind of thing. But it turned out that wasn't what he had in mind at all. It was much more simple than that. And actually kind of clever. We had set up the door leading into the garage from the outside with a dead-bolt lock that you could control with an app. But the brilliant part was we had installed it backwards. That way, Justin would walk into the garage, the door would close, we'd trigger the dead bolt then *bam!* Trapped.

But before we moved the stuff to Freddie's, we double-checked all the cameras outside, so we could see someone coming from pretty much any direction, and we set up a video baby monitor in the garage, so we could talk to the guy, you know, once he was trapped, and before the police arrived.

Then we made a really big show of moving the stuff from the gazebo and Candace's shed to Freddie's house. A hot, irritating show. Taking lots of trips. We also got Candace to post pictures of the entire ordeal on her social media just in case we weren't being watched.

So all in all we thought it was a pretty good plan, and we had put a lot of work into it.

The only problem was nobody was trying to break into Freddie's garage.

Nope, aside from getting the heads-up that pizza had arrived on the computer monitor, so far, the entire operation had been a failure.

Tonight, it was just Freddie and me on watch. Once again, Rhonda wanted to get a few more photos of our insurance target first thing in the morning, so she needed her rest. I was going to have to stage an intervention for her soon.

"I really think maybe we just have to let it go," I said from Freddie's couch. "We need to get some sleep. Candace's parents are flying in tomorrow, and we have to make sure everything is ready for the rehearsal dinner."

"You go to sleep," Freddie said, face aglow from the light of the computer screen. "I'm going to keep watch for a couple more hours."

I pulled a blanket over me then scratched Stanley's head. The little bulldog was sleeping at my feet. "Okay, wake me if anything happens."

We were quiet for a few minutes before I said, "Freddie?"

Stanley groaned.

"What?"

"You know when you were at Grady's the other night?"

"Uh-huh."

"What did you guys talk about?"

I never did make it over to Grady's after the whole thing at the gazebo. I had been telling myself it was because I needed to help watch the trap, but I knew that wasn't entirely it. When I had heard Mary's story, the way forward had all seemed so clear, but as time passed, I lost my nerve. I didn't know what was going on with Grady. What if I said the wrong thing? What if I made things even worse? I was still planning on talking to him. I just needed to do a bit more intel gathering first.

"You mean you want to know if we talked about you?" Freddie asked, arching an eyebrow.

"No, I want to know if you discussed the weather." I chucked a pillow at him. "Of course I want to know if you talked about me."

"Hey, watch where you're throwing those things,"

Freddie said, petting his computer. "And the truth is . . . I can't answer that question."

"What?"

"Grady and I are finally buds," he said, peeking at me around his screen. "I can't go telling you his secrets."

"Grady has secrets? What secrets?"

"Okay, that was a poor choice of words. It's more like—"

"So you did talk about me."

"Well, yeah, but—"

"Did you talk about this crazy vacation of his?" I propped myself up on my elbow, making Stanley raise his head. He was unimpressed by my lack of sleep.

"We did. And it's really not so crazy once you understand . . ." Freddie shook his head. "I've said too much."

"You haven't said anything!"

"Look, after this whole thing happened with Sean . . . well, it made me think that maybe I have perhaps"—he tapped the desk with a pencil—"in the past . . . caused some trouble for you and Grady by being *too* involved. And I don't want to do that anymore. I'm staying out of it. Weren't you the one who said we needed healthy boundaries?"

"I don't remember," I said. "But so . . . wait, are you saying that this vacation has something to do with me?"

"I'm saying nothing," Freddie said. "Don't you want us to be happy? You know, with separate people . . . while still having a relationship that is all our own?"

I slumped back into the sofa and Stanley lowered his head. He still had his eye on me though. "I guess so." A moment later I added, "I can't believe you've chosen this very moment to establish *healthy boundaries*." I sighed. "But you're right. If Grady has something to say to me, he should say it to me. Not you. In fact," I said, snuggling deeper into the blanket. "I don't want to know."

"You're serious? You don't want to know?"

I closed my eyes. "Nope. Healthy boundaries."

"Well, now I kind of want to tell you."

My eyes shot open. "So tell me."

Freddie looked me up and down. "Never mind, the feeling's passed."

"But you just said you wanted to tell me."

Freddie sighed. "That was when you didn't want to know, but now that I know you were lying . . . it just doesn't have the same appeal."

"You're evil."

"I know," Freddie said, chuckling to himself.

I snuggled back into the sofa and Stanley let out a breath that flapped his gums before closing his eyes. I didn't think I was going to be able to fall asleep with all this new Grady noninformation to speculate on, but within minutes, my mind had drifted off . . .

I was in a beautiful meadow. Birds were singing. The sun was shining. White chairs were lined up in the distance in front of a pagoda draped in white gauze. It was perfect . . . beautiful . . .

Terrifying!

Little brides and grooms—wedding toppers—had come to life and they were running toward me! Tiny little knives in their hands! They were coming for me! Cutting little trails through the grass! They were going to stab me with their little blades and—

"Erica!"

I jerked against the couch.

"Erica, wake up!"

I shot up. "What? What's happening?"

"One of the motion sensors is going off," Freddie hissed.

I wiped some drool from my mouth. "Are you sure it's not just another raccoon?"

"No, it's him! And he's going for the garage!"

Chapter Thirty-nine

I pushed myself off the couch, landing hard on my knees.

"Watch Stanley!" Freddie shouted.

Stanley was fine. He was still on the couch looking annoyed.

I popped to my feet and raced over to Freddie at his computer desk.

"Where? Where is he?"

Freddie pointed to the top right video feed on his computer screen.

"Holy crap!" I shook Freddie's shoulder. "That's him!" I mean, I couldn't exactly be one hundred percent sure given that I had only seen him twice under less than ideal conditions, but that was totally him. Who else would be sneaking around Freddie's garage?

"This is it. He's going to do it," Freddie whispered. "He's going for the door."

I leaned closer toward the screen. "Do you have the dead-bolt switch ready?"

Freddie nodded and pointed at a lock icon on his other computer screen. "Now, we just need him to go inside and . . . wait . . . no! Why is he stopping?"

He had stopped right in front of the door, hand outstretched. "He's looking at the handle!" I gripped Freddie's shoulder even harder. "He knows something's up. He . . ." He was turning the knob, so I shut up. But not for long. "I can't believe this is working."

"Shut up. Shut up. Shut up," Freddie hissed. "I have to concentrate. Time it just right. I need to click the lock as soon as the door closes behind him."

We were watching the screen that had the feed going from the inside of the garage. He was stepping inside.

"That's it," I whispered.

"Shut up," Freddie hissed.

"Keep going."

"Shut up."

"The door's shutting."

"Shut up."

"I don't need to shut up! All you have to do is click the button . . ." I watched the garage door shut behind the man. "Now!"

Freddie clicked it. The man jumped just as all the lights in the garage went on.

"It worked!" Freddie shouted. "He's trapped!"

The man was shaking the door handle. It wasn't budging!

"Oh my God! We did it!" I shook Freddie's shoulder some more and jumped up and down. "Turn on the monitor thingy! I want to hear what he's saying!"

Freddie clicked around the screen.

"—out of here!" the man shouted. "What is this?"

"He's freaking out," I said. "Turn on the two-way so we can talk to him."

"Hang on," Freddie said, eyes darting around the screen.

"I'm not sawing off my own leg if that's what you're thinking!" the man shouted.

"Saw off his own leg?" I asked Freddie. "What's he talking about?"

"You know that horror movie where the people are trapped and they have to—just freaking Google it! Later. I need to focus. I can't get the two-way—"

"Wait, what's he doing now?" I asked, looking at the screen.

The guy was tearing around the car now. Oh boy, he tripped . . . but now he was back up and . . .

"You locked the door that leads to the inside of the house, right?" I asked.

Freddie shot a look at me. "Of course I did. But you locked it again after you got those Popsicles from the freezer in there?"

"I . . . I think I did. What about you when you got us those beers?"

"I . . . I think I did too."

We watched the man tear across the garage, up the steps that led to the door that accessed the kitchen, and then . . .

. . . we heard the door open.

Chapter Forty

"Weapons!" I screamed. "We need weapons!"

We could totally hear the guy in the kitchen. Even over all our screaming.

"Here!" Freddie ran to the fireplace and tossed a fire poker in my direction. I jumped out of the way and it clattered to the floor. "Erica, when are you going to learn how to catch?" He picked up the little shovel that went with the poker as I scrambled to pick the poker off the floor.

The noise in the kitchen stopped.

Where is he? I mouthed, clutching the iron to my chest.

Freddie shook his head.

We tiptoed across the floor so that we were standing side by side then we took a couple of steps toward the hallway that connected all the rooms . . . including the kitchen.

"Maybe we should just let him leave," I whispered.

"Or leave ourselves," I said with a jerk of my head to the sliding glass doors.

"But we've come this far," Freddie said.

"This far to die."

"But this may be our one chance to—"

We heard a crash in the hallway.

"So help me if that was my collector's Elvis bust," Freddie said, "he is going to die."

I couldn't care about that though because all that clatter meant he was coming this way!

I pointed my poker shakily out in the front of me. Freddie did the same with his shovel.

Seconds passed like years then—

Everybody was screaming again.

I was screaming.

Freddie was screaming.

The guy standing in front of us was screaming.

But even though we were all screaming at each other, I couldn't help but think that it didn't look like he was going to kill us with that rolling pin in his hand. I mean, one, he was screaming like *we* were the ones who were going to kill *him*. And two . . . well, he obviously wasn't all that smart because he had grabbed a rolling pin in a room full of knives. Not that I was judging. We hadn't locked the door on our trap.

Eventually all of our screams dwindled away. Freddie let out one last little yelp, but that's because he always needs to have the last word.

"Okay, everybody calm down," Freddie said. "You're scaring my dog."

I took a look back at Stanley. He didn't look that

upset. In fact, he had just put his chin back down on his paws.

"What do you want?" the man asked. "Why are you trying to trap me in your house?"

"Justin?"

He just stared at me.

"We . . . we just want to talk to you," I said, holding up my hands in surrender—while still holding on to the poker. "We're friends of Candace's. We want to know what happened to Lyssa."

"I didn't kill her," he said, shaking his head violently. "I know that's what you guys probably think. But I didn't kill her."

Neither one of us answered.

"I loved Lyssa. I would never hurt her."

Chapter Forty-one

"Talk to us," Freddie said. "Tell us what happened. Maybe we can help."

"I just want my money, so I can get out of this place. I can't even think about Lyssa. I can't even . . ." He raked his hand through his spiky hair while shaking his head.

I looked him over quickly. His jeans were torn and he was covered in dirt. He also looked half starved and dehydrated. "Have you been in Otter Lake this whole time?" I asked. "Where have you been staying?"

He nodded quickly. "Different places. I found an abandoned lodge in the woods, but the police came. I slept on the ground one night."

"Why are you hiding from them?" Freddie asked. "What did you do?"

"They're going to think I did it! Because of what Lyssa and I *did*. But we didn't do anything wrong! It's not illegal." He was gesturing a little too wildly for my liking. "But don't you get it? It's going to look like I cut her out of the deal. I just want the money, and I'll go. Start a new life. Start the life Lyssa and I wanted."

"We're not following," Freddie said. "What did you two do?"

"Nothing," he said, voice tightening with emotion. "That's what I'm trying to tell you. That guy knew why she was with him."

"What guy?" I asked.

"The guy who gave her the money!" Justin grabbed his hair with his free hand. "That's how it works. She gives him companionship. He gives her gifts and money. She never slept with him. But I looked out for her, you know? She—"

"Some guy gave Lyssa forty thousand dollars to hang out with him?" I asked.

"Forty thousand . . . ?" He took a step back and pointed the rolling pin at us. "No. It was only a couple of grand. Enough for us to get down to the Keys. Lyssa said we could get jobs at one of those tiki bars. Maybe run our own one day. Why did you say forty—"

Suddenly there was a loud bang at the door. "Open up—Police!"

Justin dropped the rolling pin. "No, man. No, don't let them in." He clutched his head.

"It's okay, Justin," I said, holding out a hand. "I think . . . I think you might have an alibi."

He was rocking now. "What are you talking about?"

"The guy you punched. He can maybe tell the police you weren't with Lyssa at the gazebo when she died." I didn't know if that was true or not, but I needed to keep him calm. Sheriff Bigly was right. He was not stable.

Freddie was inching his way toward the hallway.

"But I went back!" Justin yelled. "She wasn't there. I couldn't find her. She was probably in the water." He fell to his knees. "I could've saved her. If I'd known she was in the water, I could have saved her."

Freddie made a run for the door, but Justin was beyond hearing him now. He was sobbing.

A moment later, Sheriff Bigly and Amos rushed in the room. Handcuffs at the ready.

This was awful. I didn't know why exactly, but part of me believed Justin's story. He was just so desperate and miserable.

"Sheriff, I know this sounds crazy," I said quickly, "but I don't think he did it. He—"

She looked up at me from under her brow. "It's all right, Erica. You don't need to worry about that."

I took a step toward them. "But he seems genuinely confused about the money and—"

She kept her gaze leveled on me. "We'll find out the truth back at the station. You two have done your part."

"Done our part?"

"You've been watching my house," Freddie said, coming to stand beside me. "You've been watching us."

Sheriff Bigly and Amos pulled Justin up to his feet. He looked so done. He wasn't crying anymore, but . . . he just looked done. "Well, I didn't want you sabotaging our plan again, so I thought we might as well piggyback on yours. We would have gotten to your door sooner, but . . ." She shot a look at Amos. He was covered in dirt. It was hard running through the woods at night.

I shook my head. I don't know why I was so upset.

Maybe it was how pathetic Justin looked . . . or the pain emanating from him.

"Listen," Sherriff Bigly said almost gently, "I don't know what he said to you, but one of the first things you learn early on in this business is that people lie. They just do." She looked at Amos and nodded. They turned Justin to leave. "Come by tomorrow to give your statements."

"You have to talk to Tommy too," I called out after them. "He might be able to give him an alibi. He followed him—"

"Erica," Sheriff Bigly said almost kindly. "Get some sleep."

"But—"

"You two look like you could use it."

Chapter Forty-two

"Well," I said, folding my napkin over my lap. "This is nice."

It was nice. As nice as it could be given the circumstances. Yup, I couldn't help but think Freddie and I had done a pretty good job putting the rehearsal dinner together considering the constraints we were working under.

We had spent the first part of the day giving our statements to Amos and the rest of the day trying to get the wedding details finalized. I kept going over and over in my mind every detail of what had happened the night before, but no matter how many times I heard Sherriff Bigly say *people lie* in my head, I just couldn't shake the feeling in Justin's eyes. He loved Lyssa. He didn't want her dead. Okay, granted, it did kind of sound like he was acting as her pimp, which didn't exactly speak to his character, but . . . again, going over the details wasn't helping anything. And

Freddie and I had work to do. And we were kind of doing it backward.

We were having the rehearsal dinner tonight before the rehearsal in the morning because the tent we had rented last minute still wasn't set up, and until that was set up we weren't entirely sure where we were going to have the actual ceremony, and . . .

Well, it was just depressing to think of all the work we still had to do.

The table looked beautiful though. Although it wasn't actually one table. We had lined up some picnic tables end to end. It was a little awkward watching Candace's mother get herself seated with her really lovely taupe pencil-shaped dress. But she had made it in the end. That's right, Candace's parents had shown up after all, but they kind of had the air of people going to a funeral not a wedding.

As for Joey's side of the family, Antonia and Nonna were back in town too. I still hadn't found the right time to talk to Antonia. But it was on the list. As there was no way we could safely get Nonna into the picnic table, we sat her at the end in one of the throne chairs Freddie had found for the bride and groom to use at the reception. She looked pretty cute all swallowed up in it.

Overall, Freddie had managed to create a pretty nice atmosphere for the dinner. He had taken poles from a couple of tents and actually made a pergola over the table, draping gauze over the top. I didn't think it was going to work, but he surprised me. It was actually kind of dreamy with the sun getting lower in the sky. If this was any indication of what the wedding was going to be like, well, it might be . . . okay.

That was really the best we could hope for given . . . everything.

Despite the nice surroundings, the tension in the air was thick. Suffocating almost. You could tell by all the throat clearing going on when the attempts at polite conversation failed. I was hoping things would pick up when my mother and Zaki joined us for dinner. My mother was oblivious to most social awkwardness and people just liked Zaki. He was very likable . . . you know, when you weren't picturing him in bed with your mother. Yeah, they might help. They just needed to get here already. I figured it might take a while since they were also helping make the meal.

"Evelyn," Freddie said from the other end of the table. "Would you like more wine?"

"Yes, please."

Oh boy, she had already downed one glass, and we hadn't even started eating. Not sure that was a good idea.

"So, Erica, Freddie," Candace's father, Michael, said. "Candace tells us that you two are not only the wedding planners, you're also looking into who murdered Lyssa?"

"Oh well . . ." I began.

"We like to keep the two topics separate," Freddie said, making a spreading motion with his hands. "No murder talk at the dinner table. That's our rule at Otter Lake Security."

"Right. Right," Michael said, leaning back and templing his fingers. "Of course. But the one does affect the other. I mean, we wouldn't want anyone else getting murdered the night before the wedding."

"Dad," Candace said tightly.

"No, I think he's got a point," Antonia said. "It could be dangerous. Maybe we should—"

"Antonia." It was Joey giving the warning this time.

We all fell back into silence.

"Maybe I should check to see what's going on with . . ." I had started to get up, but when I saw the look on Freddie's face, I sat right back down. "I'm sure it will be out shortly.

"It's nice having the tables all set up like this," I went on. "I don't have a big family, but I'm guessing this is what it's like."

Joey nodded. "This is how we ate in prison . . . too."

Candace's dad clutched the sides of his plate, as his wife put a hand on his forearm then said, "Certainly is buggy in New Hampshire, isn't it?"

"I'll light more lanterns," Freddie said, jumping to his feet. We already had five or six lit around the perimeter of the table. If Freddie lit any more of them we all might die of toxic fumes.

Just then a noise caught my attention.

Was that . . . chittering?

I looked over my shoulder. Oh crap, it *was* chittering. A red squirrel was staring at us and swearing a blue streak by the sounds of it. I darted a quick look over at Nonna. I was sitting at her left at the end of the table. It didn't look like she had noticed. In all the planning for this dinner—which, admittedly, was not very much—I had forgotten about the squirrels. It was a good distance away, but it seemed superannoyed that we were in its squirrel space.

"Erica?" Freddie called out.

My eyes darted back to the table.

"Is there . . . ?"

"Nothing's wrong. Everything's good. Oh boy, I'm hungry."

Just then I spotted my mother come out from the lodge's front door. A couple of the vegan caterers from the retreat were following behind her with dishes. Oh, and there was Zaki too. With a dish of his own.

"Oh dear," Evelyn said. "I don't usually eat Indian food. Too spicy." She looked at Freddie. "Sorry."

"Why are you looking at me?" Freddie asked. "My family's from Hong Kong."

"That's close to India, isn't it?"

Freddie frowned. "Probably not as close as you think."

Another awkward moment passed before Evelyn added, "I don't like Chinese food either."

"Mom," Candace snapped.

"What?" her father answered. "Your mother's never been good with geography. Or spice."

"Oh no . . ." Evelyn said with a gasp. "Was that racist?" She was looking at Freddie again.

"I don't . . . can you ask someone else at the table?"

"I . . . I'm mortified," Evelyn said, bringing a tissue to her eye.

Antonia nodded. "Oh yeah, I can see where Candace gets it from now."

"Please don't cry," Freddie said, leaning over to pat her hand. "I don't like Indian food either, and I failed tenth-grade geography. I probably couldn't find Canada on a map." Freddie looked at me and mouthed, *Do something*. What was I supposed to do?

"Um, so . . . it's been a pretty warm spring."

Weather. Yup, you could always count on the good ol' weather small talk. "It's nice to be outside after a long winter."

"Do you like the outdoors, Joseph?" Candace's father asked.

Or not . . . weather was bad. Freddie shot me a "how could you?" look. But really, I didn't think there was any winning this.

"I do." Joey nodded.

"I see," Michael said, nodding too. "Did prison—being locked up—strengthen that appreciation?"

Candace shot her father a pretty terrifying look. "Dad."

"Just making conversation."

Antonia dropped her hand heavily by her plate, making her cutlery clatter. "Is there something you would like to say about my brother, *Michael*."

"Oh, I have a lot I'd like to—"

"Here's the food!" Freddie shouted. "Oh, and it looks wonderful. Not too spicy at all."

My mother and Zaki and the caterers placed dishes all over the table. They were all smiles. Once my mother thanked the caterers she turned to the group and said, "Sorry for the delay, everyone. I am Summer and this is Zaki."

"Hello," Zaki said. "Thank you so much for inviting us to share this beautiful dinner with you."

Everyone nodded.

Yes, that's what we needed. My mother and Zaki. They didn't know what was going on, so everyone would have to behave themselves.

The caterers left, and my mother was just about to

sit down beside me when she said, "Oh! I forgot the sprouted grain bread and hummus. Zaki, could you come with m—"

Without even realizing it, I had grabbed my mother's wrist.

She looked down at me.

"Don't go," I whispered through my teeth.

She patted my hand. "I'll be right back," she said with a nervous chuckle. Then leaned in and whispered, "Don't be awkward, dear." Then she pried her arm from my grip and she and Zaki left.

"Was that *the* Zaki?" Evelyn asked Freddie. "Guru Zaki? The author?"

Freddie nodded.

"You won't tell him what I said about not liking spicy food?"

"What will you pay me?" he said deadpan.

More tears came to Evelyn's eyes.

"Oh no!" Freddie said. "I was joking. Trying to lighten the moment. I . . ." He looked back to me for help.

I didn't know what to do! I cleared my throat. "Well, the food smells wonder—"

Just then a crash sounded at the other the table. Nonna's wineglass had spilled onto her plate.

She must have knocked it over when she had made a grab for the knife.

"No!" I shouted, getting to my feet. Yup, that a-hole red squirrel had crept nearly right up to the table.

"Nonna!" Joey yelled. "Put down the knife."

Nonna didn't drop the knife. No, instead she pinched it by the blade and whipped it right at the squirrel.

I screamed. Couldn't help it. But I quickly recovered. "It's okay!" I shouted. "It's okay. She missed."

I charged the squirrel, waving my hands at it, shouting, "Shoo, tree rat. Shoo." But the little jerk was holding its ground, up on its back legs, chittering.

"Give me your knife," Nonna said, waving at me.

"No!"

"I won't miss this time," she said, struggling to get to her feet, but the wedding throne was so heavy, she couldn't move it back so she could stand. The most she could do was rock it on the uneven ground.

"Nonna," Antonia said. "Just sit. We'll take care of the squirrel."

"You never take care of the squirrels. You say you're going to take care of the squirrels, but—"

She tried to push herself up again, but when it didn't work, she gripped underneath the seat and tipped it up—

"Antonia!" I shouted. "The chair!"

It was tipping . . . and Nonna was falling back into it!

Antonia lunged across the table to grab the armrest, but it was too late.

"Nonna!" Joey shouted, jumping to his feet.

I ran to Nonna. Joey, Candace, Antonia, and Josie were already helping her to her feet, with my knife still clutched in her hand.

"Is she okay?"

"I think so," Joey said.

"Candace," Michael said, getting to his feet. "It's not too late. This can't be how you want to spend the rest of your l—"

"Dad, please—"

"No," Antonia shouted. "Let him say what he wants to say. He thinks his little princess is too good for my family."

"No," Candace said. "No, it's—"

"She is!" Michael shouted.

"My brother is too good for her!" Antonia shouted back.

"Everyone!" Freddie shouted. "The food is going to get cold if we don't—"

"Evelyn, we're leaving," Michael said, throwing his napkin on the table and stomping off.

Evelyn swiveled her way out from the picnic table and hurried after him. Candace wasn't far behind.

"We're going too," Antonia said, grabbing her nonna's elbow.

"Toni . . ." Joey pleaded.

"No."

"At least let me help you get to the boat."

Freddie and I stood in front of the pergola and watched the fractured family head off across the lawn.

"Do you think they realize they're all headed to the same dock?" I asked.

Freddie shrugged. "You know, I'm starting to think Candace might be onto something with this whole curse thing."

"You think?"

Freddie just sighed . . .

. . . and smoked?

Well, he wasn't smoking. The smoke was rising up behind him.

I shook his arm. "Freddie! Fire!"

Someone must have knocked over a lantern when

they left—it had caught the bottom edge of the gauze hanging over the pergola and flames were now racing up the side.

Freddie took a quick look over his shoulder. "Let it burn."

The gauze did burn itself out pretty quickly. Being spring, everything outdoors was still pretty damp.

Candace's side of the family left the retreat first in her boat while Joey and his grandmother sat on the porch with Kit Kat and Tweety.

"Where's Antonia?" I asked as I headed over. Freddie decided he was going to enjoy the meal despite the burned-out-pergola.

"She's down at the water," Joey said. "She wanted a moment."

I nodded. "I'm going to go talk to her."

"I doubt she'll listen," Joey said with a sigh.

"You go try, Erica," Kit Kat said. "We'll take care of Joey and his grandmother."

"Yeah," Tweety said. "I think they could both use a drink."

I sighed. Hopefully it would just be iced tea again and not the twins' homemade whiskey.

I meandered my way over to the steps leading down to the water.

Okay, maybe now wasn't the best time to talk to Antonia, but it was *a* time, and I was thinking that was as *good* as it was going to get.

I found Antonia sitting on the swing seat by the water. It was pretty buggy with the sun going down. She must be in a bad state if she was willing to sit out here. I walked over the rocks to get to her. The swing was back near the treeline. There wasn't a lot of room by the shore.

I didn't exactly know how to start this conversation, so I just sat down beside her.

"Listen," Antonia said after a moment, "I know you think I'm a terrible person—"

"I don't think that."

"Joey means everything to me."

I nodded. I believed her. Unfortunately I also believed that he meant everything to Candace. I caught her looking at me from the corner of my eye.

"You know he went to prison because of me, right?"

I nodded. "I heard something about that. But I don't think you can blame yourself for that. Joey made his own choices and—"

"Did you hear what it was? Why I was sick?"

I shook my head.

She stared at me a bit longer. I think internally debating whether or not she should tell me her story. "Eating disorder. Anorexia. Joey went to jail because I was starving myself to death."

"Oh."

"Yeah."

"But still . . . you can't blame yourself for being sick. Anorexia is a disease."

"Right." By her tone I was thinking she didn't buy that at all. "Anyway, the point is after Joey got out of prison I made a promise that I would look out for him. He's got such a big heart. It gets him into trouble sometimes."

I looked out to the water. "Candace has a big heart too. I can promise you that."

Antonia scoffed and dropped her hands between her

knees. "I'll have to take your word on that, but either way, that's not my problem with her."

"Okay." I was really hoping she wasn't going back to the crying thing because—

"Joey needs someone who can look out for him. Help him make decisions with his head. Not his heart."

I frowned. I didn't want her to bring up the crying thing again, but I also hated it when I didn't have my arguments ready. "Candace isn't stupid. I think together—"

"Come on," Antonia said, dropping back against the swing, really screwing up our rhythm. "We both know that Candace is one of those chicks who needs taking care of."

"Not true."

"She's crying all the time!"

Aha! I was ready for this one. "That's not fair. Her maid of honor was murdered the night before her wedding."

Antonia turned her head to look at me. "Erica, come on. She cried the first time we met. Because she was so happy to meet Joey's family. She cried the second time because we told her about Nonna, and she felt like she already knew her. She cried when—"

I put a hand up. "Okay, I get it. You have a list. But . . . so what? She expresses her emotions with tears. It doesn't mean—"

"She's needy. Joey will spend his life trying to meet all those needs."

Frick. I should have known I came unprepared to this fight. Antonia had obviously been thinking about this for a long time now. She'd had months to prepare her arguments.

"She's going to kill him."

"Kill him? Okay, that's a wee bit dramatic." I shook my head, but kept my eyes on the lake. That kind of ridiculousness didn't deserve eye contact.

"It's not," she said, straightening up. "I mean, she's not going to kill him, kill him. Like Lyssa." She made the sign of the cross. "You know, God rest her soul and all that. But my brother is like this big, lovable, dumb dog. I mean, he's smart—but look at all these accidents he's been having trying to get her to stop crying."

"I was under the impression that when Joey can't fix things, he"—I moved my hands around like tinkering with something . . . or kneading bread? I don't know what I was trying to do—"he, like, fixes things."

"Well yeah, but he doesn't usually drive nails through his hand," she said. "I think it's because he's distracted and upset, and he knows he will never be able to make Candace happy."

"Again, that's not fair. I've known Candace for a lot longer than you. She's usually a happy person. Almost, you know, unbelievably happy. She frequently bakes cupcakes just to share with other people. Who does that?" I mean, I might make cupcakes for myself, but not to share with other people.

"Look, I know she's your friend, but would you want her marrying your brother?"

I squinted. I had no idea how to answer that. I couldn't actually imagine my mother having more children. Let alone a boy. I mean, there was Caesar of course. A picture of Candace marrying Caesar popped into my head.

"See? Even you think it's ridiculous."

"No, I—" Dammit, Erica, focus. "I just wish I could

change your mind about Candace." I was racking my brain trying to think of something that I could tell her to change her mind. Some story or example where Candace was really badass that might make her see things—see Candace—in a different light. But the pressure kept making the cat wedding pop up in my mind and it was really hard to think. Maybe I was suffering from smoke inhalation. My brain did feel oxygen deprived. "I think if you got to know her a little better, you might . . . ?"

The look on Antonia's face shut me down.

"Well, maybe you could, for the wedding, just try to . . . ?"

And there was that look again.

"Maybe just for the photos? I mean, for the photos you have to . . . smile? No?"

She didn't even shake her head that time.

"Okay, here's the thing though." I turned my body to face her. This was my big gun. Full force. She needed to pay attention. "Candace and Joey are going to get married. It doesn't matter if you don't want it or her parents don't want it, they are getting married. They love each other, and Joey wants your nonna at the wedding, so Candace will move heaven and earth to make that happen—even if they do it at the courthouse."

Antonia didn't say anything, but I could see I was getting to her.

"Now it will break their hearts if you are not there, but they will do it." Didn't know if that was true, and I was probably overstepping, but I couldn't stop now. "*But* if you do decide to come and you ruin their wedding, well, that will break your brother's heart too."

"Erica, I get that you want me to promise that I

won't do anything to disrupt the wedding, but I can't do that. If there's anything I can do to stop my brother from making the biggest mistake of his life, I'll do it."

"But it's *his* mistake to make," I said. "And it's not a mistake." I probably should have led with that. Not that it would have made any difference.

"I'm sorry," Antonia said, getting to her feet. "Just . . . I'm sorry."

I sighed. I couldn't let her go yet. I didn't want to tear any more rifts into the wedding, but I just had to ask her about the night Lyssa died. I didn't want to believe she had anything to do with Lyssa's drowning in some crazed attempt to stop the wedding, but someone other than Justin and Tommy had been at the gazebo that night. "Antonia, did you go to the gazebo at all the night of the bachelorette party?"

"No." She looked me hard in the eye. "Why would you ask me th—" Realization hit her. "You think I . . . ? Nice," she said with a nod. "God, I hate this town." She turned and walked back to the steps that led up to the retreat.

Yeah, we weren't going to be friends.

I rested my head back on the swing. That had been a pretty firm no, but as Sheriff Bigly had pointed out, people lie.

Not too much later, I spotted Candace's boat coming across the water.

Once she killed the engine, she called out to me. "Erica?"

"That's me," I said with a wave. "You get your parents back to the mainland okay?"

"They're going back to the hotel. What are you doing down here?"

"Oh, I just had a chat with Antonia."

Candace got out of the boat and secured it to the dock. "I'm guessing you didn't have any luck convincing her I'm not the worst thing that has ever happened to her brother."

I sighed.

"Didn't think so."

She sat down beside me on the swing and I swiveled my head to meet her eye.

"You have any luck with your parents?"

She shook her head.

"You know what? I'm starting to think you have to approach this whole wedding thing differently."

Candace frowned. "I do?"

I smiled. "You said *I do*. It's funny because you're a bride and—" I shook my head. "What I mean is this is your day. Yours and Joey's."

She smiled, but kind of sadly for my liking.

"You two are in love. This is your wedding. Screw everybody else."

"I'm sorry, did you say—"

"Screw 'em!" I threw my hands in the air. "Try it. *Screw 'em!* It feels good."

Candace blushed. "I don't think I could say that. I mean it's okay if you say it. I'm just not really comfortable with that particular phrase—"

"Oh my God—"

"That one either," she said.

"Sorry."

She smiled . . . devilishly.

"Wait . . . were you teasing me?"

"A little bit," she said.

"Oh look at you, making the funnies," I said, nodding. "Now you're getting it. So say it with me now. Screw—"

"I'm still not really comfortable with that phrase," Candace, said, wrinkling her nose.

"Okay, the point is your family loves you. Antonia loves her brother. But that doesn't give them the right to ruin this day for you. Don't let them ruin *our* day."

Another smile came to the corner of her mouth. "*Our* day?"

I nodded. "Freddie and I have put a lot of work into this wedding."

Just then Freddie walked down the stairs. "Hell yeah, we have."

I looked back at Candace. "You probably don't like the *h, e,* double-hockey-sticks word either, huh?"

"It's okay, Erica," Candace said. "I get what you're trying to say and thank you."

"Does that mean you'll try out the screw—I mean, the attitude?"

She shrugged sweetly. "I'll try."

"Not the conviction I was looking for."

Suddenly she was hugging me. "Thanks again, Erica." She got to her feet. "I'll try for you, okay?"

"Don't do it for me. Do it for . . ." She was already headed for the stairs. She looked back at me and smiled, but those dimples were definitely at half-depth.

"From now on OLS is strictly crime. No more weddings," Freddie said, coming up to me. "Am I right?"

"So right."

Chapter Forty-three

I woke up pretty early the morning of the day before the wedding—wedding eve, I guess. There was too much on my mind for sleep. There was too much on my mind for anything really. It was going to be a miracle if Freddie and I pulled this off. I knew that at the end of the day, all that should matter was that Candace and Joey loved each other—not whether napkins were folded just so into little swans. But for someone who wasn't that into weddings, I *really* did want them folded just so. Like really, really wanted that.

And I suppose I should have been happy that someone was in jail for Lyssa's murder. Freddie had called over to the sheriff's department, and Justin had been charged after all. I guess there had been enough time for Justin to follow Tommy and then go back to the gazebo, but it still wasn't sitting right with me.

I pulled on some clothes and headed toward the kitchen. Maybe some coffee would help get me in a more festive mood or—

I spotted the top of Zaki's head on the other side of the common room window. He was meditating on the porch again.

Hmm, here I was struggling with all sorts of conflicting feelings and overwhelming stress . . . and there was the guru who was dating my mom sitting on my front porch. How many people could say that? I didn't want to bother him though. I mean, yes, he had invited me to meditate with him before, but that didn't mean he wanted to meditate with me now. Hard to say what the etiquette was on this. Then again he should be trying to impress me.

I padded my way over to the door and peeked my head out.

He didn't open his eyes.

I cleared my throat.

Still nothing.

"Hey Zaki."

He still didn't open his eyes, but he did say, "Good morning, Erica," with just a tiny little smile.

"Morning."

"Would you like to join me?"

I scurried outside and grabbed the extra mat. "Don't mind if I do." I sat in front of him and crossed my legs. He looked so serene. I wanted me some of that.

I adjusted my position a little bit and closed my eyes.

I lasted about twenty seconds before I said, "I always feel like I'm doing this wrong."

"You cannot do meditation wrong," Zaki said. "That is why we call it a practice. The skill is never completely mastered. The act of trying is the ability itself."

"Cool," I said.

We were quiet again. For about twenty more seconds.

"It's just I've never been able to quiet my mind. Like not even for a second."

Zaki opened his eyes. "Perhaps you would like to talk about what it is that's bothering you before you meditate."

"You don't mind?"

"Not at all."

"I have a lot of things that are bothering me actually. Number one, I think the police have arrested the wrong person for a murder that happened in town. You probably heard about it."

"You feel as though it is your job to fix this mistake."

"I do." Seeing as Freddie and I had trapped Justin in the first place.

He nodded.

"I mean, I know it's not my job to fix everything . . . but I kind of feel like it is. It really bothers me when people I care about are suffering."

He nodded again.

"I'm also kind of worried that Freddie and I won't be able to pull off this wedding tomorrow. At least not in a way that the bride deserves."

Again with the nod.

"And while we're talking about what brides deserve, I'm not sure if I'm being honest with myself about why I'm so uncomfortable with weddings in general. I've been saying it's because of all the stress, but I don't know . . . it's like I have always just thought weddings weren't meant for people like me."

Still no words from him.

"And I've got to know . . . that message card you gave me," I said, "why was it blank? Like why give me one at all? Were they all just random like *Look at this inkblot. What do you see? A flattened frog? Or your first-grade teacher lighting fire to the school?"*

He smiled and looked like he was about to answer right away, but then needed a moment to process that last part. "All questions are individual. How can they be anything but? Although your mother and I agreed that if she had a part in your question it would influence the reading of it."

I nodded. "You are wise, Guru."

"Zaki, please."

"Everyone refers to you as Guru though."

"That . . . was a marketing decision."

I smiled. "A guru's got to eat."

He smiled back at me. "I don't have all the answers, Erica. I will always be a student. Your mother and I have that belief in common."

I nodded. I kind of wanted to ask him what his intentions toward my mother were at that point, but seeing as I didn't know hers, I thought I'd better leave it alone. "But I kind of want to know while I'm still single."

"Then that is your question."

"But I don't know the answer. That's what I'm saying." I mean, I think my mother had a point about Freddie and me shielding ourselves from asking the hard questions, but I didn't want to be shielded any more.

"The beauty of meditation," Zaki said, "is that by releasing our thoughts, new possibilities arise. Would you like to try again?"

I shook my head. "I don't think I will be able to do it."

"Again, the doing is in the practice, and I promise none of your problems will disappear if you leave them unattended for a little while."

I took a deep breath and closed my eyes.

I tried. I really did. But despite what Zaki said about the trying being the actual practice, I was still pretty sure I wasn't doing it right. Lots of thoughts popped in and out of my consciousness, but every time one came to my attention, I did my best to release it. Whatever that meant. I also tried the whole "focusing on my breathing and nothing else" technique too, but every time I did that I suddenly felt like I was breathing funny, and then I would wonder why I was breathing so funny and then how it was that our brains knew how to make us breathe without even thinking about it, and our hearts beat for that matter and—

Let it go.

I took another deep breath.

I am thinking nothing. I am thinking nothing. Nope, I was totally thinking about the wedding and whether or not Freddie had told Big Don when the reception dinner was supposed to be. Yup, he had agreed to provide some meat options for the guests, and my mother's caterers were going to supply the vegan options. This place was turning into quite the money-maker for them. I hadn't decided what I was going to hav—

Let it go.

Hey, it's just like the Disney song "Let It—

Let it go.

We also really had to get one rehearsal in. Everybody needed to know where to stand. And we had to settle on a spot for the wedding arbor. We needed to find a pretty even spot of ground for all the chairs, and a path for Candace to walk down. At least she had her father to—

Her father to walk her down the aisle.

Hey, maybe that was why I wasn't into traditional weddings? I had never had a traditional family and—

Let it go.

And we needed to make sure we had rented enough chairs. It was possible some of the women for the retreat would want to watch the ceremony, so I still had to ask Candace if that was okay with her. It might be weird to be gawked at by a bunch of strangers. It might be good for Eeyore—I mean Mary—to see the wedding though. Cheer her up a little. Or not. A couple of weeks was not a long time to get over the death of the love of your life.

My breath caught.

No . . . a couple of weeks was not a long time at all to deal with a death like that . . . then sign up for a retreat?

That was actually kind of weird.

Really weird.

Why would Mary, in the depths of grief, sign up for a retreat asking the question *Why am I still single?* She already knew the answer to that question. And she really didn't seem interested in participating in any of the sessions I had witnessed. Unless . . .

My eyes popped open and I jumped to my feet.

"Erica, are you all right?" Zaki asked, also getting up.

"I'm not. I'm—"

Just then my mother opened the door. "There you two are. Erica, what a nice surprise to—"

"Mom, when did Mary arrive at the retreat? Did she come with a group or—"

"No, no. She was by herself. First to arrive. Red brought her over."

I put a hand to my head. I just realized something else that was very strange. Mary was always wearing a white shirt and a pair of khakis. I think maybe the exact same ones. Every day. I had thought she was depressed, but—

"What's going on, guys?" Freddie asked, coming outside too with a mug in his hand. He had stayed the night so that we could get an early start—it didn't matter. None of it mattered except—

"Mom, which cabin is Mary staying in?"

"Number seven, I think. Erica, what is going on?"

I couldn't answer. I just jumped off the porch and headed down the gravel path that led to the cabins. Lyssa had been dating someone for money. Someone that she had gotten a lot of money from. What if . . . what if it was Mary's Frank? It was crazy . . . but the timing. It just didn't make sense that Mary was here.

I broke out into a run. I ran all the way to the cabin. Everyone shouting behind me.

I knocked on the door. A woman I didn't recognize answered.

"Is Mary here?"

"No," the woman said, shaking her head. "She got up early. Said she was going to the lake."

My eyes scanned the room. Oh God . . . windbreaker! It was the windbreaker on the bed.

My head whipped around. Freddie had caught up with me.

I ran back toward the lodge shouting, "Mom, I need

you to call the sheriff's department. Tell them to get over here."

"But Erica—"

"Just do it! It's an emergency."

I kept moving to the steps that led down to the lake.

"Erica?" Freddie called out, panting. "What is going on?"

"It was Mary. Mary killed Lyssa."

Chapter Forty-four

"Hurry," I said, pushing at Freddie's back. He had gotten to the log steps that led down to the lake before me. The mist was still clinging to the water with the sun still low in the sky.

I couldn't believe it. I never once . . . it had never even occurred to me . . .

I had believed her. I had felt so incredibly sorry for her. It didn't make sense. But it did if Frank was the man that Lyssa had . . . what? Did she swindle him? And Mary knew? Oh God . . . maybe that brought on his heart attack.

If I was right . . .

"Freddie, we can't let her get away," I mumbled, watching my footing.

"She's not . . ." Freddie had stopped at the bottom of the log steps. I came up behind him. "I don't think she's trying to get away."

I froze.

No, it didn't look like she was trying to get away at all.

Mary was sitting in the canoe with her back to us not moving.

Freddie and I walked slowly toward the dock.

"Mary?"

She didn't turn.

I moved closer. "Mary?"

"The money's gone, isn't it?" she said in a flat voice.

I slowly walked down the dock until I was at her side then lowered myself to my knees. Freddie joined me. "The police have it."

She nodded. "I wasn't trying to take the money for me. It was for Frank's daughter."

"What . . . what are you doing out here?" Freddie asked.

"I think I was going to paddle out to the middle of the lake and then just . . ." She looked at me then, eyes empty.

"What happened?" I asked.

She didn't answer at first. The only sound was the water lapping gently against the side of the canoe.

"I never meant to . . ." Mary looked down at her hands. "I didn't know she existed until after Frank died. He never told me. I think he might have been embarrassed." She looked up at the distant treeline, barely visible in the mist. "His daughter, though, at the funeral, she told me Frank had been dating this . . . gold digger. That she had cleaned him out. That money was for Frank's daughter's college."

I felt my shoulders drop. So it was . . . what I had

thought. You'd think there would be relief in that, but there wasn't.

"I kind of lost it a little bit after that," she said, looking back at her hands and nodding. "Got every bit of information I could on who this woman was. She told Frank so many lies. Didn't even use her real name, but I found her. She was on a Web site. For sugar babies."

"Oh man," Freddie said.

"Younger women wanting to date rich older men? I still don't believe that's how she met Frank. It must have been some other way." She shook her head. "But maybe he *was* that lonely? I don't know. And I guess it doesn't matter now." She took a long breath. "I contacted her. Tried to pretend I was a man interested in meeting her, but she said she was leaving town. I was desperate then. I don't know what I was desperate for—why I wanted to see her—but I knew I had to. Maybe make her understand that that money Frank had given her . . . it had to be a loan. He never would have taken that money from his daughter. She meant everything to him. It just wasn't right," she said, looking at me. "None of it. It wasn't right that he was dead, it wasn't right that she didn't care, and it wasn't right that the last thing he would have wanted to give his daughter was gone."

Mary clenched her hands together, knuckles white.

"So I went to the bus station. I thought there was no way . . . the odds were completely against me finding her, but I went anyway, and she just walked in." Mary shook her head like she still couldn't believe it.

"Did you talk to her?" I asked.

"No. I just followed her. Bought the same ticket she did. Then got on the bus. She never once noticed me.

Never once looked at me. I followed her all the way
here. Bought clothes at one of the rest stops. And when
we finally got here, I watched her meet up with your
friend, and I followed them. I waited down the road
from her house. Then I watched her go to the party. I
could see her through the window, riding that bull.
Having the time of her life." She again looked up at
me as though I could explain to her how that could be.
"After that I watched her go with that man to the
gazebo. Frank was dead, and she was . . . *hooking up*.
None of it mattered to her. The man who meant everything to me, meant less than nothing to her. My world
had been split open . . . and she just carried on. I just
couldn't . . ." She shook her head.

I dug the heel of my palm into my chest. For a
moment there, I had gotten just the tiniest taste of
her sadness, and it was enough to make it difficult to
breathe.

"What happened?" Freddie asked.

"I waited. The man left, and I went to the gazebo."
She shrugged. "Do you know what she told me?"

I shook my head.

"She recognized my name and laughed. She told me
that Frank had always loved me, but thought I only
liked him as a friend. But that when *she* came into
Frank's life, it all made sense to him. That things happened for a reason. He believed that we," she said,
patting her chest, "didn't get together because he was
meant to be with her. With *her*?"

Part of me wanted to tell her I was sorry, sorry for
her pain, but I couldn't. Not when . . .

"I didn't mean for her to fall into the water. But suddenly she was. I don't even remember pushing her. I

just remember watching as she struggled and—" She shook her head. "The next morning, I was just sitting on a bench in town when this man asked if I was headed for the retreat."

That must have been Red.

"I said yes, and . . ." She shrugged. "At first I was in shock, but I thought maybe I could still find the money. Get it to Frank's daughter. It was the only thing I could still do for him."

She must have been the one taking the canoes. Going to Candace's . . .

"Maybe don't say anything more to anyone yet," Freddie said. "You need a lawyer."

"And you need to turn yourself in."

Mary did turn herself in.

Didn't make any of us feel any better though.

The rest of the day had a brutally somber feel to it. I couldn't bear to tell Candace the whole story Mary had told us about Lyssa. I just told her that she had been arrested and that yes, we were sure she was the one behind Lyssa's death. It was enough for now.

After Mary had been taken away, Freddie and I just set about getting down to the business of the wedding—not saying a whole lot. Normally we felt pretty awesome when we solved a case, but this didn't feel good at all. It's not that I felt Mary should go free, but . . . it just all felt wrong. And sad. Really, really sad.

On the bright side, the wedding was really coming together. The tent for the reception turned out better than we had hoped. It was beautiful—big, white, elegant. And we had found the perfect spot for the arbor—

right in front of a little clearing in the trees that allowed for a view of the lake. We decided not to set up the chairs until the morning though. The weather was supposed to be good, so I didn't think they would blow away, but I was concerned about the amount of bird poop we might find on them if we left them out.

"Okay," Freddie said, coming up to me as I was doing a walk around the tent. "I know this morning was . . ."

I nodded. "It was."

"But we need to rally. I can hardly believe it myself, but this wedding is actually coming together."

I nodded.

"So we have to show a little . . . joy," he said, punching me on the shoulder.

"Ow."

"For Candace."

"I know. You're right. I'm trying."

"No you're not."

"Well, I will try. It's just . . ." I stopped walking and put my sunglasses on my head. "How is it possible that someone's life can go so wrong? I mean, if two people love each other, shouldn't they be together?"

"Are you asking me or Grady?"

I frowned at him. "Grady's not here."

"Indeed."

I shook my head and started walking again. "Life's just too short, you know. I mean, everything would have turned out so differently if Mary had just told Frank how she felt twenty years ago."

"That's no guarantee that they would have worked out."

"But that's my point exactly. Life is short. We need

to . . ." I grabbed my forehead. "I don't know what I'm trying to say."

Suddenly Freddie was shaking his fists in the air. *"Carpe diem!"*

"Are you seizing the day or strangling it?"

"Whatever works." He dropped his hands. "The point is we get to be part of something tomorrow. Two people who are really, really in love are getting married. And we get to witness that. And what's more, it's going to be beautiful, and everyone at that ceremony will know that it was me who—"

Suddenly we heard someone very angry shout, "That's it! I've had it!"

I blinked at Freddie. "Was that . . . ?"

"It sounded like . . ."

We looked at each other. "Candace."

Chapter Forty-five

Freddie and I scurried over to the reception tent, waving and smiling at all the retreatgoers and volunteers who were helping out.

"It's okay," Freddie called out. "Everything's fine. The bride's just . . ."

"Practicing a dramatic reading," I called out.

"A dramatic reading?" Freddie whispered.

"I didn't hear you coming up with anything better."

We hurried into the tent. The entire wedding party was inside except for Joey. They were supposed to be practicing their entrances after the ceremony. Candace was standing in the middle of the group in jeans and T-shirt and a veil. Antonia and Candace's parents had backed up to give her some distance. Nonna was there too but she was wandering around in the back corner of the tent, and it looked like she had trapped herself in some chairs again.

"Candace," Antonia said, putting her hands up. "I just meant—"

"I know exactly what you meant!" Candace snapped. "And I am not having it, do you hear me? I am not having it!"

"What do you think is happening?" I whispered to Freddie.

He shook his head. "I could be wrong, but I think we might be witnessing the birth of a bridezilla."

"You know what?" Candace shouted. "I love you all. I really, really do."

"I sense a *but* coming on," Freddie whispered.

"*But* I have so had it!" Oh wow, Candace was getting very . . . red. "I've had it with you," she said, pointing at her father. "I've have it with you," she said, pointing at her mother. "And I've really had it with you!" she shouted, pointing at Antonia.

"Hey," Freddie whispered. "It's like *You get a car! And you get a car! And you get*—" He stopped when he caught my look. "But you know, really messed up."

"This wedding has faced a lot of setbacks," Candace announced in the fake calm voice people use when they are really, really upset.

"That's because it's cursed," Antonia muttered.

Candace turned her head exorcist-style to look at her future sister-in-law—who finally had the good sense to keep her mouth shut.

"Cursed or not, this wedding *is* happening."

"Candace, sweetheart—"

"Mom," Candace said, whipping around to face her. "Stop talking now."

"But—"

"Stop talking!" she barked.

Everybody froze.

"And you know what? This wedding is not cursed. You know how I know that?"

I shook my head quickly side to side, but she wasn't really looking at me. I kind of had the feeling we all might be in trouble though.

"Because Joey and I love each other. Mom? Dad? Do you hear me? We love each other," she said, pounding her chest. "Antonia? Your brother loves me. And I will cherish him the rest of my life."

"He's her home!" I called out.

Everyone turned to look at me.

"What?" Freddie whispered. "What does that even mean?"

"It means . . . just never mind," I muttered. "It was really sweet the way she explained it."

"So listen up, people," Candace shouted. "My friends," she said, waving a hand in our direction, "have been busting their asses . . ."

"Oh no, she swore," Freddie said with a gasp. "Somebody's gonna die."

". . . to give me and Joey our special day."

"That's right!" Freddie shouted with a general point.

"Even if they did come a little late to the game."

Freddie's hand dropped. "Kind of stings when she turns it directly at you."

I nodded.

"So this day is happening!"

"You know," Freddie whispered. "I haven't seen this side of Candace since—"

"Oh! That's the story I was trying to remember," I said, flapping my hands. "Hey Antonia—sorry to interrupt, Candace—remember when I was saying that

Candace knows how to take care of herself? But I couldn't think of an example?"

Antonia—and everybody else for that matter—just looked at me like I was crazy.

"Well, Candace almost flattened the entire town with a giant billboard raspberry once."

No reaction. Just the crazy eyes.

"It's true," I said, nodding big. "Plowed right into it with a truck."

Antonia's disbelief transformed into concern.

"Oh, don't worry," I said, waving a hand in the air. "We totally deserved it."

"Maybe it's not Candace," Antonia said to . . . herself really. "Maybe it's this town."

"Who's getting married?" Nonna asked, suddenly coming up to the group.

"Joey!" Candace shouted. "To me."

The woman turned her watery eyes up to me. "Does he know she yells like that? What happened to that sweet girl he was going to marry?"

"Same girl," I said with a nod.

"Do you like squirrels?"

I shook my head no.

She patted my arm. "That's good."

"So here's what's going to happen," Candace shouted. "The wedding train is leaving the station whether you all like or not."

"All aboard!" Freddie called out.

"So if you can't be happy for us, then there's the door," she said, pointing at the tent flap.

Just then Joey walked into the tent carrying a long ladder tucked under his arm. "Hey guys, sorry I'm late.

Someone said a string of lights was . . . what's going on?"

Nobody answered.

"Is everything okay in here?"

Antonia stepped forward. "Yeah . . . everything's okay."

"Really?"

She nodded.

"Well . . . good," he said, dropping the feet of the ladder onto the ground and unfolding the top.

"Uh, Joey," I called out. "Maybe you shouldn't be the one working on the ladder. The wedding's tomorrow and—"

"Oh, it's no big deal," Joey said, gripping the sides and putting a foot on the bottom rung. "I'll just—"

"She said *no ladder*!" Candace shouted.

Joey's eyes went wide. "No . . . ladder?"

"No ladder," Candace said more quietly but just as firmly.

"Okay then." He quickly picked it back up again. "Right." He looked back at Candace. "Are you sure everything is . . . ?"

"Everything's great," Antonia called out. "Candace is . . . great."

"Really?" he asked with a hopeful smile.

She smiled back and nodded.

Joey, looking happier than he had in weeks, turned around and left the way he came.

"Love you, baby," Candace shouted after him.

"Love you too!"

We all turned back to see Candace smiling and

clutching her hands together. "Okay, now that that's all settled . . ."

"You're getting married!" I shouted.

"I'm getting married!"

Chapter Forty-six

Otter Lake woke up to a perfect day.

I was really getting the whole thing of why people had weddings in late spring. It was warm but not hot. Sunny without a cloud in the sky. The water was sparkling on the lake. It was the kind of weather that made you think that happy endings were possible.

Rhonda, Antonia, and I were all in my bedroom at the lodge getting Candace ready.

"You look beautiful," Rhonda said, putting one last dab of pink gloss on Candace's lower lip. "You look just like one of those brides on top of a wedding cake."

"Thank you," Candace said, her smile deepening her dimples. "It's almost time to go though, isn't it?"

I checked the time and nodded.

"Yeah," Rhonda said, hurrying to the door. "I'd better get going. My date's probably wondering where I am. I'll send your dad to come get you in ten."

I hurried after her. "Um . . . Rhonda?"

She turned around.

I scratched the back of my neck. "You didn't tell me you had a date. What date are we talking about? Is it anyone I know?"

She put up her hands. "It's not what you think, Erica."

I dropped my voice. "Tell me right now that you did not bring the tree rat—I mean, tree man—to the wedding."

"It's not what you think. Don't worry. Everything's cool," she said, backstepping quickly.

"Rhonda," I growled through my teeth. "Don't you—"

"Bye!"

I closed the door and turned back around, smiling at Candace.

"Hey, Erica, my mom isn't out there, is she? I was kind of hoping she'd get to see me before, you know . . ."

"Um, not right this second she's not, but . . ." I grabbed my phone off my dresser and typed a quick message. "I'll go get her for you in just a moment. But before I do . . ."

Candace's eyes darted over my face. "Is something wrong?"

"Well," I said, looking up from my phone. "I'm not exactly sure how to say this . . ."

"What? What is it?" She brought her hand to her chest. "Just tell me."

I sighed. "I've been thinking about it, and I know I said I would . . . but I don't think I should be your maid of honor."

Candace's hand dropped to her side. "What? Why?"

I looked down at the floor and shook my head.

"Well, like I was trying to tell you before, it's hard to put into words exactly, but I'm not really a wedding person and—"

"Erica," Candace said, voice tightening. "Please tell me you're not saying this right now. You don't mean it, right? You're just—"

"You know what?" I said, looking up at her. "I think it might be better if I just showed you what I'm trying to say."

I walked back over to my bedroom door and swung it open.

Nobody was there.

"Show me what? Why—"

"Freddie!" I hissed into the hallway.

Just then Candace's mother came to the door, beautiful smile on her face . . . with Candace's sister.

"Bethanny?" Candace whispered. "Bethanny!"

Suddenly the two sisters were hugging and jumping up and down in that excited way women wearing heels do.

"But how?" Candace asked.

"Freddie's got about two million frequent flyer miles," I said just as he walked into the room. "It's his family's card."

"What?" Candace shrieked happily.

"It was nothing," Freddie said. "Consider it your wedding present."

"Freddie!" Candace shouted, still jumping. "You are the best wedding planner ever!"

"I know," he said happily. I elbowed him in the ribs. "Erica helped."

A couple of minutes of excited chatter passed when a knock sounded on the door.

"All right. All right," Freddie said, holding out his hands. "Everybody stop crying. You're going to wreck your makeup." He then clapped his hands in the air. "Places!"

I came up behind him and whispered, "You did good."

He looked back at me. "*We* did good."

I smiled.

"But especially me."

I nodded.

"Okay, everyone! Let's get this girl married!"

Chapter Forty-seven

The wedding was beautiful. I know everyone says *the wedding was beautiful* . . . kind of like everyone says all newborns are beautiful . . . even when they aren't . . . because only terrible, terrible people think otherwise . . . but Candace's wedding really was beautiful.

My mom really did a wonderful job. She had a lot of nice things to say about love. I didn't know she could be such a sentimentalist. And I was only a little disconcerted by how often she looked over to Zaki during the ceremony. I mean, I liked Zaki . . . but the whole thing was still weird.

The reception looked like it was going to go off without a hitch too. As the sun set, we tied back the sides of the tent to let the night air rush across the dance floor. The inside glowed with warm yellow lanterns and twinkly lights.

I found a spot just outside the tent to get a clear view of the dance floor. Doug was just about to get the music

started, and I wanted to be sure I had a good view of
Candace and Joey. I took a sip of champagne. I didn't
think we were going to be able to pull it off, but—

Just then a dog let out a howl from one of the tables
and the crowd laughed.

"Carmen!" Mrs. Roy snapped.

Yup, Mrs. Roy had brought Carmen to the wedding.
She was wearing a lovely corsage on her collar.
Mrs. Roy had brought a boutonniere for Stanley too.

She caught me looking at her, so I shot her a
thumbs-up.

It turned out the tree branch bouquets were gor-
geous. Mrs. Roy had tied fat white satin ribbons around
small evergreen branches, ferns, and just enough white
roses and lily of the valley to make it work. She even
made the pinecone accents look pretty. I never should
have doubted her for a moment.

Yup, everything had turned out pretty perfec—

Just then I noticed a woman in a lovely lavender
dress headed my way. I didn't recognize her at first all
dressed up, but . . . Sheriff Bigly?

I was kind of surprised Candace had invited her, but
then again, no I wasn't. Candace liked everybody. She
just couldn't help herself.

"Erica," Sheriff Bigly said with a nod.

"Sheriff," I said.

"It was a beautiful ceremony," she said, coming to
stand beside me.

"It was," I said with a nod. "They're a great couple."

A moment passed before she added, "And who
would have thought you and Freddie would make such
a good team?"

I met her eye.

She smiled. "Well, Grady did try to tell me that actually. It was just hard to listen given all the stories."

I frowned at her. "Grady told you that?"

She nodded. "We talked most nights. He wanted to be kept apprised of the investigation. Mentioned several times that . . ." She frowned. "How did he put it?" She wagged a finger in the air. "That you and Freddie had a way of shaking evidence free."

I smiled. I knew Grady never would have abandoned the town.

"He also said that you two would drive me nuts, so he was right about that too."

"I am sorry that—"

She waved a hand out and cleared her throat. "I thought you'd be interested to know that we have Mary's confession. She's being transported upstate."

"Oh."

She nodded. "And Justin has been released. Said he's headed down to the Keys."

"Well, I'm glad it's over." I took a deep breath. "I've been wondering though, what's going to happen to the money? Is it going to Justin?" I was kind of thinking that was a bad idea if it turned out to be the case. He didn't seem to be the type to do well with that much money upfront, and I kind of got the impression that he had some sort of substance-abuse problem.

She shook her head. "No. I don't think so."

I frowned. "Lyssa had family after all? Candace thought—"

"None that I could find," she said, looking up at the

stars. "The way I see it, the money was given freely to Lyssa, so it was legally hers. Lyssa then put that money into Candace's gift box. Sounds like a wedding present to me."

My eyes darted over her face.

"Candace being the sweet girl that she is, well, she's already asked for the name of Frank's daughter."

"She has?"

"She has." Sheriff Bigly smiled again. She was a really nice-looking woman when she didn't look like she wanted to throttle you.

We stood watching the dancing for a while longer in silence before Sheriff Bigly said, "Well, I think I'm going to head down to the dock, and see if I can catch Red's next trip to the mainland. You have a nice night, Erica."

"Sleep well, Sheriff."

She smiled. "I think I just may do that." She nodded and ambled away.

"Oh! Don't forget to say bye to Don!"

She shot me look and wagged a finger.

I shrugged. What? They were both widowers.

I turned my attention back to Candace and Joey dancing. She was so little in his big werewolf arms . . . and the way they were looking at each other? It was enough to make a girl tear up.

I blinked a few times. When I could finally see straight, I spotted Rhonda . . .

. . . with her date!

It *was* him.

Topless insurance guy!

Although he was wearing a shirt tonight.

What was she thinking? Freddie was going to freak

out! He might even flip a table. Granted, flipping a table at a formal event was on his bucket list of things to accomplish before he died, but—I waved a hand at her to come over.

"Hey," Rhonda said, coming up, her hand in our target's. "Erica, I want you to meet someone." She put her hand on her date's chest. "This is George."

"I know who George is, Rhonda," I said tightly then frowned. "Wait . . . I thought your name was Jake? Didn't the file say Jake?"

Rhonda and George slash Jake laughed.

"Actually, we wanted to let you in on a little secret," Rhonda said with a smile.

I raised my brow. "What little secret?"

"George works for the insurance agency," she said, patting his chest again. "He's quality control. They were testing us to see if we could get the job done."

"What? How did you—"

"Well, after our little talk, I knew I had to go with my instincts about George here. So I started doing some checking. Like who owned the property we were scoping. If there was anything funny linked to his license plate. I still have my contacts from my police days, you know."

"Then she followed me home one night," George said. "To my real address. I just needed a change of clothes and—"

"I told him I knew what he was up to," she said, gazing at him.

"I was impressed by her thoroughness," he said, gazing right back.

Nobody was looking at me. Which was good. My jaw was hanging down.

"Anyway, he's going to give us a great recommendation to the insurance company."

"I think you should expect a lot of business to be coming your way," he said with a nod before looking back at Rhonda. "Not a lot of investigators want to come out here. Certainly none as talented as Rhonda."

"Wow, that's . . . awesome!"

"I know," Rhonda said, leaning in to give me a hug. Once her mouth was at my ear, she whispered, "George did his research on us ahead of time. I think that shirtless show was for my benefit. He likes the gingers."

"And he is a ginger," I whispered.

"I know. It's a lot of *spice*."

Rhonda leaned back and George asked, "Do you want to dance?"

"I'd love to," Rhonda said, putting her hand in his.

Just then I noticed Freddie making a beeline through the crowd to get to us.

"Tell me that is not who I think it is," Freddie said when he got to my side.

"It is," I said, shaking my head, "but it isn't." I told him the story.

"Oh thank God," Freddie said when I was through. "And holy crap! That's awesome!"

I smiled. "I know."

"It's like my whole life is coming together all at once," Freddie said, shaking his head. "I've got you. I've got Sean. I've got the business . . . with Rhonda as my star employee. No offense."

"Not employees, Freddie. Partners."

"Right. Right," he said. He took a deep breath. "And I think the wedding's a hit."

"I agree."

We both looked back to the dance floor. Everyone was getting in on the action now. Even Candace's parents were dancing . . . and smiling.

"It wasn't easy though."

"No, it was not." I looked over at him. "It almost broke us up."

Freddie scoffed. "Like that's ever going to happen."

"Hey, you're the one who said it. Our relationship caused trouble between me and Grady, and now it has caused trouble between you and Sean. We have to figure out a way to make room for other . . . significant others in our lives."

"Totes," he said with a nod. "We'll put it on the whiteboard. You can write."

"I'm being serious."

Freddie shot me his most serious face. "I don't joke about the whiteboard, Erica. We'll make a list of things we can do to improve our other relationships. Tomorrow. Or the next day . . . I've got company," he said, jabbing me in the ribs.

"Speaking of Sean, he does seem to be fitting in well," I said, holding my champagne flute out in his direction. He was laughing and talking with a whole bunch of people. I was guessing everybody wanted to get the lowdown on Freddie's boyfriend.

"He does, doesn't he?" Freddie said, smiling. "But how are you doing with everything?"

"What do you mean?"

"Well, I know it's a wedding, and you're not a wedding person, so . . . ?"

"Yeah, I've been giving that some thought," I said. "I had a minor epiphany when I was meditating with Zaki."

"You did?"

"Just before I figured out the whole thing with Mary." I took a breath. Suddenly I was nervous. Like if I said this out loud it would become real.

"Well?"

"I kind of had this weird moment where I was picturing myself walking down the aisle—"

"And let me guess, Grady was waiting for you."

"No," I said, shaking my head. "I didn't see who was waiting for me. I just . . . more felt who was missing."

"What?"

"My father," I said, looking at Freddie. "I think I really want to know who my father is."

"Your father?" Freddie shook his head. "Whoa. That's . . . big."

I nodded. It was big. I had always acted as though not knowing who my father was wasn't that big of a deal. But it was. I had a story to me that I knew nothing about. I hadn't pressed my mother hard on it in years, mainly because even a mere mention of the topic caused her pain, but . . . I had a right to know, didn't I? And the more I thought about it, the more I was starting to think that that whole issue was the answer to my question. Of why I was still single. Or at least part of it. Not that I needed to know who my father was to complete me. No, it was more like I couldn't believe that I deserved all those traditional things like a husband, a wedding, a white picket fence . . . a baby, if I didn't think I was worth it enough to demand answers.

"But in answer to your question," I said. "I'm happy. Really happy seeing that." I pointed to Candace and

Joey. "I think she really liked your tribute to Lyssa by the way."

We both looked over to the far side of the property—the spot right where the stairs led down to the lake—at the mechanical bull.

Yup, it had taken some doing, but we had rented the same mechanical bull that Lyssa had gotten for the bachelorette party and placed it on the lawn surrounded by pictures of Lyssa.

"Yeah," Freddie said, rocking on his heels. "Lycra might not have been the best person but—"

I slapped him on the chest. "You have to stop doing that."

"What?"

"Lycra."

Freddie looked at me miserably. "I can't. Because if I do, that will be like admitting I'm a really bad person, and"—he dropped his voice to a whisper—"I don't want Sean to know what a bad person I am. So I decided just to roll with it and act all tough like it didn't bother me, and then maybe other people wouldn't think it was so bad if I was like . . . owning it."

"That doesn't make any sense, Freddie."

"Do you know how bad I felt when I found out she died? Out of all the people who had to die, why did it have to be the one person whose name I made fun of?"

I blinked. "Now I think you might be a bad person."

"I'm so ashamed."

"It's okay," I said. "I think you made up for it with the tribute, but no more Lycra."

Freddie nodded. "Anyway, she may have done

crappy things, but she didn't deserve . . . what happened to her."

I nodded.

We turned back to the dance floor.

"Well," Freddie said. "All in all I think we've learned a lot these two weeks about love, and relationships— Oh! There he is! Grady!" Freddie was waving his hand in the air.

"What are you doing?" I hissed, yanking it down. "What about the boundaries we talked about?"

"I thought we weren't doing that yet. Whiteboard, remember?" He looked back to the dance floor and shouted, "Erica wants to dance!"

Grady didn't move from his chair.

"I hate you. I hate you. I hate—"

"He's getting up."

He was getting up.

I swallowed hard.

"Okay," Freddie said, turning to me and leaning in close, "And I've decided this whole not telling you what Grady's been doing is stupid. You two don't know how to communicate. You never have. So here it is. He's trying to like change and grow as a person in hopes that maybe you two could actually get together. When he found out you kissed Matthew, he was upset, but he also realized he could lose you forever, and he doesn't want that. He's even been talking to your mother, and—oh! He read Zaki's book."

"Are you serious?"

He whacked me on the arm. "Of course I'm serious. Stop interrupting. He's also been doing stuff like yoga and knitting to cope with the stress of being this wackadoo town's sheriff. And he's trying to remember what it was like to be the guy he was before he was this wackadoo town's sheriff. But here's the thing, he's not entirely sure that people can change—or that you two can change how you are together—but he's trying really hard, so don't screw this up. Any questions?"

"I . . . um . . ." That was a lot of news to digest. "How . . . how do my bangs look?"

Freddie's eyes flicked up to my brow. "Awful." He then licked his fingers and smoothed them to the side. "Now they look cute, young Audrey Hepburn."

"I . . ."

"No time for that. You're welcome. Gotta go." Freddie zipped away. Not that I really noticed. I suddenly had tunnel vision. All I could see was Grady walking across the dance floor.

He held out a hand to me.

I put mine in his.

His hand was so warm. Chills raced up my sides.

"Sorry," I said quickly. "It was Freddie's idea to call you over."

He stopped his lead of me to the dance floor. "So you don't want to . . . dance?"

"No. No. I totally do."

"Oh, okay." He smiled. "Good."

We carved our own little space in between all the couples. I suspected a lot of them were watching us, but I only had eyes for one thing . . . and I stepped into its arms . . . *his* arms . . . whatever.

Once my hand rested on his shoulder with my other hand in his, every part of me sighed. It had been so long.

"So," he said, moving his palm from the side of my

waist to the small of my back. "I thought you might be interested to know I went over to see Tommy today."

I leaned my head back a little so that I could look him in the eye. "You did?"

He nodded. "I heard you guys were going over there tomorrow to help him clean up."

"Yeah, it's no big deal."

"I wanted to come and help," he said, looking down at me with those blue eyes that were even prettier up close. "I think my family needs to keep a closer eye on him, and I've got one last day of vac—" He stopped himself short.

I laughed. "It's okay. You can say *vacation*. I won't freak out. I'm not sure why I was so . . ." I just shook my head and closed my eyes.

"I get it," Grady said. "I mean, from your perspective it was a big change. It must have seemed—"

"Change is good," I said quickly—while nodding quickly. "I'm a big believer in change."

He cocked his head a little and smiled. "I'm also sorry for the other night with all the stretching and . . . whatever that was."

I looked up at him. He was blushing! Oh my God, Grady was blushing. "You never have to apologize for stretching without your shirt on. There is absolutely nothing to be sorry for."

He laughed. "Yeah, but I'm kind of embarrassed. I've just been trying to figure some things out . . . about me. And us . . ."

Oh boy. Oh boy. Oh boy. Don't screw this up, Erica.

I cleared my throat just to make sure I had a voice. "Us?"

"Erica," he said, locking eyes with me. "I don't want to be done."

I shook my head then switched directions and nodded up and down. "Me neither. I'm not done. Not even a little bit. I'm still rare. Like so rare, I'm still bloody and—I think you know what I mean."

"I don't care anymore if everyone in this town thinks we're crazy," he said. "I just . . . don't want to be done."

"Me neither." I keep my mouth firmly shut after saying those two words this time.

"We have to do things differently though."

"I know. I know. I was thinking the same thing."

"Maybe take things really slow."

"Exactly," I said. "Like we've never even really dated."

He frowned. "I was thinking even slower than that."

"There is slower than dating?"

"Friends."

"Oh." I nodded. "Friends?"

"Well," he said, tipping his head side to side, "friends who maybe don't date other people."

I nodded. "I think . . . I think I'd like that."

"Good," Grady said, pulling me in closer.

We danced in silence for a little then Grady put his mouth close to my ear and whispered, "Have you noticed all of the music so far has been from the seventies?"

I nodded. "It's a long story."

"This is town is so weird sometimes," he said, leaning back to look me in the eyes. "But I love it."

"I love it too."